Fatal Frailties

Peter Davidson

Fatal Frailties

tellwell

Tellwell Talent
www.tellwell.ca

ISBN
978-0-2288-7288-7 (Hardcover)
978-0-2288-7287-0 (Paperback)
978-0-2288-7289-4 (eBook)

Table of Contents

The breeze waved through the tall green grass in the fallow field. Autumn chills were not yet fully upon the land, yet there was still a briskness that showed on the white-capped waves washing up on the seashore where the land tapered away. A stone dyke protected it from three directions, but the sea was enough of a barrier to the south.

Three crows, seeking respite from the wind, landed and perched on top of the rocky wall and scanned the field for something to eat. They had not been there long when they noticed the flattened grass and an incongruous blue and brown not far from their perch. The blue parka and brown corduroys were inhabited by a man who lay face down, spread-eagled before them. His blue eyes were fixed open, glazed and dead. Drops of rain started to fall onto his body; the crows took flight and sought easier pickings elsewhere.

"Prepare a face to meet the faces that you meet." – T.S. Eliot

Chapter 1: Dodderin' Doddie

"Pist-ol! Pist-ol!" There was no reply to the shouted call.

"Where is that bloody dog now?"

The man stumbled up the hillside through the rough, matted heather. The cold bit at his lungs. His breath steamed in front of him. He gasped for air. Below and abovc him was a light dusting of snow, and there were iced puddles that crunched and gave when he stepped upon them. He swore as his right boot broke through, and his leg disappeared into the glaur up to his knee.

"I thought the fucking globe was supposed to be warming." Disgusted, he glowered down at the mess.

It took some moments for him to extricate his foot. It wasn't made any easier by the fact that he carried a belly that had fallen victim to too many early-evening pints and frequent late-night curries. Finally, with gasping reluctance, a sucking slurp saw his leg released. Out of breath, he sat down on a rock and contemplated his sopping foot. His sharp, blue eyes strayed from his body back towards the bare hillside. The glen, about five hundred feet below, was shrouded in a damp mist, but through wispy gaps, he could pick out the ripples on the loch beneath him. Loch Ruthven was narrow between its eastern and western reaches yet long from north to south. Here on the northwest slopes, he could look down on the white-washed walls of the old farmhouse that was his home. He looked on the loch too as his own property, although he had no claims on it other than emotional ones.

Childhood fishing trips had drawn him to buy the property that was now his home. The days of his strife-ridden marriage and rented bachelor pads were long since gone. He was now content to live alone with his dog. He would never call himself a loner; he thrived on the everyday banter and camaraderie of his work. But the end of the working day gave him the aloneness that allowed him to wash away the filth of his police work.

Detective Superintendent Doddie Macfarlane worked in the Inverness branch of Police Scotland about thirty minutes north of his home. Behind his back, he was known as "Dodderin" Doddie. He presented a grumpy, unconventional exterior to his colleagues, who frequently smirked at his dishevelled appearance. He dressed like a burst sofa. Everyone at the station knew he had an "outie" for a belly button because it frequently appeared buttressing its way through shirt buttons for which Doddie's beer-laden, take-away curried paunch were a triumph of hope over reality. He was a laundry pile of a man, but his clear, strikingly blue eyes penetrated faces with fearless focus when the need arose. His sharp common sense, his shrewd human perceptions, and, most of all, his frequent abandonment of the rule book made him a risk. But his results convinced the powers that be that Doddie was a risk worth taking.

He looked up and saw the black and white streak traversing the heather, getting ever closer to him. The dog soon reached him and sat before his master awaiting his treat.

"Where have you been, ye daft dog?" He reached into his pocket and pulled out the expected biscuit. Together, man and dog trudged down the hill as the sun ebbed slowly to the west; the early autumn twilight, known locally as "the gloaming."

"Life is a hospital in which every patient is obsessed with changing beds."
– Anonymous

Chapter 2: A School Visit

"You two get yourself over to Chisholm Secondary School, stopping on the way at Patel's corner store. The proprietor has been robbed by one of their pupils."

Chief Superintendent Brian Rowlands peered over his desk at Detective Sergeant Monica Richards and her immediate boss, Doddie Macfarlane. He looked directly at Monica because he daredn't look at Doddie. His workday suit had shrunk, or he had been given the wrong one back at the dry cleaners. On arrival at work, his offsider, Monica, had expressed her opinion.

"What happened to you? I thought shrinkage only happened when ye swam in the North Sea in winter."

"It's they dry cleaners; hanging's too good for them," thus did Doddie express his opinion on capital punishment and dry cleaners in the same breath.

"Grab Pistol and let's away tae the school."

They took the elevator down to the entrance. Doddie led off to his car, battered and dated on the outside, a heap of discarded food wrappings on the inside. Monica was familiar with the smells and the mess. She tossed the packaging into the back seat, much to the rummaging delight of Pistol, and put on her seat belt as Doddie edged his way out of the car park and into traffic.

Tamiz Patel greeted them with the long-suffering cynicism that was his demeanour.

"Whit did they take this time, Tamiz?"

"A bottle of vodka and a Mars bar. Nae hope of getting them back, I suppose."

"Pistol will find the culprit. He never fails." Doddie pointed at the dog, sniffing around the place, searching for clues. Mr Patel looked doubtful.

Back in the car, Monica phoned the school, told them they were on their way and asked if they could meet with the Headmaster, Mr George Sinclair.

The school was on lunch break as they pulled into the car park. Teenagers milled around on the tarmac, and groups kicked footballs about on the field. The two police officers received interested glances as they walked toward the front entrance.

Sinclair was a little man with an expensive suit. The desk in his office was large and, no doubt, forbidding if a pupil was called to task before him. Sinclair sat down behind it, nudging his swivel chair back and forth, looking for all money like he enjoyed having the two police standing before him like thirteen-year-old miscreants. They were offered no seats.

"What can I do for you?" He looked relaxed. His attitude and demeanour showed that he relished his position. He was a small man behind a big desk. Suddenly, he changed his smiling facade and screwed up his nose. He looked under his desk where Pistol had taken a large dump. Doddie noticed and patted the dog affectionately on the head as if in congratulations for a job well done.

"One of your pupils stole a bottle of spirits and a Mars bar from Mr Patel's shop. It's lunchtime. May we take a walk around the school so that Pistol can apprehend him?"

"The wee bastard, eh? Will the dog really find him?"

"Or her. Aye, he will."

Sinclair looked sceptical. Meanwhile, Pistol had wandered over to a bookcase and repeated the process, leaving a large turd nestling up against the bottom shelf.

Sinclair stood up, peacocked his suited plumage, and asked the two detectives to follow him. They found themselves in the hallway with all the hustle and bustle of teenage youth. Locker doors were slamming, empty lunch garbage was finding its way to the floor, and school uniforms were not being worn with pride. The youth turned as they walked by. The police officers had long ago realised that, despite their plain clothes, people always saw them as what they were. There was no disguising their profession.

In Doddie's experience, the boys' toilet was always a good place to begin when searching a school. As they reached the door, they had to step back as an acne-clad seventeen-year-old appeared from within. He glared at the adults with insolence and disdain, showing little respect for Sinclair and less for Doddie and Monica. But interest was piqued in Pistol who had made a useful note of the human smells in Mr Patel's corner store. He stiffened and turned and followed the boy until he stopped at his locker. The dog brushed up next to him, cocked his leg, and pissed on the boy's grey pants, much to the amusement of his peers.

"Get away from me, ye daft dug." For once, he emitted an emotional response.

Monica was on him in seconds.

"Open up yer locker, son."

"Why? Why should I?" he appealed to Sinclair, who merely nodded to infer that the lad had to meet the request.

Reluctantly, he opened it up, and there stood a full bottle of vodka and a Mars bar wrapper. Monica grabbed the evidence and smiled.

"Let's head down to Mr Sinclair's office for a nice, cosy chat, shall we?"

Sinclair's office stank. Pistol's two deposits still lay on the carpet. The boy turned up his nose.

"Why's there dog shite on the carpet?"

The adults ignored the question, but Sinclair coloured up.

"What's yer name, son?" Doddie stared into the laddie's soul, and the boy shivered slightly.

"Stewart Farquarson," he mumbled.

"Well, now, young Stewart, wi' the boss's permission here, we shall take you off to be identified by Mr Patel and then awa' tae yer hame to hear what Ma and Pa have to say about this situation ye find yersel in."

At the mention of his dad, Stewart let out a moan. "No, not ma dad, he'll beat the livin' daylights out o' me."

"Should hae thocht o' that before, should you no?" And Doddie smiled a grin like poison coming to supper.

Tears started to roll down the boy's cheeks, and a new smell was added to the old as it became obvious that Stewart had shit himself at the mention of his dad.

"We'll take it from here, Mr Sinclair." Monica grabbed Stewart by the arm and marched him out of the office.

Doddie paused at the door, sniffed the air, and muttered sotto voce, "Really must think about what I'm feeding that dug."

They walked across the car park towards the car with Pistol following at the culprit's heels. Doddie reached for his car keys and hesitated.

"Really don't want you smellin' up my motor. Let's take a walk; it's not far."

It was only a short couple of blocks to Mr Patel's shop. The police officers pushed Stewart forward along the narrow gap between high shelves stacked to the rafters with cans, cereal boxes, and other household necessities. Mr Patel made his living out of what was forgotten at the supermarket; it was later bought at the corner store in the evening. The two officers ensured that the lanky, skinny, spotty-faced youth stood upright at the counter. Mr Patel was standing on the other side before them.

"Here's your thief, Mr Patel." Monica didn't mince words.

With his head down in shame and teardrops appearing again from the corners of his eyes, Stewart mumbled something towards the shopkeeper.

"Louder. Speak up, son." Doddie gave him a push.

"Ah'm sorry ah stole the vodka and the chocolate, Mr Patel. Please don't prosecute me."

Mr Patel turned up his nose as Monica placed the bottle and Mars bar wrapper on the counter.

"Get him out o' here; he stinks."

"No charges then?" questioned Doddie.

"Unless ye get that stinkin' thief oot o' here, I'll have ye afore the beak for disturbing the peace, OOT THE NOO!"

He pointed to the door.

The three found themselves back on the street.

"Awa hame and change yer claes. Ah niver want tae see ye again." Doddie slipped easily back into the dialect for effect.

Stewart, head down and tears streaming down his cheeks, turned on his heel and waddled his shitey way down the street, leaving Pistol wagging his tail at the two adults, expecting a reward for his good work. Doddie went back into the store.

"Got any doggie treats, Mr Patel?"

"Aye, on the shelf behind ye."

Doddie scanned the shelf behind him and grabbed a bag of "Good Dog Delicacies." He reached for his wallet.

"How much do I owe you?"

"On the house."

"Naw, I'll pay. Pistol cannae accept gifts."

Once they were outside the shop, Monica confronted her superior as they walked back to the school.

"You know, Boss, I would never speak against you in front of others, but why did you no apologise and clean up Pistol's shite in Sinclair's office?"

Doddie guffawed.

"Did you not notice the size of yon mannie's desk? Massive, eh? There's only one reason he needs a desk that big, and that is to intimidate any poor bugger who is hauled into his study to sit on the other side of it. No, no, Pistol did the right thing. Confucius says, 'The occasional dog shitting under your desk keeps you humble.' Yon mannie needed a quick clip around the ego. See the books on his bookshelf? Pretentious claptrap. Pistol was right to take a crap there as well."

Monica smirked.

"Are you saying Pistol can read?"

"Of course, he can." Doddie looked at Monica as if she was mad.

Immediately upon their return to the station, Chief Superintendent Brian Rowlands called them into the office. He was edgy and angry.

"Both of you are suspended as of now. Humiliation of a minor in front of his peers. Your damned dog defecating in the Headmaster's office. Sinclair is not happy. What did you think you were doing? What did you hope to achieve?"

Doddie spoke up. "Would you rather we had the lad prosecuted, hauled through an expensive court proceeding from which he is likely to learn very little? Come on, Sir, this is a far better solution."

"That's as maybe, but the Complaints Section don't see it that way. Hand over your badges and go home. I'll be in touch. You're suspended without pay."

"The rightness is located somewhere between the beauty of science and the science of beauty." – Christopher Hitchens

Chapter 3: Murder in Munlochy

Monica was livid as she drove home. She had done nothing wrong. The suspension was Doddie's fault. He hadn't even apologised to her; not a word of recalcitrance had passed his lips. Instead, he had smiled with blithe indifference, infuriating her more by his beatific grin, which always sprung to his face when he was convinced he was in the right. He was smug. She was annoyed.

Monica had been his bagman for the last eighteen months. Doddie had had a reputation for treating his offsiders like something smelly found on the sole of his shoe. But this relationship with Monica had gotten off to a different start. People suspected that Doddie was worried he would be accused of harassment and racism and had adjusted his temperament accordingly now that he was no longer dealing with young white males. But they were wrong. Although Monica was of West Indian descent and black, her Aberdeenshire accent was replete with words and phrases of the Doric dialect. Monica was tall and athletic. Her face was thin and narrow. Her eyes sparkled with cheekiness and fearlessness. Her long black hair, so frequently in a bun when she had been in uniform, now cascaded luxuriantly to her shoulders and below. She smirked often, but it was on the rare occasions that she beamed her full smile that she melted hearts. Her perfect white teeth suddenly made an appearance, her cheeks dimpled. Her co-workers, who were men, and some who were not, had been known to subconsciously break the pencil they were fiddling with when this happened. It was as if this duckling, determined on a façade of professional ugliness, suddenly became a swan. She was stunningly beautiful. One would suspect she was fighting off lustful manhood, or indeed the female equivalent, all the time, yet she maintained an aloofness, a professional distance she rarely allowed to weaken. Any prospective suitor, male or female, took this as a signal to stay away. So, stay away, they did.

And then there was her relationship with her boss, Doddie. She had bantered with him from day one, had not kowtowed, had not "yes boss, no boss-ed" him. She had told it how it was, and often she was right. Far from lack of respect, she respected him from the tip of his toes to the top of his greying temples. The feeling was mutual. Plus, Pistol had warmed to her from the beginning. On that first day of her new posting, Pistol had introduced himself to her before Doddie had reached her work station, wagging a greeting all the way from the neck backwards. The tail really did wag the dog.

"What's his name?" she asked as she made a fuss.

"Pistol, which is short for 'Pissed-All-Over-The-Place' 'cos that's what he does."

"Can't you train him?"

"Untrainable. Besides, why would I want to? He's a better detective than I am."

"In what way?"

"He can spot a rogue at one hundred yards; he runs up to him, cocks his leg, and pisses all over him. He's never wrong," Doddie said with a shrugging, subdued pride.

"I'm Detective Sergeant Monica Richards, your new bagman." She stretched out her hand. "Och, aye, and I am a black woman frae Aberdeenshire," she added with a challenging jut of the jaw.

He smiled and nodded. He was as oblivious to the colour of a person's skin as he was to his personal appearance. He simply did not care.

"How do or should I say 'fit like?' I'm Doddie Macfarlane, but these bastards call me 'Dodderin' Doddie and think that I don't know it." He raised his voice and glowered around the room as heads bowed in manufactured busyness. That was Doddie, the policeman.

On the first morning of their suspension, Monica was sat at home having a cup of tea, brooding still on the unfairness of the decision. The phone rang.

Doddie was sat in his large farmhouse kitchen. Before him, a sink full of dirty dishes and an empty glass and an emptier bottle of Chivas Regal were on the table. He had arrived home on the previous day at about 4.00 p.m. and eschewed the usual cup of tea and opened the bottle of whisky, putting the Chinese sweet and sour he had bought at his local takeaway into the fridge. The food remained there untouched, and the bottle was a pathetic, lonely reminder of a forgotten dinner. He knew that he had not made it into his bed but could not remember where he had slept, indeed if he had slept at all. Pistol was sat on the chair opposite him, head resting on the table with his left paw on top of it. For all the world, the dog looked like he was the one nursing the hangover. Doddie struggled to his feet, walked to the back door, opened it, and ushered his dog into the backyard. He broke into a sweat as he did it.

"Oot ye go."

Doddie reached for his cereal boxes and found himself gripping Bran Flakes. Screwing up his face, he thought better of it, placed it back on the shelf, and pulled up some Weetabix. He somehow found a clean bowl, deposited three biscuits, and poured some milk and sugar on top. He rummaged through the cutlery drawer and, miracle of miracles, found a clean spoon in the fork section. He sat down to eat. His spoon hovered over the mush for some ten seconds, after which he put it down and pushed the bowl away in disgust.

He heard Pistol scraping his paws on the back door. He opened it and let him in. He reached onto the floor for his doggie bowl and filled it with dog food which, he noted in passing, looked more appetizing than the Weetabix. For the briefest of moments, he considered eating it himself. He went to his lounge, swept several open newspapers off his couch, lay down, grabbed his remote, and switched on the TV.

The local news was full of the information that the salmon run up the River Ness was expected to be better than usual. An eccentric Nessie watcher had been arrested on the shores of Loch Ness, where his mission to spot the elusive monster had been interrupted by local police because he was naked except for binoculars and a pair of boots. The man appeared between two police officers with his "meat and two veggies" censored by a police cap. There was a complaint from an American tourist that the deep-fried Mars bar she had ordered at a local chip shop was not indeed a real Mars bar but rather a Milky Way, which presented as "false advertising" according to her. Inverness Caledonian Thistle, the Highland League Football team, were due to play away at Bruach Rangers on the coming weekend. The pundits expected the winner to be the team that coped best with the forecasted gale-force winds. Highland Rugby Club was conducting their annual haggis and neeps raffle. Somebody had dried their carpets in the drier at the town campsite and had broken it in the process. Mr Macleod, the owner, was demanding compensation. From whom he was demanding remained unclear. The carpet washer had done so in the wee sma' hours but not yet appeared to pick the carpet up.

Doddie's head pounded. He needed water and a strong cup of coffee. He creaked to his feet and made his way into the kitchen to put the kettle on. He rummaged in his cupboard for some instant coffee, found a jar of Nescafé, only to discover it was empty. He swore and was about to hurl the empty jar across the room when his mobile phone rang.

"What the hell are ye callin' me fur, Richards? We're fuckin' suspended."

"And a good morning to you too, Boss, who rattled your cage?"

There was silence and an intake of breath on the other end of the line.

"Aww, supper frae a bottle and nae caffeine in the hoose. Sorry about that. What can I dae fer ye, lassie?"

"We're nae langer suspended, Boss, been a murder in Munlochy. Seems they need us, want us back."

Doddie went silent again.

"Are you there, Boss?"

"Aye, I'm here. How come they rang you first and no me?"

"They tried, but you werena pickin' up. They want us at Munlochy asap. Can you pick me up at the railway station car park, by the statue?"

"Aye, aye, grab me a coffee and a bacon butty, and I'll be there in an hour."

As he emerged from the shower, which he had deliberately run cold, Doddie reflected that he was now likely to be present at a first. He doubted that the quiet community of Munlochy had ever had a murder before. Stealing women's lingerie off the washing line and wrapping lit fireworks in bread for the seagulls would have been as heinous as it would have got there. Even Doddie, with his capital solution for every crime, recognised that his slogan of "hanging's too good fer them" would have been a step too far.

He grabbed Pistol, and they both bundled themselves into his 2002 Mini Cooper. Slowly they wended their way along the narrow B-road, past The Royal Society for the Protection of Birds car park at the north end of the loch and up the hill to join the main road into the town.

As he drove into Inverness, he pondered how anybody could get murdered in a wee community like Munlochy. He pictured the village, the white houses, the small parcel of social housing, the Knockbain kirk, and the peanut-shaped bay that led out towards the Moray Firth. "Done in for shopping on a Sunday?" he voiced aloud and chuckled to himself, which produced an unwelcome rush of blood to his aching head. Those days of the Wee Frees locking up swings in the kids' playgrounds on the Sabbath were long gone. Now your religion was your own. There was no longer a community out to shame people who put their washing on the line or watered their garden when they were supposed to be devoting their day to praising the Lord.

Doddie had grown up in a household where his dad had professed that going to Church was a good thing to do. His mum had been on the same page. They had always intended to take their only son along to one of the Sunday services at their local kirk. But it was always maybe next week or next month or just around the corner of a new beginning. Inevitably, what had happened was that his dad would walk down to the local shop on thc high street of Nairn, buy a selection of Sunday newspapers, make himself a pot of tea, put up his feet, and read them. Meanwhile, his mum would busy herself cooking the Sunday lunch, always traditional roast beef, potatoes, carrots, and lashings of gravy. From an early age, Doddie had been left to his own devices on Sunday mornings. He often took himself down to the seafront to meet his pals, Calum and Colin. There they would search for crabs, chuck stones in the water, and search the bushes by the local pitch and putt for any errant golf balls to retrieve. Doddie was under strict instructions to be home for a late lunch, but he needed no reminder. He loved his Sunday lunch with his mum and dad. The conversation around the table was always lively, inevitably filled with topics from the news, but it was never totally adult-centred, and Doddie had relished the time with his parents where he felt like an equal. Afterwards, he and his dad would fill the sink and carry on their chat while they washed up while his mum put her feet up in front of the TV. There the chat would be about sport and school and high jinks with his mates and stories from his dad's school days. It was, in many ways, an idyllic childhood. Now, looking back, Doddie often wondered where and when he had acquired that hard edge of cynicism and lack of respect for authority. He figured he had been created as a beautiful jewel in his upbringing, a salad green gem, a smoothed and perfected emerald that eventually had been battered, bruised, and soiled in his early army training. He smiled at the concept of the diamond in the rough; he had had his rough edges manicured and perfected, and then the army had taken hold and sharpened a battered beauty until it was worse than its origins. He was the perfect diamond incongruously made into a rougher version. His life had been the reverse of what it should have been. Basic training was not that hard for Doddie. He gave himself extra motivation to achieve, trying to overcome the spoilt reputation of the only child. His childhood upbringing had civilised him; his career choice had undone almost all that good work.

His eyes scanned the station car park for Monica, but there was no sign. He pulled up and waited. He then pulled over behind the statue of the Highland soldier at the railway station. He peered for Monica out of the passenger side window and was irritated that she was nowhere to be seen. He failed to notice the approaching traffic warden, who was suddenly standing at his driver's side in the process of writing him a ticket. He wound down his window.

"If yon ticket is for me, then I'm goin' tae shove it where the sun don't shine, sunshine."

"You are illegally parked, Sir, and as such, I hiv nae choice," he smirked.

Doddie was tempted to reach for his ID, but instead, he smiled back at him. The traffic warden was nonplussed.

"You look very happy, Sir."

"I am, I am. I am over fifty years old, and I still have it."

"Have what, Sir?"

"I still have the ability to spot a total fuckin' arsehole when I meet one."

At that, Mr Officious Face flushed, and his visage darkened. Just then, Monica appeared from the station entrance, balancing two cups of coffee, one on top of the other, her chin pressing on the top one to keep it stable, and holding two bags of food in the other hand. She came around to the driver's side, where the uniform was standing. Doddie reached out, grabbed the top coffee, and took a sandwich bag.

"Thanks, Detective Sergeant Richards," he said with emphasis on the "detective sergeant."

"No problem, Detective Inspector," she replied with equal emphasis on his rank; she guessed what was happening.

Doddie turned his attention to the traffic warden.

"Now piss off and find another victim and, next time, before you reach for your pen and wee book, engage in some pleasantries and human contact."

"I'll report you for this," the red-faced gauleiter spluttered.

"Be our guest, and don't forget to take yer foot oot of yer mouth afore ye dae so. We're in a rush; we have a crime to solve."

They drove slowly out of the car park.

"So, whit do ye know aboot it?"

"Not much. Male in his late-thirties. Found face down in a field. No ID. No weapon as yet. Looks like a blow to the head and a stab to the heart."

They were entering the south end of the Kessock Bridge with the Inverness Caledonian Thistle football ground on the right.

"Hopefully, some of oor people are already on the scene. Don't want some teuchter plod tramping all ower the evidence, do we?"

"Dinnae worry. SOCO is there. As is the boss."

Doddie groaned. "That's all we need, Rowlands with his by the book ramblings and his size twelve ego getting in the way."

Chief Superintendent Brian Rowlands was not the man to skimp on the rules. That was why he had no option but to suspend Doddie and Monica on the previous day. But he knew he needed all hands on deck for the upcoming murder inquiry and that it would look bad on him if his two best detectives were both suspended when a murderer was on the loose, particularly given the reason for their suspension. Rowlands was an angst-ridden individual who would have inwardly debated his decision for some time before doing the right thing and calling them back in. Rowlands, known to all as "Barney

Rubble," had a bare, polished and tidy desk, the victim of an undiagnosed Obsessive Compulsive Disorder. A pencil, eraser, and ruler were set out on a blotter like a table set for dinner. There was also a picture of him on his wedding day with "Betty Rubble" looking far too bonnie, slender, and smiling. She was a catch and no mistake. The surprise was that Rowlands had caught her since he was not exactly George Clooney. He had two cauliflower ears, victims of a less than stellar rugby career, spent propping Highland RFC 3rd XV. These could have remained innocuous and unnoticed had they not been Prince Charles like in their protuberance, TV satellite dishes. Then there was the broken nose that had never been fixed matched with the one cross-eye. In sharp contrast, his pearly white teeth were so obviously not his own. Doddie had once muttered to himself when he thought nobody was in earshot that he had "a face that launched a thousand shits," a phrase that had gone the rounds of the station for some time before it had finally petered out. Yet he had courted and eventually married Belinda Rowlands. Pigs did indeed fly.

Doddie had no time for psychological bafflegab. To him, his boss was too neatly "by the book," a mind too cluttered with things that didn't matter, which got in the way of seeing things that did. It was hard to respect him because he had married the boss's daughter several years before. Belinda Rowlands, nee Urquhart, was the daughter of Stewart Urquhart, the high heidyin of the Highlands and Islands section of Police Scotland. Marrying Belinda had not exactly resulted in promotion up the ranks, but it certainly had helped. A silver spoon in one's mouth is never a bad move, even if it is somebody else's.

As they turned east towards the village, Monica watched as Doddie gobbled his butty and drank his coffee, all the while driving far too fast.

"You had your supper oot o' a bottle last nicht, did ye no?"

"You should be a detective," Doddie remarked sardonically, then loudly cursed as coffee spilt onto his lap. He changed the subject.

"The Black Isle, huh? Says a lot about the inhabitants that they don't even know that it isnae an island, let alone black. The Cromarty Firth tae the north, the Moray Firth to the south, and a fuckin' main road hammering up and down to the west. Maybe they couldna spell bloody 'peninsula.' God save us frae teuchters. You put they country bumpkins in a barrel of breasts, and they'll come up sucking their thumbs."

They neared the village.

"Where's the body?"

Monica looked at the Google map on her phone.

"Doon the road to the bay. Turn off to the right at the next junction."

As they slowly bumped their way down the farm track, they spotted all the trappings of a crime scene in a field—two boys in blue on the farm gate, a crime scene tent, and white-suited boffins appearing now and then from behind the curtain. Rowlands was sat on a shooting stick like a conductor on a podium, although it looked like the orchestra could manage perfectly well without him. Everyone was going about their business. Their car pulled up.

Monica and Doddie got out. They nodded at the shooting stick and synchronized their greeting.

"Sir."

"They don't know when he passed away, but he has a blow to the head and a stab to the heart."

Doddie and Monica moved towards the tent and out of the Rowlands's earshot.

Doddie muttered to Monica, "Passed away, passed a-fuckin'-way! What does he mean? He caught a bus and passed away somewhere else? The guy was bloody killed, brutally murdered; no gentle death in his bed for this guy. Gimme a break, 'passed away' indeed. He's dead, broon breid, deid as a fuckin' doornail. Passed away?" And he lapsed into disgruntled silence as they donned their crime scene suits and pulled back the tent flap.

"Wait there, Pistol. And leave Rowlands alone."

"Deadpan" Dick McIvor greeted them both with a nod.

"Before ye ask, not sure when he died. Heavy blow to the head with a stab wound to the heart to make sure. Must have rolled him over post mortem for what reason, I do not know. Only thing I found on him was this ticket to the game between Caley and Bruach, in which case, the killer probably did him a favour. That was a joke. Sort of gallows humour we, in the profession, call Celtic noir, but you would call it 'gallows humour.' It helps us deal with traumatic situations." McIvor gave them a wide grin, a smile like poison coming to supper.

Before them, face down with arms and legs akimbo, lay the body of a young man of not yet forty years of age. His eyes were still open expectantly, his mouth gaped wide, and there was a notable absence of blood. Monica was quick to sense that this murder had taken place at a different scene.

"Thanks, McIvor. Let's you and I tak a dander and get a feel for the scene, Richards."

With that, they left the tent, discarded their crime scene suits, and walked down to the seashore. They needed to know several things, most of which would come out from the coroner's report. But Doddie and Monica saw the science as a support for their instincts and experience as a mere confirmation of their intuitions. They had played their hunches over the years and found that although these attributes had moved them in strange and mysterious ways, they often found themselves in an endgame that resulted in a prosecution and a prison sentence for some poor sap who had failed to take account of every eventuality.

Rowlands was still sat on his shooting stick, giving the impression that he was a true leader when he might as well have been a bird on a wire for all the attention that anybody in this now-crowded crime scene was giving him.

Doddie and Monica strolled the five hundred yards or so down to the seafront, casually scanning the ground as they travelled. Of course, larger numbers of their colleagues would soon arrive to comb the area in an orderly and scientific manner, but who knows what a cursory glance might turn up.

"Could do wi' findin' a murder weapon," Monica voiced what they were both thinking.

"Pistol's a great asset wi' findin' people, but I dinnae ken aboot knives and the like," Doddie said, reaching down and tousling his head. Pistol looked up with what approximated a smile.

They were soon upon the strand, strolling aimlessly amongst the rocks and the rock pools, looking for a bloody rock or, better still, a knife.

"We don't even know whether he was killed in situ," muttered Doddie despondently.

"I noticed no blood, Boss. I think he was killed elsewhere and brought here."

"Things will look up when McIvor gets his claws into him back at the morgue. Let's head back over the bridge and head into the station and, at least, see if we can get our badges back from Rowlands."

"Reading between the lines, listening between the lines." — Robert Ludlum

Chapter 4: Demons and Deceit

Monica and Doddie arrived at the station to find it in a buzz of activity. People were walking and talking with purpose, and there was an intensity about the computer activity that befitted the beginning of a murder investigation. Doddie almost collided with a colleague as they came through the doors onto the main floor.

"Is Rowlands here?" asked Monica.

"Aye. He's in his office. Just got in ahead of you."

They knocked on his door, and a voice beckoned them in. They entered but could not see anybody. They looked around and suddenly heard a chant emanating from behind his desk. On peering around the edge, they found their boss in the lotus position.

"Helps me think," he said as he unravelled himself.

"We've come to get our badges back, Boss," Monica spoke.

"Help me up, Macfarlane."

Doddie reached down and grabbed Rowlands's outstretched arm. He groaned as Doddie pulled and fell back down again. Monica raced in, grabbed the other arm, and they both pulled Rowlands upright. As soon as he was standing, he groaned some more and put both his hands on his hips as he eased himself into a more erect position. He grimaced and grunted.

"Yoga keeps you supple and flexible. You should both try it."

Doddie and Monica looked at each other unconvinced.

Rowlands sat down at his desk.

"Here's yours, Richards. Sit down, Macfarlane. Richards, you can go," he said as he handed her badge and ID to her.

Monica frowned and hesitated. Doddie looked confused but sat down. Monica left the room.

"Well, now, Macfarlane, how are you doing?"

"I'm fine. Get to the point, Sir."

Rowlands looked and sounded ill at ease.

"You have to get counselling before you get your badge back, Macfarlane. Message from on high. Your demons are there for all to see. They impact your judgment. You're not back at work until you've sat down with our resident shrink. Dr Martin Nunn is in his office on the sixth floor awaiting your arrival as we speak. Let "Mental" Martin lay to rest some of your demons, Macfarlane, and then you'll get your badge back. Off you go."

Monica was waiting for him as he left.

"And the verdict is?"

"No badge fur me until I have had a wee chat with Mental Martin. You're on yer ain, lassie."

And with that, he turned on his heel and headed off to make his peace with the main "trick cyclist" of the Inverness Constabulary.

On opening Mental Martin's door, Doddie was confronted by a newspaper behind a desk. Two arms were outstretched, the face hidden behind the newsprint. Doddie was brought up short. He didn't know whether to wait to be asked to sit down or to take a seat anyway. He did not know whether he should announce his presence, return to the door and slam it to show that he had entered or what to do. Eventually, Mental Martin's face appeared from the other side of the paper, left eye twitching a la Patrick Moore on *The Sky at Night* or Police Chief Charles Dreyfus driven wild by Clouseau in the *Pink Panther* movies.

"Try to attract my attention," he said, then disappeared back behind the paper again and resumed reading. Doddie would typically have shown no patience with such psychobabble, such puerile attempts at analysis, but he desperately wanted his job back, so he felt he had to go along with the farce. He ran his fingers through his hair, pondering his next move and put his hand in his suit pocket. There he found the cigarette lighter he had confiscated from a schoolgirl smoker they had run into during the thieving incident. The temptation was too much. He pulled it out of his pocket, flipped it open, and lit a corner of Mental Martin's paper.

The effect was remarkable; the paper quickly flared. Mental Martin screamed in alarm and leapt out of his chair. He thrust the fiery newspaper into the nearest garbage bin and stamped vigorously on it like a Zulu warrior dancing on thorns to harden his feet, all the time shouting at the top of his voice, "I loved your reaction, DI Macfarlane; just what I would have expected from a man of your type. Excellent, excellent, excellent. Ouch, ouch, ouch, 'fraid I've burnt my fingers. The fire alarm didn't go off. Be so good as to tell my secretary that everything is fine. Thank you."

Doddie went to the door, stuck his head around it, and explained to his male secretary, a young intern by the name of Umbago Lombard, that there was nothing to worry about. He had not been concerned in the first place, but now he was confused and more than a little concerned.

Doddie returned to the inner office to find Mental Martin with his hands under the cold-water tap. He was obviously in some pain, so Doddie felt a smidge guilty.

"Can I help, Doc?"

"Aye, just reach into my right-hand drawer, and you'll find some alcohol and Blistex. Arrrgh, I think I may have blisters on my fingertips. Ow! Ouch!"

Doddie reached into the drawer, found the First Aid kit, put it on the desk, and opened it. He looked up to find Mental Martin dabbing his hands and fingers dry. Doddie examined the kit's contents and pulled out some antiseptic cream and plasters.

"Can't find any alcohol." Doddie had expected a small container of medical alcohol.

"No, no, it's separate from the kit. Go back to the drawer."

Doddie returned to the drawer and found a bottle of Dalwhinnie 12-Year-Old.

He held up the whisky.

"Is this what you meant?"

"Aye, aye, bring it over."

Mental Martin reached under the sink, carefully managing and dabbing gingerly at his damaged fingers with the towel he had retrieved from below. He then reached up into the cupboard above and produced two glasses of the finest crystal. He poured himself a large glass and downed it quickly.

"Let's have a dram, and we'll get down to business."

He poured two generous measures. Mental Martin again downed his and poured himself another.

"This will save bothering with the antiseptic and the plasters. Go grab a chair, and we'll do the chat thing."

Doddie had heard about the doctor's eccentric behaviour but was nevertheless reluctant to betray his innermost secrets when he had burnt the guy's fingers, and he had downed a couple of doubles and was, by the looks of it, pouring himself more. But Doddie wanted to be back at work, so he saw no alternative. He made himself comfortable and prepared to bear his soul.

"Tell me about your military experiences."

"From the beginning?"

"Aye, aye, we'll have some laughs."

Doddie was taken aback by this statement but rationalized that all he wanted out of this chat was the piece of paper allowing him to go back to work.

"Basic training was good, but there was an incident that has remained with me."

"Take your time and tell me about it," Mental Martin said, trying to look seriously interested while pouring them both another whisky.

"Well, it was our passing out parade. My parents were there. As a close-knit group of young soldiers, we were proud of our achievement. We were on parade in our dress uniforms. We marched with precision. We were finally dismissed and allowed to visit with our friends and relatives. A wonderful evening ensued. At the end of it, I was walking back to the barracks and needed to take a crap. So, there was a porta-potty handy, and I dove in there to do my business. I was sat still. I was reflecting on the day. Suddenly, I felt the outhouse move. I heard the noise of an engine. I heard ropes banging on the outside. I shouted, but the noise from the equipment muffled my words. I felt myself being hoisted into the air. I couldn't open the door. I soon realised that I was on the back of a truck, and we were about to move. I waited until we were at our destination. Then I shouted and banged on the door but to no avail. The truck was parked and locked in, and I had to come to terms with the fact that I was there for the night. Morning came. I heard the gates open and somebody whistling. I started banging and shouting again, and eventually, somebody came, and I was released. I will never enter a porta-potty again unless you hypnotise me away from the fear."

There was silence for a long moment. Looking over at Mental Martin, Doddie realised he was desperately trying to focus his sight and fumbling for words.

Eventually, he said, "No shit, Doddie."

"Well, actually, I did, but I had no intention of spending the night wi' it."

"Aye, aye, aye, I guess, I guess, you must, you must have PTSD."

"Yesss, yess, Doddie Macfarlane can now add to his medal tally and put PTSD after his name," slurred Doddie. "Post-Toilet Stress Syndrome," he added.

Mental Martin started to chuckle. He tried to control himself, but soon a belly laugh could be contained no longer. He stood up and stumbled over to Doddie, who staggered to his feet. Mental Martin put his arms around his shoulders, and both were bent double with tears and laughter emanating from them. Soon they were dancing around the room shoulder to shoulder.

"Post-Toilet Stress Syndrome. Heh! Post-Toilet Stress Syndrome. Heh!"

They kicked up their feet and danced and sang. Eventually, they fell back onto the couch, and Doddie whispered in Mental Martin's ear.

"I, I love you. Will you, can you sign me off?"

"Yessh! Yessh! Let me find the form."

There was a knock at the door, and Umbago camc in, at which point Doddie and Mental Martin were sat on the floor, leaning on the desk, with their legs splayed in front of them and glasses of whisky tipped at a dangerous angle.

"Your next appointment is here, Dr Nunn."

"Tell him or her, I'm, I'm 'Nunn' too well. 'Nunn' too well. Get it, Umbago?"

A fit of giggles and an appreciative slap on the back from Doddie, "And shhhhhh, hhhe has to fuck off and come, come again anither, anither fuckin' time," Mental Martin slurred.

He then stood up with difficulty, stumbled over to his desk, and rummaged amidst a sea of papers. Triumphant, he held it up.

"Here it is. HAH! Here too is a pen. And here, D-D-Doddie, is a signature."

He signed with a flourish.

"I pronounce you man and job; you may kiss the certificate."

He gave Doddie his licence to work, put his arms around him, and accompanied him to the door.

Umbago, smart in his suit, was sat at the reception desk typing up reports when the drunk middle-aged men appeared arm in arm before him.

He looked a bit fazed by what he had just witnessed but was resolved to be professional.

"Um-Um-Umbago, thissssh ish the finesht mental doctor that ever lived."

"And, and Ummmmmbago Lllllombardon me, this is the politest, perfectest policeman that ever plodded the str, str, the roads of Inver—Inver—ness. Good luck, danderin' dodderin' Doddie."

And Doddie left.

"Try to see what everyone has seen and then think what nobody has thought."
– Lester Sinclair

Chapter 5: Identity Crisis

First thing on the following morning, Doddie presented himself, certificate in hand, at Rowlands's office. He stood before Rowlands's desk and held out his handwritten certificate. Rowlands read it aloud.

"I, Dr Martin Nunn, hiv interviewed and examined Detectiveive Inspector Doddie Macfarlane and have found his sound mind to be of sound mind. He is, herewith and forthwith, to be deemed fit for duty, for fit for duty he is.

Yours lovingly, Dr Martin Nunn (Signature)."

"This is the weirdest, misspelt, badly-constructed professional letter I have read, but I do recognise the signature, so I guess I have to accept it. Welcome back, Macfarlane. We need you."

With that, he handed him his ID, and Doddie went off to find Monica. She was huddled over her computer screen.

"Coroner's Report. Neither the blow to the head nor the knife wound killed him. The wounds were likely inflicted post mortem. Looks like he died of a heart attack. Still no news as to his identity?"

"We'll post a picture and ask for the public's help." Monica nodded wisely at Doddie's plan.

"Did our guys turn up anything at the scene?"

"They found a blue silk scarf and a Safeway sandwich with a bite out of it. McIvor has organised for the sandwich to be tested for DNA."

"Anything from Missing Persons?"

"Aye. Three fellows of similar age. Two are accounted for. One of them turned up on the North Sea rigs; the other turned up shacked up with a stripper he met while on holiday in Edinburgh, so he never returned home. The third is an Irish footballer called Aidan Cullimore. He has just been signed by Bruach Rangers and has not appeared for training."

"That sounds like a good lead. Let's follow up with blood type and a chat with the family."

Suddenly, standing next to them was a blue uniform. Doddie jumped involuntarily, and Monica took a step backwards.

"Jesus, Chris, I wish you wouldnae dae that. Make some noise and gie us a warning."

"Sorry, Boss, but I have the phone number of Aidan Cullimore's parents in West Belfast if you want to phone them," "Crawlin" Chris, the station sycophant, did his best Uriah Heep imitation and ever so "umbly" took himself off back to his station, almost bowing, beatifically gifting all with a view of his yellowing teeth with the gap at the front.

"Pull up a chair at my station, and we'll give them a call," Doddie said to Monica.

"Have a word wi' Chris, Richards, and fix him up wi' a dentist; might help wi' his bad breath and his appearance."

"That's suddenly become my job?" Monica gave him a look of "no way."

"Okay, okay, I'll tell the bugger. Just thought it might be better coming from a woman."

"'Chris would get the wrong idea. I wud rather find a body in a sewer than have Chris slobberin' and lustin' efter me."

Doddie reached for the phone and dialled. Monica heard the pick-up.

"Hello, this is Detective Inspector Macfarlane of Police Scotland; who am I speaking to?" Doddie spoke clearly, doing his best to lose the dialect and as much of his accent. The effect produced a grimace from Monica.

"Ah, yer spekkin' wath Sean Cullimore an' no mistik."

"Are you related to Aidan Cullimore?"

"Rye aiftre spikkin to Aidan, hee's not hair, he's efter gone to Scatland. Ah'm his daaa, so ah am."

Doddie held the phone away from his ear, put his eyes to the heavens, and looked at Monica.

"Are you his father, Mr Cullimore?"

"Aye, ah jest sed so, sure ah did. Do they hand out braaaains in the Scattish Constabulary?"

"Can you speak more slowly, Mr Cullimore? I'm having difficulty understanding you."

"Ah thaat ye spak English over there in Scatland, so ye did."

"I'm going to hang up now, Mr Cullimore, and get somebody else to speak to you in a few minutes. Don't move far from the phone."

"Shar an' ma phone is always in ma back pucket, so it is. Whar else wad it be?" And he hung up.

Doddie spoke to Monica. "We need a translator. Can you get me one?"

"What, Mandarin, Urdu, Cantonese?"

Doddie looked at her as if she was crazy.

"No, fuckin' Northern Irish! Ah' cannae unnerstan' a word the bastard's saying."

"Ah," Monica smiled. "I'll see what I can do." She stood up and moved away. In moments, she was back accompanied by a red-haired, freckle-faced twenty-something. "This is Constable Dermot Long. He's from Belfast."

Doddie explained what he needed from him, so Dermot sat down and dialled the number. Doddie and Monica decided against listening in on the speakerphone but became frustrated at what was obviously a chat about the weather, the local economy, the recent football results, and local characters. Both were laughing at some colourful in-joke when Doddie tapped him on the shoulder, indicating that he should get on with it.

The outcome was that Mr Cullimore had not heard from his son for several days now. He was not worried about this because he was not the most communicative of his children (he and his wife had five). So, they were not concerned. What was all of this about? Could Mr Cullimore send them over a recent photo of Aidan so that they could take him off what could eventually be a Missing Persons list? Yes, he would do that right away, and it was "nace talken'" to all ye friendly peple from Scatland, so it was. And he hung up.

About thirty minutes later, a picture came through on the station's fax machine. Monica picked it up, smiled, and walked over to Doddie.

"What are you grinnin' at?" Doddie was irritated.

"He's not our victim, Boss." She showed him the picture. Aidan Cullimore was a turbaned Sikh, an obvious product of the sub-continent, with thin brown features, a black beard, and sparkling eyes. He was obviously an adopted son while their dead victim was white, most clearly, a Caucasian.

Monica saw Doddie's blood rise as he grabbed the picture and walked briskly to Dermot's desk.

"Did ye not ask Cullimore for a description of his son?"

"Yes, Sir, I did." Dermot saw and was taken aback by the anger in Doddie's features and voice.

"Does this photograph match it?"

Dermot looked long and hard at the picture and muttered to himself, "Sikh religion, yes, Indian extraction, yes, adopted son, yes." He handed back the picture. "That's pretty much the description I was given over the phone, Sir."

Doddie blew up.

"You're a fuckin' eejut. There are pictures all over this station of our murder victim. It's a bloody wallpaper design, for Christ's sake. We've just wasted valuable time trying to find out if this guy was him or not." And he punched the picture before screwing it up and throwing it into the rubbish bin. He stomped back to his station, hearing the plaintiff Ulster accent following him.

"Ye never told me who and why we were looking for the murder victim, Sir. I thought this was just a Missing

Persons case. How was I to know?" he said with arms spread wide in exasperation.

"Were you standing in the wrong queue when they handed oot the brains? You, fuckin' Irish bampot."

Doddie turned his back on him, then suddenly stopped and turned to face Dermot again.

"Sorry. That was racist. Apologies. I'll try again. You fuckin' bampot."

"Sooooo," Monica intervened, "we picked the wrang tree up which to bark."

"Aye," Doddie was pensive. "Let's go visit McIvor at the morgue; might cheer me up," he said loudly, as he pointedly glared in Dermot's direction.

*"Never touch mud with gloves on;
the gloves get muddier; the mud
doesn't get glovier." – Molnar*

Chapter 6: A Breakthrough

Monica had a heart of gold. When she loved, her passion was intense. When she cared, her commitment went deep. She always had friends because she knew how to be a friend. She was loyal and showed her loyalty by having the backs of all her colleagues, especially Doddie. It was not just because he was her boss; it went deeper than that. She could not have explained it if she had been put on the spot. She knew, however, that she enjoyed his blunder and bluster. She knew too that she was not attached to a rising star; those days were long gone for Doddie, but certainly to one who always, unlike many of her other colleagues, came up with an arrest and almost always a conviction when he saw that a court case was inevitable. She was pragmatic and realistic and knew that she had the opportunity to learn from the best. But apart from all that, she sensed that here was a man who was sensitive, scarred, and basically unsure of himself. Her inner self wanted to reach out and protect him from himself, primarily, but from others as well. Deep down, she looked upon Doddie as the dad she had once had but who had left her far too soon.

Before Inverness, Monica had been a uniformed policewoman in the small Aberdeenshire town of Turriff.

Not much to police there except the odd "dine and dash" from the local cafés and the occasional domestic or party feud that often resulted in a car being keyed and a whole lot of shouting and swearing. Even as a young PC, she had not looked at the book of rules as a Bible but more as a guideline and, latterly, a script to be ignored. So, the dine and dashers, mostly teenage rebels, were caught and carted off to the local café and set to work washing dishes for a couple of days. The key scrapers became gophers for the local car body shops. There were no criminal records for these kids, just a watchful eye, a word of warning, and a consequence that came from the book of common sense. Not without affection did she become known as the "Turra Coo." Mothers used to threaten their naughty children, saying, "Behave yersel or ah'll send the Turra Coo efter ye."

It would be wonderful to say that Monica's fame spread far and wide, except there was no far and wide in Turriff. It was a sleepy wee place in a county famed for its farmland, its prison at Peterhead, the oil industry in Aberdeen, the fish at Fraserburgh, the Royals at Balmoral who used to disembark from the now-defunct Royal Yacht in Aberdeen Harbour ("The Queen cam' in wi' the fush this morning"), and part of the Cairngorms National Park.

The statue of the "Turra Coo," the Turriff cow, stood between two shopping streets. Monica knew that being called a "coo" in Turriff was not an insulting defamation. This was a statue of a true hero, one likely to outlast those of Edward Colston and Winston Churchill in the virtue-signalling days to come.

So, Monica had done all there was to do in Turriff, but then a new-born bairn had done all there was to do in Turriff. She sat her sergeant's exams and moved to the steamy, seamy town of Inverness, where major crimes were graffiti and salmon poaching on the River Ness that ran through the centre of the town. There she had settled, and there she had met Doddie.

On the disturbing side of the profession, she had learned to accept that death was part of the job. She had seen, in Turriff, the result of a road traffic accident. Two young men speeding on a rural road, a swerve too late, and the terrible destruction of the branches of a tree through the windscreen was gruesome indeed. These had been the first dead bodies she had seen. She did not know what to expect when she entered the mortuary. She was surprised when she saw the dismemberment and the disfigurement that she had not lost control of herself. At that moment, she had forced herself to be the model professional, immersed in the administration of the job; she had successfully overcome her feelings of faintness and nausea. She had reached for her notepad and penned notes she might use later. She had left, returned to the small police station in Turriff, dropped off her stuff, stopped at the local Indian takeaway on the way home, and followed this by picking up a bottle of wine. She settled down in her small flat, drank her wine, ate her food, and watched an old tape she had of a tribute to the Swedish pop group, ABBA. She had danced alone through "Dancing Queen," frenetically and frantically pushing chairs over. She had wept and hugged herself through "Fernando." She had passed out on the couch as the last chords of "Knowing Me, Knowing You" faded into the distance. In the morning, with a throat like a wrestler's jockstrap and a head like being in a church bell tower on a Sunday, she had greased herself a fried breakfast, black coffee, and a cold shower. She was ready for work. She arrived at the office for all intents and purposes looking like she had been a judge at the Turriff Flower Show the day before and not a viewer of dead youth gone before its time. From that moment, she had resolved to become a homicide detective. She had not known why a traffic accident had pushed her in that direction except that while looking at the torn flesh and crushed bones on the slab, she had an undiminished curiosity to understand what part of the crash was responsible for which wound. Was it the steering wheel that had crushed the ribs and heart? Was it the windshield that had fractured the skulls? She realised then and there that she was capable of an indefatigable curiosity that by far overrode any sadness at a tragedy, any dismay at mangled flesh.

Doddie had seen so much death. But death in war seemed so much different from that in peace. Bodies by a Basra road, soldiers on a Falklands moor did not shock like the body of an unidentified male found in a quiet backwater in the north of Scotland.

Their John Doe was naked on the slab as they entered. His torso and head had been stitched back together after 'McIvor's post mortem. McIvor was hosing the surfaces. He greeted them with joyful bonhomie.

"Ahh, Macfarlane and Richards. Live people with whom I can talk. The beauty of the dead is that they don't answer back; the beauty of the living is that they do. I have news for you that you may or may not like. Using my eagle eye, my remarkable attention to detail and my incurable curiosity, I found some pieces of a plant under yer man's nails. Lab identifies it as saxifrage, an Arctic high ground plant. John Doe here had been dead for about a week when he was found. Saxifrage Paniculata, 'broken rock tufts' to anglicize the name, will grow on high ground. It is self-pollinating. It hugs rocks 'cos it doesn't like to be too wet. Important to you, I think, is that it is likely to be found on high ground in an Arctic climate. May I suggest a bit of a trip to the Cairngorms National Park in your hunt for the killer?"

It was Doddie who spoke first. "So what are you suggesting? That he was killed in the Cairngorms and dumped in Munlochy?"

McIvor shook his head. "This man was not murdered. Absolutely not. He died of natural causes—a myocardial infarction—a heart attack to you. The blow to the back of the head and the stab wound both occurred after his death. The post mortem wounds appear as if the perpetrator or plural were frustrated at his death and felt cheated of some form of vengeance."

He finished his explanation and turned to find that Pistol had wandered into the room.

"What the fuck? How did that creetur get in here? He'll mess up my whole environment. Get his nose oot o' my entrails!" Pistol had found a blood-filled, gut-filled galvanized bucket on the floor.

"This is a place of humanity, nae a place for canine carnivores," McIvor said, hurling a small hammer at the dog. He missed, and Pistol looked up with a quizzical yet impish grin and pissed on the leg of the table.

"See, see, he likes you." McIvor was clenching his fists, and his red face looked ready to erupt.

Doddie put up his hands. "Okay, okay, we're goin'. Come awa' ben, Richards, let's tak a dander up the Cairngorms, shall we?" He said this in his best Aberdeenshire accent, his attempt at the Doric.

Monica and Doddie hastily retreated to the car park. Doddie was chuckling.

"Nae so 'deadpan' at the end was he?"

"Boss, we're just off suspension; do you not think we need to tread gently for a while?"

Doddie dismissed her with a wave.

"Och, McIvor will never be a problem. He and I go back a long way. He doesn't know that I know, but he was having a bit of a fling with my ex-wife afore she left me. Us, treading on eggshells? I think not. I know he feels guilty about it. Personally, I understand. Sheena and I were finished, and she still is a very good looking woman. Let's get permission to climb the Cairngorms. It's a beautiful day for a drive to Tomintoul. I know somebody there who can help."

"Tis known by the name of perseverance in a good cause and obstinacy in a bad one." – Laurence Sterne

Chapter 7: A Mountain of Evidence

Monica and Doddie received permission and funding to travel to the Cairngorms National Park for a couple of nights. Monica booked herself into The Glenavon Hotel in Tomintoul while Doddie enigmatically said that he had "other arrangements." Uncharacteristically, he was whistling as he left Rowlands's office.

"No time like the present, Richards. Let's hit the road."

Dermot was heard singing sotto voce, "And don't you come back no more, no more, no more."

They reached the car park, the sun was shining, the blue was in its heaven, and there was a faint skip in Doddie's step. Everything was seemingly right with his world. Monica followed in his footsteps, pondering the unaccustomed jocularity.

Doddie unlocked his car door. They had been offered an unmarked police car, but Doddie opted for the petrol allowance and to use his own. Monica dropped her overnight case on the back seat amongst the chip papers and Macdonald's wrappers. Pistol hopped in and nestled himself comfortably among the detritus.

Doddie dropped his rucksack in the boot. Having negotiated the early morning traffic, they soon rose above the town, past Culloden Muir and en route to Carrbridge. As they found the freedom of the open road, Doddie asked Monica to search the glove box for some music to play. She found a dozen CDs, all of them Bruce Springsteen.

"Only 'The Boss' here, Boss," she wrinkled her nose.

"Is there anybody else?" quipped Doddie. "*Born to Run*, please, would seem appropriate. Never say 'only' when Bruce Springsteen is involved."

And so, they made steady progress up the winding road to Carrbridge until they reached the meandering road to Grantown-on-Spey and upwards to Tomintoul, the highest village in the UK—population seven hundred and sixteen at last count.

Monica had many questions, but she waited until they were well on their way before she framed her first one.

"Where are you staying tonight, Doddie?"

"We, Richards, are going to meet a close friend of mine. Wullie McPherson, born and bred in Tomintoul, knows the Cairngorms Plateau like the back of his hand. Knows the moods of the mountains, the highways and byways, the lore and the flora, the locals and the wardens. He looks as though he is forty years old, but I'll bet he's over seventy if he's a day."

"How would we use him to find a murder victim?"

"First, we talk about any local gossip, any unusual goings-on in the area, then we narrow things down to likely places where accidents or worse could happen. We look at vehicles that are still in the various car parks after days or weeks. All will be revealed. Oh, and I nearly forgot, we use his knowledge to tell us where that Arctic plant of McIvor's is most likely to grow. What's it called again?"

"Saxifraga paniculata."

"Aye, that. Sounds like a fancy loaf of bread."

They approached the entrance to the village and soon found themselves on the greensward that formed a square around its centre. Monica took a deep breath and suddenly felt a calm flow through her veins. Upon seeing the old stone houses that surrounded the square, the trees that guarded the edge, the grocery store, the little museum, Monica resolved then and there that when things became too much at work and when the town burdened her with its hustle and bustle, she would escape to Tomintoul as a retreat from her busy life.

Monica suddenly shook herself from her reverie when she spotted the hotel where she was due to stay. They stopped and, grabbing her case, she dashed in and registered while Doddie waited in the car.

She was back in ten minutes.

"Just a wee leg stretch afore we meet Wullie. Follow me."

Pistol and the two policemen walked along the high street a little way until they reached The Whisky Castle.

"Wait here, dug." And they went in.

Monica looked around the crowded shelves, examined the many varieties, and couldn't help voicing that if there were a whisky from Scotland not represented there, then she would be surprised. In minutes, Doddie was at her shoulder with a bottle of Tomintoul, a 25-year-old single malt.

"Let's go meet the guru."

They drove to the north side of the green and down a narrow road to the outskirts of the settlement, then right onto a dirt road along which nestled an old stone cottage with smoke wisping from the chimney. Parking close to the front door, they smelt the aroma of burning peat before they reached the entrance. Before they could knock, the door was flung open, and a small, white-haired lady in her sixties flung it wide, ran forward, and threw her arms around Doddie.

"Doddie Macfarlane, as I live and breathe. What's kept ye away all this time? And who is this bonnie lassie?" She stretched out her right hand, and Monica was surprised at the firmness of the grip.

"Come away in. Tea and scones. Wullie's up the hill at the moment, but he should be back soon."

She offered them both chairs in the quaint tiny kitchen where Doddie and Monica had to duck if they were not to bump their heads. The AGA cooker gave off a real and comforting warmth, only matched by that of the woman of the house. The uneven flagstones scraped as they pulled back the chairs to sit down.

"Sit down and tell us your news. What brings you here to our lonely wee spot?"

"Murder most foul, Martha. Nothing less, nothing more. We need the help and expertise of yer man here to solve a mystery."

They heard the front door open behind them. There stood the tall, ramrod straight, weather-beaten man, Wullie McPherson. Monica noted his piercing blue eyes and the twinkle and the wisdom that lay behind them. She felt, rather than saw, the power in his arms, legs, and chest. In an instant, she saw courage, fortitude, and stamina. Every wrinkle and furrow suggested a tough as teak life but a healthy one. If he were to walk along a street in Inverness or any other town, he would have looked as incongruous as one of the River Ness's famed salmon riding along the pavement on a bike. He and the land were one. The mountains and glens owned him, and he offered them the respect of apprentice to master. In the town, he would have looked as much an alien as the mountain goat he was.

"Welcome, welcome, welcome. You've been away too long, Doddie." He extended his hand to Monica, who shook it and introduced herself.

"Thanks for the message. I'll see what I can do." He heard the kettle boil.

"If that's the kettle for tea, Martha, do ye mind if we head off to the shed for some fly tying first?"

"Awa ye go. I'm makkin' shepherd's pie, the twa o' ye shall be here for supper."

This was not a question.

"Have you ever tied a fish fly before, Monica? There's a real art to it. Let's the three of us head to the shed to learn how."

Monica started to protest, explaining that they had limited time and needed to get to work.

"Aye, aye, lassie, but unlike you, city slickers, we bumpkins can tie a fly *and* talk *and* listen at the same time."

About two hundred yards from the main house, they found themselves outside a wooden shed measuring about eighteen feet by ten feet. On entering, they found a desk area with two book shelves brimming with books on either side. Papers were strewn across a desk in organized disarray. Two large threadbare sofas formed an L shape behind the desk. An orange shag carpet that had seen better days lay deep and thick on the floor. The shed looked like an old man about to brush the crumbs from his chest, yet it smacked of productive bustle. Monica suspected that Wullie instinctively knew where everything was. If he had been asked to lay his hands on an important document, then it would be a reach into a pile, and it would appear. Monica did not see the fustiness and dusty unkempt nature of the room; all she saw was warmth and comfort and evidence of a busy and passionate existence, a plethora of bustling enthusiasm for all aspects of being.

"Sit ye doon, sit ye doon. I'll go dig out the fly tying equipment." He rummaged in the desk drawers and produced three tumblers and a bottle of Laphroig.

"Fly tying made easy," and he winked at Monica.

"So, whit have you got fur me?" Wullie settled himself on the couch next to Doddie, having poured three large drams.

Doddie went through how John Doe had died. He asked Wullie how he could help. Monica took out the picture of the body and the picture being circulated around the news media and local authorities on that day. The people of Scotland were alerted to help find a missing, murdered man.

"So, we need to visit the Cairngorms Mountain Car Park and go through their CCTV files. Inverness has sent them a picture of the body, so they should be on it as we speak."

"Dead about a week, you say? How do ye know he was killed around here?"

Monica explained about the Saxifrage, and Wullie nodded his agreement. He knew that they had come to the right place.

"Furst light, we'll head over to the Cairngorms and look for oursels. For the moment, we have to make anither discovery, and that, Detective Sergeant Monica Richards," and his eyes twinkled with merriment, "is whether Martha's famed shepherd's pie can beat anything that Aberdeenshire has to offer."

With that, he was on his feet, grabbing the now empty glasses and ushering them out the door.

Monica was a young woman. She kept herself fit and slim by running and exercising frequently and eating well. She believed that her regime kept her alert for the long hours that the job sometimes demanded. So, it was a surprise to her when after they had eaten the most delicious shepherd's pie, green vegetables and rich, succulent gravy, followed by a cheese platter with stilton, gouda, and the most delicious brown sweet/savoury Norwegian cheese she had ever tasted, that she felt herself nodding towards sleep. She kept having to bring her head up with a start as she felt herself drifting away. The subdued lights of the kitchen, the post-prandial malt, the gentle heat from the AGA, the gentle conversation, the comforting melody of the natural storyteller all were a lull and a balm. She felt as much peace and calm as she had known in a long time.

Martha stood up and smiled. She walked around the side of the table and put her hands on Monica's shoulders.

"Ye twa auld farts can blether the nicht awa,' but yon sweet lassie here is needin' her bed. Get aff yer backside, Wullie, and walk her up to the hotel so as I can hiv Doddie tae myself for a bittie."

Monica shook her head and protested that she could make the walk on her own. Martha insisted. Wullie already had his coat on and was at the door. Monica pulled on her shoes, conveyed her thanks, and made for the door.

"Dinnae tak any messin' from that hotel staff. Don't let them fob you off with a puny bowl of cereal and a piece of toast; you're entitled to the Full Scottish for breakfast. Tell that auld besom, Morag Brodie, that she'll hae me to answer for if she taks the lazy way out. Off ye go now."

And they were out into the night.

"So, Doddie, auld friend, tell me about your demons."

Doddie shook his head, "How long have you got, Martha?"

"Och, a guid while yet, yon lassie, o' yours has been tellt to keep my Wullie away for a while. They'll be havin a long deuch an'dorris in the hotel bar."

So, Doddie opened up, and Martha listened, and Doddie felt his shoulders relax and the tension leave his body.

"Message from the mountain: It's my job to take up space and look fucking magnificent." – T-shirt slogan

Chapter 8: The Secret Mountain

Wullie drove his beaten-up Land Rover from around the back of the house and picked up the waiting policemen. Monica was dressed in hiking boots, long shorts, and a lightweight blouse. She carried a day-pack that included waterproofs, water, snack bars, and the bagged lunch that Martha had thoughtfully packed. Doddie wore suitable footwear and long corduroy, brown trousers, an old Scottish rugby jersey, his old military tam o'shanter, and a walking stick. He carried a bigger pack. Wullie was dressed in what he always wore—his boots and walking gear were his everyday being. If he had been suddenly kitted up in a suit and tie, he would have looked like some alien being. Pistol knew they were in for an adventure and skipped into the back of the vehicle like he was off to dog heaven.

Monica settled herself into the passenger side of the vehicle, and Doddie got into the back with Pistol. They drove out of the driveway.

"You go with Wullie up the hill, Richards. I've arranged with the Cairngorms's manager to spend time going through the CCTV footage. If necessary, I'll phone you and come and meet with you later. The funicular will take you up to near the top. Wullie will have some possible sites to visit."

They drove through Aviemore and turned left off the A9. They passed the Coylumbridge Hotel and the nearby campsite from which many walkers set off to hike the Lairig Ghru, the "gloomy pass," a day's walk that took walkers through the massif, past the Pools of Dee, where the River Dee had its source. There it trickled down towards Deeside before becoming a bigger flow, the river which flowed into the North Sea in the City of Aberdeen, the "mouth of the Dee."

Monica and Wullie were silent companions in the front of the Land Rover. She loved the old Scots Pines they passed, remnants of the old Caledonian Forest, which had been so much a part of the landscape before human beings raped and pillaged and turned the wood and landscape into a home for peat and heather.

Eventually, they reached the shores of Loch Morlich, which, despite the earliness of the hour, had sailing dinghies out making the most of the morning wind, along with the occasional kayak, vigorously attacking the wavelets. Exercise regimers, fitness fanatics whose templed and tanned bodies took life far too seriously, had risen with the dawn chorus and were out and about in force. Wullie had probably never done a day's "fitness" in his life, yet he was likely a lot fitter than any of the athletes who scientifically dieted and built their stamina through regimens of rigour. Wullie did not go for walks. He went to find Saxifrage, to search for a missing hiker, to rescue an injured tourist and, in the process, covering miles and miles of rough terrain using only shanks' pony.

If Wullie had been asked to go for a walk, he would have looked askance. Monica, however, worked at her fitness. She often cycled to work from her flat up the hill near Raigmore Hospital. It was an easy ride in but a hard ride home. The end of her working day was a time to sweat through the issues she had encountered, a welcome period where she allowed the endorphins to flow through her body, giving her a natural high and a better perspective.

Wullie spoke, "Ach, Doddie, there's nae fool like an auld fool. Am I not chust the stupidest man who left the hoose and kissed the coo instead o'his wife. The top of a treeless mountain is nae place to hide a body with all the visitors there these days. Trees and bushes are needed. Monica and I will drap you at the railway, and we'll drive back doon the road, park up and hike towards the Chalamain Gap. That would seem more likely than a mountain peak to me."

So, they dropped Doddie and Pistol off at the office in the Cairngorms Mountain Car Park, saw him shake hands with a parks board uniform and disappear inside a wooden building. Monica thought Pistol was gazing back at the Land Rover wistfully, thinking he was getting the short straw of the deal and he would rather be with them. Wullie turned the vehicle around and headed back down the hill.

"Well, lass, this is a MacPherson hunch. Ah've had a lot of them over the years. Some of them have worked out, some less so. We shall see."

Far below them, Loch Morlich glistened in the early morning sun. They could just make out the hotels of Aviemore in the distant haze; it was unseasonably warm for an autumn day. Wullie found the car park some way above the foot of the hill. They walked a little way down the road, found the entrance to the path, and began their exploration. The trees were not tall, and the bushes were prevalent; gorse, broom, and ferns added a pleasant variation to the side of the moor. There was a steep descent to a bubbling burn, not the full spated roar that would prevail during a spring thaw but nevertheless demanding of the sturdy bridge they found as they reached the lowest point of the trail. They did not pause but were soon climbing the other side, reaching a good height where the trail levelled off. When they reached the top, Monica was in a light sweat; Wullie was barely breathing. All the time, he was peering side to side, looking up and looking down; very little seemed to escape his notice.

"Look for a flattening of the heather, Monica, a trampling of boots, evidence of human activity. Could be somebody just popping off to the side to let nature take its course, or it could be something more sinister."

Inwardly, Monica thought this was an impossible task; a needle in a haystack would have been a piece of cake by comparison. Maybe they should have brought Pistol along to help, but Wullie had been reluctant so to do, believing the dog would lead them on too many wild goose chases to be useful. Wullie knew life but didn't understand Doddie's dug.

"If we find something oursels, then is the time to bring in that dog's nose. Have you ever been to the Chalamain Gap?"

Monica shook her head. "We'll stop when we get there. To drag a body through that rocky pass would be a balancing act too far, in my opinion."

So, the two of them trekked along the well-groomed path steadily onwards, gently upwards. They stepped aside to accommodate the occasional mountain bikers who encroached on their space. They greeted fellow hikers who approached them. At this point, the path was easy walking. It was well-groomed. It undulated waves on a peaty sea that were gradually steepening. The tree cover was now sparse. It was more rough heather, growing through sandy glacial tilt.

Above them, on their left, they saw the large car park, the building that housed the train, the tee bar ski lifts blowing gently in the breeze.

About two hundred yards ahead of them, Monica saw the unmistakable rock spillage, the pass between the gulley that constituted the hazard to hikers—the Chalamain Gap.

"That above should be for anither day, Monica. I find it hard to believe that people could carry a body through there without somebody noticing. Gie yer boss a call and see how he's getting along."

Monica reached for her mobile phone. Immediately, there was an answer.

"We have footage of oor man here on his own. However, there's naething to confirm that he went up on the railway, so I think that ye are in a good place. Pistol and I are going to start walking down the road now; we'll walk along the trail to meet you."

Wullie and Monica started back along the path. They had just crossed a bridge and were coming up a short but steep rise when Wullie spotted something in the heather. The sun had glinted off a shiny object about ten yards off the beaten track. Wullie stopped and pointed.

"Ye had better earn yer keep here, lassie. Don't want a big glaikit bastard like me trekking all over a possible crime scene."

Monica suddenly forgot her tiredness and felt the adrenal rush that always came to her when there was something to discover. She dropped her pack, unzipped a side pocket, and pulled out a pair of gloves. She put them on, pinpointed the reflection, and gingerly circled the location, keeping her eyes peeled for anything else that may be worthy of note. Wullie sat on a rock, munched a sandwich, and drank from his water bottle. All the time, his sharp eyes never left the jewel or failed to follow Monica's movements. By this time, she was on the far side of the shining article; she had not yet approached it. Wullie watched as she flopped onto her front and gradually started to crawl forwards, stopping every foot or so to look and observe. Eventually, she reached her destination. Wullie noted her reaching in her pocket, pulling out a Ziploc, and placing the glitter into the bag. Monica stood up and walked back to Wullie. She showed him her find. It was a small, silver engraving of a haloed man with his right hand resting on the shoulder of a baby boy and his left on that of a little girl. Underneath was engraved the words "St Albert." It was a necklace. The clasp was obviously damaged as if it had been ripped off.

She showed it to Wullie through the bag. He showed his recognition.

"Albert the Great, a polymath if ever there was one." He nodded. "He was one of many patron saints of children." He smiled. "Who do ye think we need here most of all right now, lass?"

As one, Wullie and Monica smiled, "Pistol," was the loud chorus. Monica phoned Doddie and explained where they were and what they had found, trying to keep the excitement out of her voice. Doddie and Pistol were on the path but some thirty minutes away from them.

"Dinnae fuckin' move," was Doddie's instruction.

"As if I fuckin' wad?" was Monica's indignant response, and she hung up.

Wullie had made himself comfortable. He was lying back on the heather with his hands cupping his head. He laughed out loud at Monica's response.

"The loonie and the queanie, the boy and the girl, as ye would say in your native Doric. You two make a great team, lassie, an' no mistake. I've known yon boss of yours since he was in short troosers. In fact, I knew his parents afore him. War and the army changed him. He carried his traumatic experiences with him everywhere thereafter. His fuse was short. Naebody in that circus they call a police force in Inverness could work with him. He never was clear about what he wanted, so many of his sergeants did not know. Then he became irritable, and he flew off the handle when they made mistakes. They were intimidated, and, to a man, they sought postings elsewhere. Despite his brilliance, Doddie could not have lasted much longer; the list of former employees was gettin' too long. Then you came along, and it somehow changed."

"That's nice of you to say so, Wullie." She smiled broadly, the dimpled smile that broke pencils and hearts. "I grew up in Aberdeenshire, as you have rightly observed, but you have neither noted, observed or commented on the fact that I am also black. It wasn't always easy being a black kid in the rural farming communities of the county. But they are, we are, warm people, kind people who respect an honest day's work, a forthright opinion and the commitment of a friend's loyalty. I think the world of Doddie. I know he will always have my back; he will never, ever let me down. He is and always will be the father I wish I still had."

Monica had surprised herself at her openness and the long explanation of her feelings. She sat down on the heather and turned her back to Wullie. She had a lump in her throat and did not want Wullie to see the tear she knew was rolling down her cheek. Wullie spoke to her back, and he spoke gruffly, "Aye, weil, he's lucky to have ye, and I hope the auld bastard appreciates that and niver taks ye fur granted. Wha's yon hound coming 'round the corner?"

Pistol appeared, tail wagging, and jumped on the horizontal Wullie, slopping his wet tongue all over his face.

"Git aff me, ye daft dug," he said, laughing as he pushed him to one side. His master appeared, wheezing and gasping behind, a rural gait made more pronounced by the wallowing ship of his belly. Doddie flopped down on the heather next to Wullie and tried to catch his breath. Wullie laughed.

"You need to come and spend a fortnight with Martha and me; too much hard living in that town of yours."

Monica and Wullie shared what they knew. Doddie reached in his backpack and pulled out a Ziploc with a sock in it. He opened the bag and gave Pistol a sniff. Doddie looked sheepish.

"Stole it from the morgue when he was making a fuss about Pistol being there. It belongs to John Doe. Off ye go, Pistol. See what you can find."

Pistol was off. He circled the three in ever-widening circles, sniffing at everything of interest—be it rock, bush, or tree.

"If there is anything of use, he'll find it," Doddie said, laying back, crossing his feet and putting his hands under his head. Monica stood up and tried to follow Pistol's movement. She walked up the trail back towards the Chalamain Gap, then retraced her steps past the two men whom she noticed were now eyes closed and snoring gently. She walked about one kilometre towards the head of the path. Pistol was still dashing hither and thither. Suddenly, he stopped and stuck his nose into a tuft of heather. He stood up and started to bark. Wullie and Doddie awoke and immediately followed Monica, who had already started a slow jog towards the spot. They reached Pistol, who was pawing a tuft of heather. Doddie reached down and pulled it back.

"We have our knife." Doddie reached for a Ziploc and his gloves. "Contact Inverness, Richards; we need SOCO here right away. Tell them they'll need a helicopter. I'll phone the guys on the mountain. They need to close off this trail."

As he spoke, two mountain bikers came up the path heading to the Gap. Monica waved them down. They were not happy as she blocked their passage. She showed them her ID.

"What the fuck? Who dae ye think ye are? We're headed across to the Lairig Ghru and back doon tae Aviemore. No way are ye stoppin' us."

Wullie and Doddie appeared at her side.

Doddie said, "You guys are oot o'here. Turn around and awa' hame."

They began to wave their arms and shout. There was no way a couple of dumb coppers were going to spoil their day. However, they failed to notice Wullie moving in behind them, swiftly reaching into his belt and the air hissing from their tyres. But they did notice him suddenly reappear back with his two friends. At this point, one of the bikers was losing his temper, spewing tales of living in a free country, some comment about "fascist bastards" and an apoplectic wagging of his finger and stomping of his feet. Wullie put his hands up like a wee student at the front of the class, determined to impress his teacher.

"Ye hae something to say, then go ahead and speeak, ye old bastard. Shouldn't you be in yer rocking chair by the fire?" But he stopped and gave Wullie his chance.

"Gentlemen, your tyres appear to be flat," he said sotto voce but with a wide smile.

The two cyclists turned and dashed back to their bikes to find their tyres slashed in several places. Wullie tipped his head modestly, the smile diminishing to a grin.

"Now, back the way ye've come afore I ask my colleagues to arrest you. YOU are at a murder scene. YOU are trespassing. Get out of here."

The belligerent one's mouth opened in surprise and his blood rose further; he was about to make matters worse when his quieter friend put his hand on his arm and turned him back to the bikes. Huffily and with righteous indignation, they muttered something about not hearing the last of this and walked their sorry-looking steeds back down the way they had come.

"Thanks, Wullie, that may have saved us a suspension but risked a prosecution for criminal damage for you."

"Dinnae fash yersels aboot me. Get one of yer boys in blue to the trailhead. I found baggies of cocaine in their saddlebags. Seems it wasn't just a high mountain that was to be their only high this day. We'll no be hearing from them again."

They settled down to await the arrival of the SOCO team. Having been rewarded for his find, Pistol continued to nose around the area.

"That dug let us down," Doddie noted ruefully. "Too involved munching on his treat. Should hae pished all over they wee niafs o' cyclists. Hanging's too good for mountain bikers," thus did Doddie give his opinion on biking and capital punishment in the same breath.

An hour later, they heard the whirl of helicopter blades and eventually the downdraft as they appeared overhead. Monica directed them away from the possible crime scene. They eventually landed on a plateau of heather about five hundred yards to the south of the path. Doddie debriefed the team leader whom he had never met before, and the three then headed back out along the path to the car park and drove back to Tomintoul, stopping at the local police station on the way, where Doddie phoned Rowlands back in Inverness, filling him in on the details.

"Post nubila Phoebus, meaning After clouds, the sun." – Horatio Nelson

Chapter 9: An Identity

Despite the urgency of the murder inquiry and the need to follow up on the new information, Doddie decided it was too late for them to drive back to Inverness that night, so they resolved to have a good night's rest back in Tomintoul.

It was Monica's turn to ride in the back of the Land Rover with Pistol. The two old friends were reminiscing as they drove home through the gloaming of an autumn evening. The motion of the Land Rover plus the gentle conversation at the front lulled Monica, and she found herself drifting off to sleep as they wended their way back up the road to the village. She did not awaken when the vehicle pulled up at Wullie and Martha's place, she never stirred as they slammed the doors, and she never moved as the conversation disappeared through the front door. She had the warmth of the sleeping Pistol for a pillow and the dreamless comfort of a day's accomplishment.

Thirty minutes elapsed, and she started to stir. She opened one eye and was confused by her surroundings. As if on cue, Pistol, too, opened his eyes. They were head to head staring at each other. Eventually, it dawned on Monica, and she sat up and stretched.

"C'mon, Pistol, let's go see whit they twa auld characters are up to," and she opened the door and dropped down onto the ground. Martha greeted them both at the front door.

"A productive day, I hear. Well done, lassie. Wullie and Doddie have headed down to the shed to do some fly tying. It's no Sunday, I know, but I've decided on a Sunday dinner for ye all. It will be ready in about an hour. Head down the shed to see whit those two auld buggers are dae'in, and give me some room to work here. No, lass, I don't need help," she said, seeing Monica about to protest.

Monica changed out of her hiking boots, slipping on the less cumbersome trainers she had thoughtfully placed in the back seat when they had departed in the morning. Martha lent her a torch, and she headed down the path to the shed.

"Ach, you're awake, Richards. You youngsters have nae stamina. Pour yersel'a dram and set doon," Doddie said, pointing to the bottle of Tomintoul he had gifted to Wullie earlier.

They discussed all they had learned. They were convinced they had found the scene of the murder. Of course, they felt they had found one of the murder weapons. Regarding the absence of any detailed CCTV footage, only a glance of a face on a screen on John Doe, Monica had remarked.

"Often, the absence of evidence is evidence."

This statement had given Wullie and Doddie pause for thought.

"The picture of our mannie here is on the TV, *Crimewatch*, and such, and is posted about the country.

Surely we will get a hit of recognition soon. Main task is to get a guid nicht's kip and for Richards and me to head back to Inverness early tomorrow morning."

"Wrong, Doddie," Wullie said, shaking his head. "The main task is to get back tae the hoose and sample whit Martha has cooked up fur oor supper. Drain your glasses and muster your appetite."

With that, Wullie was on his feet and collecting the empties.

Once again, replete with Martha's cooking, the comfort of the company and the house's ambience swept over them. The roast beef, roast potatoes, turnips, Yorkshire pudding, and gravy had worked their magic. They were now sat around the table sipping their after-dinner drams and enjoying relaxed somnolence in front of the heat from the AGA. Doddie stood up. Monica joined him, and they proceeded, despite protestations from Martha, to wash the dishes. When they had finished, and Wullie had put everything away in their proper places, Doddie and Monica grabbed their belongings and headed for the door. Wullie and Martha reached out their hands to shake their farewells, but Monica was having none of that and opened her arms wide to give a hug. Doddie shook Wullie's hand and hugged Martha. Doddie walked Monica back to the hotel and asked her to forego the hotel breakfast so that they could be on the road for 6.00 a.m.

"Nae bother wi'that, Boss. Much more o' this Highland hospitality, and I'll no fit in the car!"

The sun was some way off making its appearance when Doddie drove up to the front of the hotel in the morning. One of the many things Monica and Doddie had in common was their regard for punctuality. Both would be early for appointments rather than late. For them, people who were always late were always diminished in their eyes. Tardiness was selfish. Monica was standing outside the hotel. She grabbed her bag, opened the back door of the car, and gave Pistol an early stroke, to which he responded with a rhythmic thump of his tail. She settled in next to Doddie, seat-belted herself, and they slowly departed the deserted village square. As they left, Monica observed almost to herself, "I will return to this beautiful place."

The journey was quick and uneventful. No music, no talk, no radio, just a companionable silence as they entered the limits of the town. Early morning rush hour traffic was just starting to build as they pulled into the police station car park.

"Too, too early to start, Richards. Let's head to the café, and I'll buy you breakfast. Too, too much bustle to face on an empty stomach."

They left the sleeping Pistol on the back seat and wandered over to the greasy spoon—the haunt of so many of their colleagues. As they approached, Doddie suddenly stopped. "Ho-hum."

Rowlands was sat at a table, slurping a cuppa tea and reading the paper. They entered as the great Scottish fry up was being placed before him—two fried eggs, rashers of bacon, black pudding, baked beans, mushrooms, fried bread, and toast and jam. All the ingredients that made Scotland number one in the coronary stakes in the Western World—an overworked cardiologist's nightmare— were on show. Rowlands saw them enter and pushed back a chair, indicating they join him.

"Glad you are here. I received a call about fifteen minutes ago. Our man here has been identified. His name is Dr George Ross, and he's an eminent paediatrician who lives and works in Welwyn Garden City in Hertfordshire in England. His wife has just returned from a girl's trip to Amsterdam and has recognised his picture on the media. Local police are interviewing her now."

Rowlands conveyed all this whilst whacking back his food as if he had not eaten in a week.

"Order what you want. I'll pay. I'll finish up and head back to the office."

He reached into his wallet and gave Doddie enough cash to cover all three breakfasts. He finished his meal. Doddie indicated the crumbs nestled into one of the corners of his mouth, and he hastily wiped them away.

"The breakfast is a bribe for your silence, by the way. Mrs Rowlands has me on whole grains and fruit, a ridiculous diet that takes all the pleasure out of living. Any word of this reaches her, and I'll have your balls on a platter." He looked across at Monica and reddened, "Well, not yours, obviously, Richards."

He indicated to the waiter that Doddie was paying and headed for the door.

The station was buzzing when they entered. The picture of John Doe now gave him his real name and told a brief history of Dr Ross—forty-two years of age, married with no children, trained in Edinburgh, and lived and worked in England for seven years as a practising paediatrician. His wife's name was Elsa, and they were happily married but took separate holidays. He had a fine reputation in the town—he had an excellent manner with parents and children, cared deeply for his patients, and could put them at ease and calm many nerves. He volunteered in the community, ran marathons for good causes, and liked to return to his native land for hikes and the outdoors, a fact which explained his presence in the Cairngorms National Park. He was Mother Teresa and a candidate for early sainthood if ever there was one; he was an all-around good egg. Doddie explained all this to the gathered throng.

At last, something to get their teeth into.

Monica went to the water cooler to fill up her water bottle before heading to her workstation. A voice behind her asked how her trip had been. She turned and found Dermot smiling and standing patiently in line.

She smiled, "It was fine. Did you hear we found the crime scene?" She checked herself, "Of course, you did; you were at the meeting. Silly me." And the dimples appeared.

Dermot was standing awkwardly beside her, fidgeting with his hands. His face had an uneasy smile. He looked as though he had something to say but didn't look like he could find the words. With her water bottle full, Monica stepped back from the cooler to allow Dermot in. He paused and thought for a moment.

"Didn't you want a drink?"

"Oh, oh aye, of course," he said, and he pulled a paper cup from the holder.

Monica took a swig of water but did not move away.

"I'm sorry I made a mess of things with the Belfast chat. I hope your boss was not too angry."

She smiled, "Oh, he's like that with everybody, including me. His bark is worse than his bite."

Dermot seemed relieved. Now, he knew, would be a good moment to move back to his station, but he continued his awkward stance.

"Was there anything else?"

"Oh, no, no, I'll head off," Dermot raised his hand to indicate he was about to move. He turned away and started to edge backwards. Monica watched him go with a wry smile. He continued to look at her and, in the process, tripped over a colleague's squash bag on the floor near his station. He went down quickly but not without an attempt to save himself by grabbing the tabletop, and down went the soup and the coffee that had just been heated for lunch. Monica grimaced, shook her head, and moved back to work on her computer. She heard the remonstrances, the "glaikits," the "bampots," the "Irish eedjuts," and then lost herself in her work.

Monica and Doddie received the message that morning that Elsa Ross, the victim's wife, was flying into Dalcross from London that afternoon, and they were to pick her up and take her directly to the mortuary to formally identify her deceased husband.

A quick lunch, which neither of them needed, found them dashing to the car park, trying to stay dry as the heavens had opened, the proverbial stair rods soaking the area. They had been ordered to take a police car because of the formality of the occasion. Monica positioned herself in the driver's seat while Doddie got in. Pistol had not been allowed along for the ride, so Doddie had asked for a volunteer to look after him.

"Funny that," he said, "that apology for a copper, the glaikit Irish guy, Constable Dermot Long, volunteered. Hopefully, he learns from Pistol and gains some dog sense."

Monica was surprised to hear this but said nothing.

They drove out of the town on the road to Nairn. It wasn't long before they reached the junction for Dalcross, drove the short distance, and pulled into the airport car park. They both sat quietly in the car, reluctant to get out. Monica puffed out her cheeks and sighed. Doddie blinked a couple of times and signalled that they should move. The breaking of the news of a death and identifying the body by a relative was the hardest part of the job. Apart from anything, it was a minefield full of the wrong things to say. There was, in these circumstances, never a right word. Both Monica and Doddie had managed to keep their speaking to a minimum and had cultivated their approaches to giving solicitous empathy. Could they offer a glass of water or a cuppa tea? They were careful to keep their physical distance and be professional but were on hand should a handkerchief be needed for a tear or a hand ready should the victim falter. They had a sign prepared with Elsa Ross's name on it. They saw that the flight had just landed, so they hurried to the arrivals gate.

Monica spotted Elsa Ross straight away. She was a large woman with auburn hair and was open-hearted with a face like a city baker's Halloween cake. Monica noted her laugh lines, but they were almost hidden in a wan seriousness. She was heavily muscled but with an athletic lope. She wore leggings that revealed legs too heavily muscled for her stature. She saw the sign and urgently marched over to them. Doddie formally introduced Monica and himself. They shook hands and explained that they were going straight to the mortuary but offered no condolences because, as yet, Dr Ross was still John Doe.

Monica guided her to the passenger seat of the car. Doddie got in the back, and they made the silent journey back to Inverness. The police officers stood silently to one side as McIvor pulled back the sheet to reveal the face of the victim. They immediately knew they could now put a name to the victim. Elsa Ross bowed her head, bent down, kissed him on the lips, stroked him on the cheek, and whispered in his ear. She then stood up, turned around to the waiting threesome, nodded, and whispered her acknowledgement that this was her husband. McIvor turned, indicated that they should move to the door and led them into a side lounge where Doddie found a kettle and tea bags available. He busied himself making a brew while Monica sat with Elsa Ross.

Suddenly, Elsa Ross spoke, “He loved children, you know. Sadly, we couldn’t have any. We had talked about adoption but then concluded that his patients were all the children he needed. He encouraged me to become involved with them as they recuperated. He was very, very good at his job. We loved each other very much. We were best friends as well as husband and wife.”

Doddie spoke, “We hope that you don’t mind, but we’ve booked you a hotel room. We would like you to stay for a few days. We need your help finding your husband's killer."

Doddie had wanted to use the plural but was reluctant to say what he believed, instinctively thinking that "killers" was much worse than "killer." A mob death was far more shocking than a blow to the head from behind by one person.

They drove her to the Best Western Inverness Palace and Spa. It was very central for their needs, on the other side of the river from the Inverness Castle, situated on the Ness Walk, very close to the town centre. On the way, Elsa. Ross spoke again.

"A beautiful town." She looked out of the window. "I don't mean to seem callous and uncaring, Detective Sergeant, but I need to go for a run, preferably uphill. Anywhere that you might suggest?"

"Culloden Battlefield is about five miles away. The hotel will give you a map. Would that work?"

"Yes, it would. Thanks." They pulled into the hotel car park. Doddie grabbed her case from the boot of the car. They both accompanied her to the hotel reception. They exchanged phone numbers, and Monica said they would be in touch and arrange a car to bring her to the station. Uncharacteristically and unprofessionally, Monica reached up and put her arm around Elsa Ross's shoulders, "Enjoy your run."

"The information content of a statement is measured as a reduction in prior uncertainty." – Anonymous

Chapter 10: A Distraction

When Doddie and Monica returned to the station, they looked around for Pistol and his guardian.

"They got called out to a disturbance on the Ness Islands, so he had to take Pistol with him," PC "Johnny" Johnson informed them. A few minutes later, Dermot and Pistol appeared. Dermot was muddied and dishevelled. His face was red and sweating. Pistol's tongue was hanging out, but he looked very happy.

Doddie was the first to speak, "What happened to you? Why is ma dug smiling?"

"Bit o' a chase, Boss."

He explained that they had had a call from a lady walking her dog on the Ness Islands. She had heard a disturbance in a wooded area. On investigation, she had seen three young men holding down a terrified looking older man with obvious intent to beat him up. She had stepped back behind a tree, dialled 999, and told her details sotto voce to the dispatcher. Within minutes, Dermot and Pistol were on the scene. Dermot had shouted his presence as the three of them were about to give the prone figure a kicking. They had run off in different directions. Pistol had decided to chase the one who ran off to the west and proceeded to run down the riverside heading south. Pistol had reached him before Dermot, but he was a sheepdog, so he proceeded to slow him up by running circles around him until Dermot arrived. Dermot had rugby tackled him, sat on him, and handcuffed him. The thug was now in the cells cooling off while his victim was up at A & E at Raigmore Hospital.

Amid a murder inquiry, it was unusual for Doddie to turn his attention elsewhere, but something did not sit right about this daylight attack, so he decided to send Monica and Dermot to the hospital to interview the victim while he had a chat with the prisoner. Pistol was given a bowl of water, a treat, and a pat on the head and was told he would be staying at the station with Doddie. Dermot had a skip in his step and a broad smile when he was asked to accompany Monica to the hospital. Monica picked up the keys to a vehicle, and together they headed to the car park.

"You drive." She dangled the keys for him to take.

There was a silent five minutes as they headed off through traffic and up the hill to the hospital.

"How come you went alone to that call? Against the rules that. The outcome could have been worse for you." The disapproval was apparent in her voice. Dermot hesitated.

"Ummm, I felt bad about the identity mistake and all. I wanted to try and make it up to DI Macfarlane and prove that I'm a better cop than he thinks I am."

Monica shook her head but said nothing. There was a traffic hold up due to road works on the hill, so they were five minutes waiting to get through. Eventually, they reached the other side and approached the hospital when Monica spoke.

"You know, if anything had happened to Pistol, Doddie would have throttled you."

Dermot reddened and looked uneasy. They pulled into the car park and got out. Monica took pity on him.

"Doddie has broken every rule in the book during his time, and look where it has got him. If you are going to break the rules, Constable Long, then just make sure you come out on top because nobody will have your back if you fail. You did well, son."

Dermot did not much like being called "son" by somebody who was not much older than him, but he balanced that with the relief he had gained from the compliment. They announced themselves at reception and were shown to a curtained cubicle. Behind it was a forlorn-looking victim. He had bruises and abrasions on his face and, he explained, worse ones on his torso. He was stiff and hurting, but nothing was broken. He felt sorry for himself, but his sorrow quickly turned to anger. He recognised Dermot but was more concerned about himself than offering him thanks for his timely intervention. His pregnant wife was coming to pick him up. They were expecting their first child in a month. He worked in the Procurator Fiscal's office, and his name was Bruce Langford. He was willing to come to the station to make a statement.

They left him and returned to the car. Monica voiced what Dermot felt.

"You'll come across a lot like him, son. All very concerned with their own bruised egos and oblivious to the needs of others. Let the lesson for the day be to develop a thick skin and let the water roll off the duck's back. Don't look so annoyed, son. It's no personal."

Dermot was about to get into the car but stopped and looked across at Monica, straight into her eyes.

"Detective Sergeant Richards, don't call me 'son.'"

Monica's mouth opened to say something, but she decided against it. They drove back to the station in silence.

Doddie was nowhere to be found, so Monica assumed he was interviewing the suspect. Pistol was asleep on his blanket in the corner by the water cooler. Dermot patted him on the head, returned to his station, and started bringing up something on his computer. There was a frown of concentration on his face. Monica looked across as though noticing him for the first time. She phoned Elsa Ross and arranged for her to come down to the station the following morning. She had booked an interview room in a distant corner so that the poor widow did not have to walk past all the pictures of her murdered husband. Forty-five minutes later, she looked up from her desk to find Dermot standing next to her, obviously very eager to tell her something.

"What is it so--, 'er, Dermot?"

"I've found out something about the attack victim." He produced a file. "Bruce Arthur Langford is known to the police. He was a dog owner and walker who all too frequently found his way to children's playgrounds. It seems he always carries a packet of sweeties with him and often offers them to the children. He had been spotted and was warned to take his walks elsewhere from places where children congregate. Our lot interviewed him, but they had found he had done nothing illegal. Nevertheless, they were keeping an eye on him."

Doddie had earlier taken himself downstairs to interview the miscreant. He entered the interview room, flicked on the tape for the record, and proceeded to interview James Nonsuch Innes, who had his lawyer present. He was slouched and sullen.

"Let's start by you telling me the names of your two mates you were with during the attack."

"There was only me," he said with defiance.

"Now, then, son, one of the first things they teach young police officers is how to count. You may not be familiar with the process being as how you have the intelligence of setting concrete. But this is one finger; if I hold up another one, there are two, and a third makes three. So, after me, 1-2-3 makes three. Get it?"

"A'm nae sayin' naethin.'"

"Correct, Jimmy boy, that means you will be saying something. Let's try a different direction, shall we? Why did you attack him?"

He shifted in his seat.

"He's a pedo, in't he? He likes sex with wee boys."

"How do ye ken that?"

"I seen him hanging around kid's playgrounds givin' oot sweeties to laddies, reachin' out to put his arm around their shoulders. Gies me the creeps. Och, aye, and I saw your boys takin' him awa' one time. Needs his balls cut aff does him and his sort, don't he?"

"So about your two mates."

"We get paid to beat up pedo, pedo-thingees. I can niver say the word, but ye ken whit ah mean."

"Who pays you?"

"We don't know. Money and pictures are put in a left luggage locker at the station. We get a phone call to check our box. There's a photograph, an address, and some money. We ambush them, mostly at night, and give them a good hiding; never enough to put them in the hospital like but enough to show them their crimes should stop."

"So you don't know who pays you?"

"Naw, I dinnae, and if I did, I wouldna tell you."

"How come we never hear about the people you beat up? No hospital or police reports."

James laughed. "You think they guys want youse to know whit they've been up to? Naw, they'll learn their lesson a different way." He punched his left palm with his right fist.

Doddie softened. "Give me the names of your mates, and you can go. Mr Langford doesn't want to press charges."

"Frankie Forsyth and Shuggie Simons. Can I go?"

"Aye. Give me the number of the station locker. Tell your mates we know who they are, and they need to stop. Pick up your things at the desk, and you can go."

James told him the number, and Doddie wrote it down.

Doddie got up and left, leaving the door ajar behind him.

"It's all there, hiding in plain sight." – Anonymous

Chapter 11: A Coming Together

Doddie instructed Monica to drop Dermot at the railway station in plain clothes on the following day. He was given the locker number, and he was to dress scruffily so that nobody would know he was a policeman. His duty was to sit at the café opposite, drink tea, read the newspaper, and maybe work on his laptop. He was to be there the whole day. Dermot phoned Monica at 7.00 a.m. to say he was waiting in the car park. She walked down into the large area but could not see Dermot anywhere. Then, suddenly, she noticed a lad with purple hair, short baggy jeans that hung precariously off his hips, a Hawaiian shirt, skateboard shoes, a skateboard, and a backpack. As she approached him, she noticed he had acquired a nose ring and an earring.

"For fuck's sake, Dermot, that's way over the top. You don't look anything like a policeman."

Dermot took it as a compliment and grinned widely.

As they drove, Monica talked.

"Don't be obvious. If the locker is opened and there is a package placed there, try to get a picture of the person who dropped it off. If it is picked up, risk following the person but don't get caught. Can you use that thing?" She pointed at the skateboard nestled between his legs in the front seat.

"Since I was a ten-year-old." It was written all over his face that Dermot was looking forward to his day.

"Anything goes wrong, don't risk your safety. Call for backup, okay?" Monica looked worried.

"We'll be busy with this murder inquiry, but don't let that stop you from making the call. Promise?"

"Promise." She dropped him off on the west side of the bridge, a twenty-minute walk through the central area to the railway station. She returned to the police HQ, where she found Doddie ensconced in an interview room with Elsa Ross. She debated with herself whether she should impose herself on the two of them, then knocked on the door and entered.

By way of introduction, she said, "How was your run?"

Elsa Ross was pleased to see her.

"Good. Funny how something so simple can help with coming to terms with something so emotionally devastating. I should feel guilty about doing something in the wake of what happened to my husband, but I know he would have understood and approved. It was just the right length and gradient, although my knees didn't like running back down the hill."

Doddie spoke, "Mrs Ross was just giving us some background on their lives together as husband and wife. Please feel free to butt in if my summary is incorrect." He looked across at Elsa Ross. "Dr Ross liked walking holidays; Mrs Ross doesn't. It was quite common for them to take separate holidays. It seems that on the day of his death, he had left his hotel in Braemar—we have confirmed that he spent the night there—and hiked up the Lairig Ghru from Mar Lodge. He did not continue down the straight path to Rothiemurchus, as he had always wanted to go through the Chalamain Gap. We have found no booking in Aviemore and environs, so we guess he was going to arrive on spec. He had no tent with him. I have told Mrs Ross that we have found the likely murder weapon, although we are also hopeful we can find what was used to hit him on the back of the head. I am sorry, Mrs Ross, that I am not more sensitive in addressing these issues, but you did say you wanted to hear it 'warts and all.'"

With that, he sat back. Monica waited a moment and then spoke.

"Do you have any emails or letters from parents who might have an axe to grind regarding your husband's treatment of their children? You know, an operation or diagnosis that went awry perhaps?"

Elsa Ross took her time before answering.

"I didn't have access to his private communications with the parents of his patients, so I can't answer that definitively, but I do believe that if he had been threatened in any way, he would have shared that information with me." Doddie and Monica nodded.

Monica said, "You know that we cannot release your husband's body at the moment, for which we apologise. We would like you to remain in Inverness for a few days so that we can talk again. Is that possible?"

"Yes, of course."

Doddie stood up and reached his hand across the table. He said, "We will do our very best to find out who killed your husband, Mrs Ross. We have your details, and you have ours. Let us know if anything that may be useful occurs to you." He looked across at Monica. "Would you be able to drop Mrs Ross back at her hotel, Richards?"

"Of course."

And they all left the room.

As they reached the car, Elsa Ross said, "Would you mind dropping me somewhere else? I don't want to go back to the hotel just yet."

"Certainly. Where to?"

"I think that the Culloden Battlefield and Museum would be a good distraction for me."

"You got it." Monica smiled as they got into the car.

As they drove, Elsa Ross asked Monica about her life—what it was like to live in the town, where she grew up with that very different accent, and her hopes for the future.

"Hope you don't mind my nosiness; it takes my mind off things."

They pulled into the Culloden Battlefield and Museum car park. Out of the blue, Monica said, "Are you sure you want to be here? Culloden was not the cheeriest of events, not exactly an uplifting historical tale."

Elsa Ross smiled but shook her head.

"History has always been a passion of mine. Sometimes you have to wade through the blood and gore to smell the roses. I'll be fine."

As Monica pulled out of the car park, her phone rang. It was Doddie.

"Get yourself ower tae Bught Park right now. Yon Irish bampot has got himsel" attacked."

"Is he going to be all right?" Monica felt a strange sinking feeling in the pit of her stomach.

"Aye, aye, he'll live. Cuts and bruises, smacked around the face a few times, and a bit of a kicking to the ribs and kidneys. They've taken him to Raigmore for a check-up."

"I'm at Culloden; why don't I just head to the hospital?"

Doddie sounded surprised, "Aye, aye, ask him whit the hell he thocht he was daein.' Nae too much sympathy, ye ken, we gave him strict instructions."

"I'm on my way."

Monica debated whether to activate the siren but then thought better of it. She would be there soon enough. She felt a bit responsible for Dermot. She had indeed given him strict instructions, which seemed like he had disobeyed. Nevertheless, she felt a puissance of concern for the young fellow, which was a little bit more than the concern she might have felt for any other injured colleague. She found the thoughts strange to her, so she shook her head in an attempt to rid herself of them.

"Strange that I should feel like that; must be guilt," she muttered as she pulled into the hospital car park.

She flashed her card at the A & E reception, and a nurse accompanied her to the cubicles off the corridor. She pulled back the curtains of one, and there, sat on the edge of his bed in his hospital gown, was Dermot looking pretty sorry for himself.

"Nae fuckin' grapes frae me. Whit the hell were ye thinkin'? You should still be sat at yon café where I left you. Tell me whit happened." Monica's hands were on her hips, and her jaw jutted forward. She pretended to be very angry.

Dermot leant forward, put his head in his hands, ran his fingers through his purple hair, and started rocking back and forth. He mumbled, "I was just-" He got no further.

"Nane of yer 'I was justs,'" Monica burst out. "Ye should have been just sat at your cosy wee café, just having a cosy wee cuppa tea, just reading your cosy wee newspaper. No more 'I was just,' Constable Long."

Dermot lay back on the bed and stared up at the ceiling, seemingly lost for words. Monica pulled up a chair and said, "I'm waiting.'"

So, Dermot told the story of his morning.

"I had settled in with a cuppa tea and a bacon and egg butty. I had only been there for about thirty minutes when a Muslim woman came to the locker, opened it up, and put an envelope in. I got a photograph."

Monica Interrupted.

"Where's your phone? Let me see it."

Dermot indicated his jeans, and Monica reached into the pocket. Dermot scrolled to the photo and showed it to her. She screwed up her face but said nothing.

"Aye, full-body black garb, no flesh at all."

"I opened up my laptop and proceeded to do some work. At about 9.30 a.m., a teenager turned up, opened the locker, took out the envelope, and headed to the toilet. This was a good move on his part because I was getting desperate to go. I stood in the cubicle next to him and just caught the title Bught Park on the front. I watched him leave the station, and I did not follow straight away. I sat down, ordered another coffee, and thought things through. DS Richards, I know you said to stay there for my whole shift, but I believed nothing else would happen that day. After all, I had seen the drop, and I had seen the pick-up. I had pictures of both." He showed her a picture of a ginger-headed teen. "So, I waited a bit longer and figured I had nothing to lose by dropping by Bught Park. I left the station and skateboarded over the bridge. When I reached the park, there were a couple of Frisbee throwers on the grass and a couple of dog walkers but no sign of ginger. Then I heard a shout from behind the stand, just next to Torvean Avenue. I went to investigate and saw two young guys kicking a guy on the ground. I shouted at them to stop but was suddenly grabbed around the neck from behind and had my face pushed up against a wall. Before I knew it, the other two thugs had joined the fray, and I was on the ground getting a kicking. I tried to fight back but was overwhelmed. Suddenly, they were gone as quickly as they had come. The other victim had vanished, and I was on my own. I must have passed out because the next thing I know, a dug was licking my face, and I heard the sound of an ambulance."

"Are you sure you saw no faces and heard no voices?" Monica asked.

Dermot thought for a moment, "They were definitely locals. I could sense they were young. And," he smiled proudly, "as the paramedics were dealing with me on the ground, I spotted something. Can you pass me my jeans?"

Monica passed them over, and he reached into his back pocket and pulled out what was obviously the stub for a ticket to some event. Monica looked at it carefully, reached for an evidence bag, and asked Dermot to place it therein before she sealed it up.

"That's it. I wonder if they will let me out of here."

"Why don't you get dressed, and I'll go and ask?" Monica said.

She smiled to herself as she left and quietly wondered whether she should mention to him that she had just been a witness to Dermot's manhood, which had been fully on display as Dermot had told his story. The hospital gown had been obliviously open as he had related his tale of woe. Monica decided to let it lie. The lad had been through enough without his senior officer letting him know that his meat and two veggies had been as clear a picture as Eilean Donan Castle on a tourist calendar.

Dermot was allowed to go with Monica so long as he went straight home and so long as Monica promised she would accompany him through the doors of his flat. Dermot's complexion was pale, and he was staggering a bit as they walked to the car. As she drove him home, she noted he was nodding and struggling to stay awake.

"Don't you fall asleep on me, son."

"Don't call me..."

"I know. I'm sorry, Dermot."

Dermot lived in rented accommodation at the rear of the house of an elderly couple. Mr and Mrs Macrae were open-hearted and friendly. Mrs Macrae saw them as they pulled up at the gate. She walked down the garden path solicitously, noting that Dermot was not the full quid. She opened the door for them and ushered them into the kitchen. Mr Macrae had been the victim of a severe stroke a couple of years previously. From his couch in the drawing-room, he watched them walk past. But his speech was severely impaired, and, Monica noted, there were many signs of paralysis.

"Take him into his flat, lass, and I'll bring you both a nice cuppa tea," Mrs Macrae looked concerned. Dermot indicated the way. They entered the one room that served as his lounge and bedroom. He flopped down on a chair and indicated another upright chair for Monica. The bedsit was neat and tidy. There was a flat-screen TV, which Dermot could watch from his bed, and there was a small bookcase with about twenty titles on it. There was a desk with a desktop computer and a coffee cup.

"I am allowed to use the kitchen for my meals," Dermot explained.

The tea arrived, and Mrs Macrae asked if they needed anything else. Monica said she would have to head back to work soon but asked if it would be okay if Mrs Macrae looked in on Dermot periodically throughout the day.

"Of course, dear, no need to worry. Like a son to us, Dermot is," and she retreated from the room. Monica sipped her tea. Neither of them spoke. On the opposite side of the coffee table, Dermot was sitting uneasily in his chair, obviously struggling for the words to speak.

"Spit it out, man."

Dermot sighed, looked down, then brought his eyes up to bear directly on Monica.

"Okay, you are going to think these are the ramblings of somebody who is severely concussed, but I have," he hesitated, "I have to ask you this. Ever since I arrived at the station for my posting from Belfast, I have watched you at work and admired how you hold yourself. At first, I thought it was the observations of one junior professional to a senior one. Time went on, and I realised that my observations were far more than professional. I know that I am your junior in years and position and cannot hold a candle to who you are. But Detective Sergeant Richards, I am totally besotted with you. I am smit. I know this is a forlorn hope, a drowning man clutching at a life raft, but I would love it if you and I could go for a drink one evening, a chance for me, well, just for a chat, a short time to get to know you better."

At this very surprising revelation, Monica felt her mouth dropping open. It was so totally unexpected.

Dermot looked down. He was red in the face. He blurted, "I know, I know, total fucking eedjut. Who do I think I am? There are three hopes in this world: Bob Hope, some hope, and no hope. But I could not, not speak. I had to get it off my chest. There was no time like the present. You don't need to reply. I should let you get back to work."

He stood to usher Monica to the door. Monica sat still, her mouth agape, her eyes wide. Eventually, she stood to leave. She turned to go but paused at the door. She heard herself speak.

"I'm free on Friday night. I'll be outside your gate at seven o'clock. Be there or be square."

With that, she left.

"Without the dark, we would not know the light. Without imperfection, we would not know perfection." – Dorothy Rowe.

Chapter 12: The Date

Dermot had to work on Friday, so he decided to give his all to the day to take his mind off the excitement of his date with Monica that night. Both had resolved to keep their evening assignation a secret from the workplace. They agreed to head out of the town not to be seen. Dermot chose the Drumnadrochit Hotel as a venue close enough to town yet far enough away to escape prying eyes and elongated noses. His suggestion of dinner was a step too far for Monica, which settled him on a couple of drinks in the bar with a bar meal if they were hungry. But the day would be never-ending for Dermot if he did not work hard. Of course, he noted Monica's arrival at work and looked across at her as they busied themselves. She looked totally oblivious about anything to do with the evening and him. Dermot would have been relieved at a smile or a catch of the eye that suggested she had not forgotten. But true to form, she gave nothing away.

Dermot filled out an official report about his morning at the station café. He looked at the photograph of the boy again. He knew that on the beat, bobbies were on the lookout for him, but nothing had turned up yet. A waste of time, though it seemed, he took a glance back at the Muslim woman. He expected to find nothing useful there, but he was idly playing with the picture, zooming in and out when his eye caught something. He sat up in his seat, suddenly alert. The woman's left hand had dropped to her side as she had opened the locker with her right. He tried to get in closer. There was something not right about the hand. He could not put his finger on it, but suddenly, he knew. To make sure of his hunch, he wanted the opinion of others, so he transferred the picture to his computer, fiddled with the technology so that only the hand was on show and sent it to his colleagues around the room with the cryptic message, "Tell me about this hand." For thirty minutes, he received no response. Eventually, he stood up and went over to Hamish Watson's station.

"Did ye get yon picture I sent you, mate?"

"Aye."

"Well, what do you think?"

Hamish shrugged his shoulders.

"Nothing really. Just some guy's hand."

Dermot said nothing but went around several of the other stations asking, nay demanding, an opinion. Now, his excitement was palpable. He found it hard to contain himself. He saw that Rowlands was seated on top of his desk with his legs crossed and eyes closed in yoga mode. Dermot went and knocked on his door.

"Enter." Rowlands never verbalized a calm, "Come in," despite the gentle implications of his much-loved yoga.

"Aye. What is it?" He tried to get down from his desk and assumed a more formal position on his chair, but he had difficulty unravelling his legs. When eventually he did, he found that one of his legs had fallen asleep, and as he put weight on it, it crumbled underneath him, and he collapsed onto the floor, dislocating one of his fingers while reaching out to arrest his fall with his right hand. He shrieked in agony. Dermot reacted without thinking, grabbed his hand, and relocated his finger with a pull and a jerk. Rowlands shrieked again at the surprise intervention and shook his wounded hand vigorously before sitting down.

"Thanks, Constable. You really should try yoga; it is so good for suppleness and health."

Dermot tried hard to hide his disbelief. From his experience of watching Rowlands at his health-giving, youth-benefitting exercise, a round with Mike Tyson would have been easier. He collected himself.

"There's something you need to see, Sir."

He showed the picture of the hand.

"It's just a hand, Constable; we've all got them. Are you sure you've nae got a concussion? Maybe a bit of PTSD, maybe a trip upstairs to see the good doctor."

Dermot was not to be dissuaded.

"Please, indulge me, Sir. Tell me what you think of this hand." Rowlands scratched his head, wincing as he did, and then rubbed his shoulder.

"Really must work on loosening up the shoulders," he said as he studied the picture intently.

"Well, it's a rough-looking hand, one used to hard labour. See those callouses. This hand has been on a building site or a fishing boat. It's not the hand of an office worker or a Caley footballer; I'll tell you that. It's a large hand. I'll tell you what, Constable Long, I would not want to be in a pub fight with the owner of this hand. He would pack a helluva punch."

Dermot could contain himself no longer. He stood up.

"Sir, I will now reveal the owner of this hand." He brought up the picture of the Muslim lady.

"Everyone I asked referred to "his" hand, as you just did, Sir. The Muslim lady who placed this package in the locker was no woman."

Rowlands, who had been resting his chin on his hands, suddenly looked up and leaned forward.

"Dermot, laddie, you're onto something here. I'm going to order a further watch on this locker. We are going to get this person in for questioning. That is great work."

Dermot returned to his desk and went about his business, although it all seemed a bit mundane after what he had just achieved.

Doddie and Monica had arranged to meet Elsa Ross in the coffee shop attached to her hotel. She arrived in a tracksuit, having just had a run along the side of the River Ness and the Caledonian Canal.

"Sorry if I'm hot, sweaty, and smelly."

She sat down opposite the two police officers.

"We omitted to tell you that we found some Saxifrage, an alpine plant, under Mr Ross's fingernails. There is no Saxifrage in the area where we found the knife. We have to extend our search because we believe that Mr Ross was killed at a different spot. We ventured into the Cairngorms, and we found this."

He produced the Ziploc with the necklace in it. Elsa Ross reached for it, stared at it, and, with a sharp intake of breath, exclaimed, "Yes, it's his."

She bowed her head and put her hand on her brow, and a tear from her right eye slowly made its way down her cheek.

"I gave it to him on his fortieth birthday, a reminder of the years of study, the financial struggles to get where he was, the good that he had done, and for the good he would do in the future. He had looked into our bedroom mirror and asked me to place it around his neck. As we looked at our reflections, the love for each other shone in both our eyes. Our passion for each other that night was like none previously."

She wiped away the tear and ventured a smile.

"I'm sorry. Too much information, I know, but our love was deep, emotional and, yes, physical."

Monica reached for her hand and placed hers on top of it on the tabletop.

After they had spoken and Elsa Ross had left to get cleaned up, Doddie phoned Wullie in Tomintoul and asked him to investigate the Chalamain Gap trail further for some other clues.

"They SOCOs are not always that great. Sometimes they miss stuff that they shouldn't," Doddie explained over the phone.

"Is hanging too good for them?" Wullie offered from the other end of the line. Doddie could sense the smile and almost hear the chuckle from Tomintoul. He hung up.

Five o'clock came, and they went home for the day.

At 6.30 p.m., Dermot was showered and dressed, ready for Monica's arrival. He had toyed with which shirt to wear and eschewed the idea of a tie; after all, they were just going to a public bar, and thinking jeans might be too casual, he had reached for some khakis and black shoes. He was tempted to pour himself a drop of Dutch courage but realised he was the driver, and that would not have been a good idea. He paced the room.

At 6.45 p.m., he moved into the hallway to be close to the front door. At 6.55 p.m., he was waiting at the front door, looking out of the glass window. He saw her silhouette open the gate and start her walk up the path. He opened the door and tried a natural smile of greeting but then abandoned it as far too goofy. Monica was dressed in tight-fitting jeans, a white buttoned blouse and a leather jacket. She wore high heels.

Dermot greeted her, and they walked down the path to his car.

"This is never your car. This is an unmarked police car. How did you get this?" she asked.

He opened the passenger side door.

"DI Macfarlane got it for me."

Monica stopped and looked irritated.

"No, no, don't worry; he doesn't know that you and I are on a date. He felt guilty about how he had treated me, so he said he would sign off on it."

Monica looked doubtful but entered the car.

Then followed half an hour of the most awkward silence that Dermot had experienced in his life. Every time he tried to open his mouth to make casual conversation, nothing would come. By the time they reached the hotel, Dermot felt miserable. This date was a bust from the moment of its inception. He should never have asked her out. It was an abject failure, and now he was going to have the embarrassment of seeing this beautiful woman every day at his place of work and knowing she was inaccessible to him. They parked in the pub car park, got out, and he opened the door of the public bar to let Monica through.

They found a convenient corner of the bar with a snug table for two, and he ordered a glass of white wine for her and an orange juice for himself. Monica and Dermot opened their mouths to speak at the same time. Dermot apologized and allowed her to go ahead.

"I don't know why I agreed to this. You've said nothing all the way here. What's with you?" Not a very impressive start. Dermot reddened, but something deep inside him stirred. If this was to be the last time he socialized with this lassie, then he was not going to be let down by lack of honesty, so he let rip and surprised himself in the process.

"When you agreed to this date, I couldn't believe my luck. I was on cloud nine. I spent a nervous few days at work wondering at your acceptance, feeling unworthy, going through the whole gambit of emotions from ecstasy to sheer terror to nervousness to worry that you would not turn up. Then when you walked down that pathway tonight, I was overawed by your beauty and felt doubly unworthy. If this is to be our first and last date, then I am grateful, but, please, believe me, DS Richards, I am overawed, but I am determined to overcome it."

He stopped, puffed out his cheeks, and sat back, reaching for his orange juice.

"Plus, I have to drink this crap all night." He managed a smile. Monica laughed out loud. Her white teeth shone, and her dimples showed. *Oh, God, the dimples!* thought Dermot.

"You call me DS Richards once more this evening, and I'm back calling you 'son,' son."

Dermot managed a slight grin.

"Tell me about growing up in Ulster."

Dermot told his story about growing up in "The Troubles" of that divided city, of the characters he had met, of the pranks, of the occasional fear but also the overwhelming character and craic in the place, of his wish to join the RUC, and his eventual transfer to Scotland because his mother wanted him "safe and away," as she put it. And then he sat back, saw by the clock that he had talked too long, and asked Monica about herself.

She talked about being Black in rural Aberdeenshire, her time at Inverurie Academy and her years studying History at Aberdeen University.

"Why History?" Dermot interrupted.

"'Cos herstory hadn't been invented."

She talked about her time as a police officer as the "Turra Coo" in Turriff and her eventual move to Inverness. Inevitably, her relationship with Doddie came up.

"We're very close. When we are not on the same page, then we eventually are. I know people shake their heads and wonder how we can operate with each other and get such good results. When asked about this, I just explain it as the pursuit of the truth, plain and simple. No bullshit will ever, ever get in the way of Doddie and me chasing down the answer."

She stopped. The bar was almost empty, and the barman was drying glasses and looking in their direction.

"He's wantin' awa hame. We should go."

Dermot stood up and helped her on with her jacket. There was a full moon and a clear night as they made their way to the car. Monica smiled at the thought of how Doddie was going to justify this to the powers that be but said nothing.

The drive back to Inverness was yet again silent. This time, however, Dermot was relaxed in his quietude. The journey to Drumnadrochit had seemed so long and drawn out, and now the trip back to Inverness was going to be over far too quickly.

As they approached Craig Dunain, Dermot said, "Can I drive you home?"

"You'd better. I'm not getting the bus at this time of night." Monica lived in a small block of flats not far from Raigmore Hospital. Dermot pulled up beneath them. They all looked like they'd seen better days.

Dermot looked dubious, "Are you going to be okay from here?"

"Of course." They sat very still in the dark, neither wanting to move, neither in a hurry for the separation.

"Well, then."

"I have had a wonderful night. Sure, I wondered what I had let myself in for, but you sure put an end to that when you let loose in the pub."

"Aye, well. The hours flew by for me. I enjoyed every second of our chat. Good night, Monica."

Dermot reached across and gave Monica a peck on the cheek, and she smiled and shook her head.

"You can do better than that, Dermot." She grabbed him by the collar, pulled him to her, and placed her lips on his. She slid her arms around his neck. Dermot ran his hands through her hair, felt her tongue probing his throat, and slipped into a feeling of the deepest, most joyous peace he thought he would ever feel. When she eventually separated from his embrace, he saw the shiny deep black eyes and their sparkle, her smile and the dimples. *Oh, God, the dimples.*

"I have to go. See you at work on Monday."

"Does this mean we can do this again?"

Monica opened her hands with a questioning smile, then looked him in the eye and pointed her finger and waved it.

"If you don't invite me out again, Dermot, I'll make sure you are on traffic duty for every shift for a month. What's more, I'll be calling you 'son' all the time, son. Now get that car back to the station afore Doddie decides that 'hanging is too good for you,' thus giving his opinion on young policemen and capital punishment in the one breath."

Dermot laughed out loud. Monica popped quickly round to the driver's side. He opened his window, and she gave him one long-lasting, luxurious kiss. He thought, *Oh, God, I don't ever want to let go of this beautiful woman,* and then caught himself when he realised he had spoken out loud.

As she walked across the car park and looked back at him, he switched on the engine and could not resist a quick blast on the siren. She smiled in mock horror and waved a finger at him.

"The hen is the wisest animal because it never cackles until the egg is laid."
– Abraham Lincoln

Chapter 13: Tomintoul Again

Monday morning found Doddie at his desk early. He and Pistol had had a sober weekend. On Friday night, he had driven home with a bag of groceries and cooked himself some pasta and meatballs. He had resisted the temptation to pour himself a dram. Distracted by thoughts of the case, he had spent a happy hour vacuuming, doing his laundry, and washing his dishes. He had enjoyed a good healthy meal and flicked the TV on to watch the news. He thought about a Netflix movie but couldn't be bothered. Instead, he grabbed one of his George Macdonald Fraser *Flashman* books from his shelf. Any one of the dozen would do. He knew the stories of the bully, the coward, and the philanderer so well that he could lose himself anywhere therein. He took Pistol out to do his business, feeling the nip in the air that only a clear star-studded night could bring in the Highlands at this time of year. When he first moved from the town, he marvelled every evening at the clarity of the night sky so evident without the ambient light of urban living. He bought himself a book of constellations and told Pistol one evening that he would become "Patrick fuckin' Moore," the iconic *The Sky at Night* TV presenter whom he had grown up watching. Of course, it was only a fad. He had found the North Star, Cassiopeia, Orion's belt, and so forth, but there always needed to be a crisis for Doddie's attention to be held. Doddie knew himself well enough to tell Pistol one night as they were taking their evening walk up a backfield, "Aye, dug, these stars have been here for thousands of years, and they'll still be here tomorrow. I need to be involved wi' things that change."

He had reached down and tousled Pistol's hair and patted the top of his head. Pistol responded with a slow tail wag.

The weather had been good, so Doddie had donned his walking boots on both days. On the Saturday, they had climbed Stac Gorm. Doddie sweated his way up, and Pistol bounced his ascent. Doddie could not help reflecting on the fit young man he had been in his army days and before. The peak was not rugged; the climb was steep in places, but the pathway was easy. He never ceased to marvel at the beauty of where he lived. The heather had passed its bloom. The day was still. The speckled rocks, ever-changing yet ever the same, embraced Doddie's soul; the rigour of the vigour dispatched his inner demons. All the way up was the comforting sight of the loch below. On the way down, he reached the trees that were nurtured by the riparian wealth on the banks of the loch, silver birch, branches leaning protectively over the loch like mothers protecting their children. There was enough of a breeze for him to hear the lap of the waters, enough of a chill to remind him that the summer's midgies would not be there, enough of the sun's warmth to allow him to lie on his back and close his eyes. The sleep which was so difficult for him at night came so easily to him here.

Only the sudden return of the roaming Pistol woke him and raised him onto his elbows. He reached for his friend, stroked, and talked to him. He decided they had to get back.

On the Sunday, they had circled the loch staying relatively low. At the south end, he found where the fishing boats were moored. He cast his mind back to his boyhood fishing trips. He remembered the day a southerly wind had blown up, and they had to battle in the early evening to get the boat back to its mooring. He remembered the day when the surface of the water had been glass. His father had given up on the fish, and he had stripped off and dived off the boat for a swim. He shook his head. A lot has happened since then. Death and war were constant companions that always trod on his happiness, a hefty reminder nipping at his heels and tripping him away from a calm existence. He and Pistol left the mooring and continued their trek around the loch, making it home in the early evening gloaming, the twilight sun dipping away to the west.

Early on the Monday morning, Monica appeared on the floor and approached his desk.

"Good weekend?" she asked.

"Nae bad, a couple of danders on the hills and nary a dram." He smiled beatifically, suddenly a holier than thou health freak. "I have a sudden favour to ask, Richards. I need Wullie to go up and look further up the pathway to the Chalamain Gap in search of more evidence. For official reasons, he needs to have a police presence. Are you able to pop up there, spend the night, and come back down tomorrow? You can stay at the same hotel. I've cleared it wi' Rowlands. Aw aye, tak' young Constable Long wi' ye, keep him oot o' trouble for a bit. He's a young guy and needs the overtime."

Monica hesitated, "Ummm, I'm happy and free to go, but surely this is something I can manage on my own. Nae need to involve Constable Long."

Doddie scratched his head and shook it.

"I've thought it through. It needs two of you. Get on the phone and book yourselves in at the hotel."

Again, Monica came back at him.

"Maybe I could stay wi' Wullie and Martha, and Constable Long could stay at the hotel."

"OK, I'll phone Wullie and Martha. Go talk to Constable Long."

She moved away.

"Oh, I nearly forgot," Doddie added, reaching down below his desk. "Return this to him. They found it in the car after the weekend. Didn't know he liked to wear silk scarves, the lad?"

Monica grabbed her silk scarf, took a deep intake of breath, and moved off to Dermot's station. She stood in front of him and muttered under her breath.

"Take my scarf, which was found in the car, and pretend it is yours."

Dermot nodded and exclaimed loudly.

"Thanks, Boss; I wondered where I had left that."

She then explained the situation to him. Dermot found it hard to contain his pleasure at the idea. They needed to get going as quickly as possible. So, they picked up a car, dashed home, hurriedly packed overnight bags, and headed up the road to Tomintoul.

On the way, they kept things professional. Dermot talked about the Muslim lady who wasn't. Monica explained about the Saxifrage, the medallion, and the knife.

Dermot suddenly exclaimed, "Wouldn't it be strange if the two things were connected?"

"Huh. Unlikely. How could that be?"

Dermot explained that he had been thinking that somebody was paying to have suspected paedophiles beaten up. He believed it was happening very frequently and that none of the instances was reported because the "culprits" were secretive about their deviance and would go to great lengths to keep things on the down-low.

"Dr Ross was anything but a paedophile," Monica said. And they had let the subject drop. Silence ensued except for the *wop, wop* of the windscreen wipers.

"This horizontal rain is going to do nothing for any potential crime scene. I hope that Wullie can work some magic." She then explained about her time with Martha and Wullie when she and Doddie had recently visited. She knew very little about the friendship between Wullie and Doddie except that they went back a long way and that Doddie was a wee bit in awe of his friend's outdoor skills. She added, "As far as he's ever in awe of any other human being."

Dermot laughed. "He certainly seemed in awe at my stupidity over the photograph."

Monica's dimples appeared, and Dermot had to remind himself to keep his eyes on the road. There had been no mention of Friday night on the whole journey, so Dermot was having doubts it had ever happened and was deep down feeling that Monica was embarrassed by the whole thing and wished it hadn't. Suddenly, there was a sad insecurity in his heart, but he was doing his best to put a brave face on.

Dermot had only been in Scotland for a few months, so it was quite natural for him to have seen very little of the countryside. He could not help exclaiming his appreciation as they entered the village.

"Have you seen the movie or read the book *The Lost World* by Arthur Conan Doyle?" Monica asked him.

He nodded.

"A high plateau in the South American jungle where the only access necessitates the climbing of sheer cliffs, where dinosaurs thought to have been extinct for millions of years are thriving. I see the connection that you are making here, Monica."

"Before we head down to Wullie's and Martha's, park up, and we'll stretch our legs."

Dermot parked on the green, and they walked towards The Whisky Castle, where Monica knew there was a café. They popped in for a pot of tea. The place was deserted, but the owner was pleased to see them. Obviously, they did not get many customers at this time of year. He was naturally inquisitive.

Monica explained that they were police officers working on a case. Dermot was staying at the hotel, and Monica was staying with Wullie and Martha Macleod.

"Don't spend too much time in that hoose, lassie; Martha will feed ye up and spoil that pretty shape of yours."

Monica let the sexist remark go, smiled, and sat down at the table with Dermot. Afterwards, they popped over to The Whisky Castle, where Monica bought a bottle for Wullie. Dermot booked into the hotel, and they headed down to Wullie and Martha's place for a Tomintoul welcome. The evening proceeded much as it had when it had been Monica and Doddie—a bit of fly tying, a home-cooked meal, the kitchen's warmth, and the discussion of the plan for the next day. Monica stood up.

"I think I'll walk Dermot back to his hotel. Can't have him getting mugged on the way hame. We'll discuss tomorrow further. Could I have a key in case you're asleep when I get back?"

Wullie and Martha burst out laughing.

"Key? Key? Nae key needed here in Tomintoul, lass. Just let yoursel' in. We'll see ye in the morn."

Dermot and Monica walked up the hill to the hotel, discussing what they hoped to find on the next day. As they entered the reception, Monica said, "Let's not bother with the public bar; the locals can be a bit nosey. Let's carry on the discussion in your room."

Dermot took his key, and they walked up the stairs. The floorboards on the landing creaked as they made their way along the corridor. Dermot opened the door to reveal a double bed, a large flat screen, two chairs, and equipment for making tea or coffee. Dermot did not ask her but put the kettle on. Monica looked pensive.

"What if your theory about a connection between the crimes is correct? This would be in danger of becoming national news," she said. "You've not mentioned Friday night, by the way."

Dermot reddened. "I thought you were embarrassed by the whole episode and that it was never to be repeated."

Monica smiled.

"Oh, God, Monica, please don't give me the dimples; I can't cope," Dermot pleaded. At that, she stood up, moved towards him, and kissed him firmly on the lips. She moved away from him and walked over and switched on the bedside lights and then to the door, where she switched off the main light. She came back before him, bent down, and kissed him again. Dermot stood up. Monica glanced down at the bulge in his pants.

"Dermot, Dermot, we need to do something about that."

She knelt in front of him and began to undo his belt. Dermot reached down, grasped her golf shirt, and pulled it up over her head. Meanwhile, Monica had revealed his erection and stood up. Urgently, Dermot reached behind her and released her bra. Her breasts were erect and beautiful. Dermot reached down to kiss them, but Monica whispered, "Wait," and stepped back. Within moments, she had unbuttoned her jeans and stood before him naked. She moved over to the bed and lay down. Dermot struggled to undo his laces and battled with the buttons on his shirt. Monica laughed and said, "Hurry up, son, get over here!"

"Don't call me 'son,'" and Dermot was suddenly naked and next to her.

He reached over and kissed her fully on the lips. Within moments, he was moving slowly down her body. He lingered over her breasts before moving to her navel and lower.

"Mmmm, don't stop." But there was an urgency in Dermot. He moved slowly back up her body. Monica saw his erection, pushed him off her, and rolled him on his back. In moments, she was on top of him. He was inside her, and slow movements began to accompany sweet moans. Dermot cupped her breasts. She leaned towards him. Her movements became more vigorous, and soon, she was in ecstasy, and then she was still. She came off him, lay on her back, and glanced towards him.

"Your turn."

Dermot mounted her. She pleaded, "Go slow," but there was an urgency in Dermot, which he had never felt before. His passion came quickly. He lingered inside for moments thereafter, luxuriating in the experience. Finally, he lay down at her side. The sweat glistened off them both. Dermot was in a dream. He could have slept right there and then. He never wanted these moments to end. Monica raised herself on her elbow and started to trace her finger in circles around his nipple. He turned his head towards her, and she smiled.

"Oh, God, oh, God, the dimples, the dimples."

Monica laughed out loud.

"I have to go. This is a small village. People will talk." She was out of bed and quickly getting dressed. Dermot watched. He couldn't help himself.

"I feel like the luckiest man in the world."

She smiled at him. She came and sat next to him, bent, and kissed him on the lips.

"Wullie and I will be here at 6.00 a.m. No time for breakfast, I'm afraid, but I am sure Martha will pack you up something."

After she left, Dermot tried to process what had just happened to him but couldn't. He set his alarm, prepared his hiking gear, and fell into a deep sleep.

Dermot was outside the front of the hotel when Wullie and Monica pulled up at precisely 6.00 a.m. He hauled himself into the back of the Land Rover, and Monica leaned back and passed him a couple of bacon and egg butties and a flask of hot sweet coffee.

"Courtesy of Martha. Wullie and I have eaten. Scoff them while they are still hot."

Dermot needed no second bidding.

It was not raining as they headed out, but there were some menacing dark clouds further to the west, which were obvious even though it was not yet dawn—an autumn morning with the prospects of rain.

As he set off, Wullie apologized. "Sorry you had to miss your hotel breakfast, laddie. Hope Martha's wee offering hit the spot."

"Aye, aye, it was grand."

The village of Aviemore was quiet as they entered. They passed the station opposite the Cairngorms Hotel, an old emblem amidst a modern conglomeration. They passed the Happy Haggis' fish 'n chipper and eventually turned left towards Coylumbridge, Loch Morlich, and Glenmore. The trees were starting to shed their leaves, but the Scots pines and other conifers stood defiant and magnificent against the elements. There was always something Darwinian in the remnants of the old Caledonian forest. The remains stood and bore witness to the events that had denuded the moors of their ancestors. Monica had always felt a special love for the old trees. She looked across at

Wullie and smiled; he was very much of that Scots pine survivor tradition. He, too, had seen it all. He, too, was at one with the moors, the mountains, the lochs, and the trees. He was elemental, at peace with all that was natural and wild. They were through Rothiemurchus, and the first light was starting to show itself in the east. From in front of them, the sun was trying desperately to make an appearance, but the dawning gloom revealed dark, Stygian clouds, filled to saturation point, waiting a moment of release.

The Land Rover began to climb the mountain road towards the skiers' car park, but they knew they were not going to the top. The three occupants slowed the vehicle to a crawl as they went up. The bubbling waters dug away in the carved-out hillside to their right. There was much evidence of violent erosion there. The vigour of Spring thaws had suddenly thrown down turbulent waters from above. The floods had ripped tenuous vegetation from the glacial till, tumbled rocks and pebbles in a clashing, bashing, rolling tumult down the hillside to the loch below.

It was an annual event and had been so for thousands of years. The trees were a mixture of deciduous and conifer. Low in stature as befits a mountain climate, they clung to banks and bushes with stoic determination, a riparian roll call of what was and is. Soon, Wullie pulled over into the familiar car park.

The three of them grabbed their day packs, crossed the road to the trailhead, and started the steep descent to the burn below. They moved quickly, reached the footbridge, and ascended the other side to the open moor above.

There, the open flats presented them with views of the ski road just above them, and, soon, the car park and the human paraphernalia of a ski hill, the offices, cafés, and entryway to the funicular railway flaunted their human impact in sharp contrast to the trail they were following on the other side of the gorge.

Dermot found himself sweating and with heightened breathing. He realised he had wrongly assumed that a walk with the old guy would have been slow progress, a gentle stroll with frequent stops to allow the oldster to catch up. Instead, the role was reversed as Monica and Wullie occasionally looked back to check if he was all right and still there. Nothing was said, and there was no suggestion they would slow their pace to accommodate his lack of fitness. Sooner than he expected, they had arrived at the entrance to the Chalamain Gap; still, the dark clouds threatened, but no rain had yet fallen. They rested, took a drink, and sat on convenient rocks.

Wullie spoke, "We know that Dr Ross was not killed where the knife was found. I am here to take note of what I know. If he was killed somewhere here amidst this rocky terrain, it would not be far off the path. To you, there is no path here, just a tumble of boulders strewn at random through this gap, but human beings are lazy; they always seek the easiest route. I know this area well. I'll lead. We'll go slowly. Keep your eyes peeled for anything that looks out of place, any sign that a rock has been overturned, any hint that something is not as nature intended. Heighten your senses."

With that, they put on their packs and moved slowly into and onto the rocks. Dermot marvelled at the change in environment. It was as if nature was toying with them. It had lulled them with the gentle moorland amble over a springy, peaty carpet. Suddenly, Mother Nature had thrown down a gauntlet. Some rocks looked solid but might teeter; there was an unevenness in the heights and size that necessitated a reach with both hand and leg. There was uncertainty about what was the safest next step. There was a need for better balance and cautious forethought. Wullie stopped every three or four steps and looked about himself, Monica peered from side to side, and Dermot looked down in front of him. Everyone was totally immersed in the process. Nobody spoke.

At about three hundred yards in, they paused. Dermot was reaching for his water bottle when he caught sight of something out of the corner of his eye, something unusual nestling between two rocks. He looked closer and noted a small bunch of plants not rooted to the ground. They looked as if they had been picked. He thought it was something of nothing, but he had been asked to bring attention to anything. He called to the other two, who were a short way in front of him.

"I think I've found something."

Monica and Wullie scrambled back to where Dermot stood. He pointed upwards to the rocks. At first, Monica did not see anything, but Wullie spotted the flowers straight away. Although not a policeman, he knew not to touch something that may be important. Monica reached for her phone, cautiously approached, and took a picture. One did not need to be a detective to realize that here was a plant that had been picked and was being carried by a human hand.

"What type of plant is this?" Monica asked Wullie. He did not hesitate.

"This is exactly what you are looking for. It is Saxifraga paniculata."

Dermot reached for an evidence bag and tweezers and passed them to Monica. Dermot's eyes had moved from his discovery, and he was now looking down below where they were standing. Big immovable boulders. No evidence of anything that could be disturbed. His eyes suddenly stopped and fixed themselves on a dark patch out of place amongst the clean weather-beaten boulders. He moved closer and found a smaller rock nesting under two larger ones that formed a pyramidal shape above it, a protective cocoon. He approached cautiously, awkwardly manoeuvred himself so that he was lying on his front, peering at his find. The other two were on the path above him, oblivious to his actions. Monica stood up from her studies, turned around, and was surprised to see him lying down. She did not call out or disturb him but tapped Wullie on the shoulder. They both scrambled down to join him. Dermot stood up and pointed at his find.

There, in the cavity, was a hand-sized rock that had the unmistakable presence of congealed blood and hair attached to it. Monica flicked off her backpack and reached for another Ziploc. Dermot took a picture of his findings.

"We need a Scene of Crime unit here asap," she said.

She reached for her phone and called Doddie. She gave their position, and Doddie said he would arrange for a helicopter to come in. She handed the phone to Wullie, who gave him details of a possible landing site. Monica turned to Dermot.

"Constable Long, I need you to stay here until they arrive. Wullie and I will head out of the Gap back to the moor and guide them in."

Dermot nodded. Large drops of rain started to fall. He pulled out his waterproofs and found a small overhang under which to sit. Wullie and Monica moved off.

Alone with his thoughts, Dermot was proud of what he had achieved. He felt he was not pulling his weight as he had trailed behind them on the way up. He felt useless and was somewhat chagrined, but now he simply grinned. The rain brought cold, and he shivered. He struggled to escape the wet and knew he would be there for a few hours. Arranging a SOCO team was not a speedy happening. Plus, they would have to fly in from Inverness.

Three hours later, the "paraffin budgie," as Doddie so colourfully called it, was waved onto Wullie and Monica's landing spot. It was not long before Dermot saw the safety vested SOCOs edging their way towards him. He pointed to the area of both finds and left them to do their work. Fifteen minutes later, he was back in the company of Monica and Wullie.

Monica greeted him.

"You and I have to get back to Inverness." This time, the hike out was quicker. Soon, they were back at the Land Rover, and Wullie speedily drove them back to Tomintoul. They grabbed their bags, said a quick farewell, and were on their way home with Dermot driving.

The sun came out as they drove down the hill towards Carrbridge. They were through the village and on the main road back to Inverness when Monica suddenly said, "Parking spot in three hundred yards." She looked at her watch. "We have time."

Dermot frowned but said nothing.

He pulled over.

"Get out of the car, Constable Long," she said somewhat aggressively. They got out of the car. They saw a pathway leading through an avenue of silver birches and ferns.

"Let's go for a short walk."

"You're the boss," and he didn't ask why.

They came to a diversion in the trail, and off to the side was a grassy bank. The sun at this stage was shining, and the wet undergrowth, although not dry, was no longer sodden. Monica slapped him on the shoulder and indicated they should pause by the bank. They stopped, and she faced him. He still looked confused. She pushed him hard on his chest, his legs gave way from underneath him, and he found himself lying flat on his back. Suddenly, she was straddling him and pulling off her blouse and bra. Dermot reached for his belt.

They returned to the car, hand in hand. Before they reached the end of the trail, Dermot stopped, turned to her, and kissed her long and hard on the lips.

"Back to being professionals," he said, smiling.

She nodded and asked to drive.

As Dermot looked back from the passenger seat to the black clouds that now seemed to be dumping their sodden load on the Cairngorms massif, he thought to himself that these two short days had been days he would never forget. He had started to prove his worth professionally, and personally, he had never known such joy. If he had been uncertain about his relationship with Monica beforehand, he now had every reason to feel confident about it. They had only made love twice, but Dermot knew they had not "had sex;" they had "made love," and there was a huge difference. He hoped that she felt the same way. In the hotel room was a pleasure, but, he felt, alfresco was a statement.

"Madness is the exception in individuals but the rule in groups." – Nietzsche

Chapter 14: A Sighting

It was late afternoon before Monica and Dermot walked into the office. Doddie was sat at his desk looking annoyed. Monica approached him.

"Whose pissed on your strawberries?" she demanded without preamble.

"Och, I sent twa eejuts tae watch yon locker at the station. I asked them to check in every hour, but I've not heard back in four hours. I've tried calling them but naething."

"Who did you send?"

"Constables Smith and Davidson. All looking wonderful and scruffy in civvies with a substantial per diem so that they could fade into the background. Tellt them tae act as if they are a couple of young lads just waiting for a train, out for a spree, if ye get my drift."

At that moment, the phone from the reception rang. Doddie answered it and signalled to Monica.

"Aye, right away." He hung up.

"They want me downstairs right away. Let's go, and we can chat about what you found up the hill. Good work, by the way."

"Wisnae me, was Constable Long."

They arrived at the reception, and the receiving officer said they needed to go and visit the cells. As they entered the secure hallway, they heard the strains of tuneless singing drifting along the corridor.

"Alllee, balllee, allele ballee bee, greetin' for a wee bawbie to buy some Coulter's candy."

Giggles and whispers came from a cell at the end. The sergeant opened the cell door. The smell of stale farts and beer was truly awful. Doddie held his nose. Monica stepped back. One spoke, trying desperately to focus his eyes. He pointed and stumbled.

"Itshhhh Tective Spector Mmmmmmmac Doddie. Hallooooooo, Shir. We, we, we didnae see abody a'd day, but we, we, we kept a a a verra, verra low profile. Did we no, Smithie?"

Smith, by this time, was slumped on the floor and leaning against the wall. He raised his thumb in agreement.

"Aye, aye, naebody n-n-noticed ushh. We wash m-m-masters of dis dis cresssssssssssssshon, so we were."

And he closed his eyes. Meanwhile, Davidson was dancing and singing.

"There's not a team like the Glasgow Rangers, no not one, no not one."

He was jigging towards Monica, who thought he would ask her to dance. She backed away with a disgusted grimace on her face. Doddie turned on his heels.

"Right, we've seen enough. Detective Sergeant, let's go."

"Whit am I to dee wi'them?" the receiving officer asked.

"Keep them in overnight. I'll see them in the morning."

The receiving officer slammed the door behind him.

"God save me from young policemen. Hanging's too good for them," thus did Doddie give his opinion on young constables and capital punishment in the same breath.

As they took the lift upstairs, Doddie kicked the side of it in frustration. Monica was silent.

"Dopey fuckin' bastards. Who was called out?"

"Barbara Dickson and Joe Barry. I'll get them up for a chat when they come off shift."

Sometime later, Dickson and Barry were sat in an interview room with Monica and Doddie. Dickson was speaking.

"We were called out to the station foyer. We found about two-dozen empty Tennant's Lager cans. They had retreated to the café opposite the lockers, where they had ordered three lots of fish 'n chips. Davidson was standing on one leg on top of a table, about to put a pickled egg in his mouth. Smith was clapping his hands, dancin' around the table and encouraging him."

Doddie swept his hands back through his hair.

"Aye weil, thanks youse two, you can awa hame."

The two police officers stood up and left.

Doddie said, "I've asked the homicide team to congregate so that we can debrief, Richards. Can you lead on what happened in the Cairngorms?"

"Aye nae bother."

They walked out of the room and into the main area where chairs had been moved. They were looking at the whiteboard with pictures of the murder victim and maps showing the Black Isle and the Cairngorms National Park.

Doddie stood up to speak.

"What do we know? We know that Dr Ross was a much-respected paediatrician. We know that he was not killed in Munlochy but was likely killed here in the Chalamain Gap in the Cairngorms. He pointed at the map on the wall. We have no motive, no idea how his body got off the hill, and less idea how it arrived in Munlochy."

Doddie's face suddenly darkened. He pointed towards Dermot, who was seated in the front row. He pointed his finger.

"Ye see yon Irish bampot sat there." Dermot coloured and sat up. Monica looked away, worried about what was going to come next. She thought about butting in, but Doddie was not to be stopped.

"He has moved this case along in a good direction, using his eyes, ears, and initiative. Well done, Constable Long. I've been in touch with Northern Ireland; they're no gonna get you back."

Dermot grinned and lowered his head in embarrassment.

"SOCO is still on the ground in the Cairngorms."

Doddie explained that he thought tomorrow would be a busy day, and there would be very little that could be gained by staying later that night. So, he dismissed them, and they headed home.

Pistol sensed the movement and approached Doddie from his corner. The autumn evening was darkening as he walked into the car park. About one hundred yards from his car, uncharacteristically, Pistol stopped and growled, then barked.

"What is it, you daft apoth?" But Doddie knew enough about his failed sheepdog to know something was not right. Immediately, he was on his guard, and they both approached the car with added caution. Suddenly, a dark mackintosh coat appeared from behind the rear as if from nowhere. Doddie caught the glow of the cigarette and knew who it was.

"Creepy" Colin Pettigrew emerged from the shadows. Doddie's dress sense was the laughing stock of the station but compared to Colin, Doddie dressed like a film actor attending the Oscars with every expectation of winning.

"How's it goin,' Mr Macfarlane?"

It had been over a decade since Doddie and Colin had first met. Doddie had been called to a supermarket where the store security had apprehended a man who was running through the car park with a shopping trolley full of groceries he had failed to pay for. The approach of the store detective was of somebody who was fully immersed in his own importance. This was always something that raised Doddie's hackles. He always reached for his ego-pricking repertoire when he came across such people and always expressed the view that capital punishment should be brought back to take them off the streets once and for all. He had warmed to Colin because he had come clean, put his hands up to the crime, even placed his wrists behind his back, ready for cuffing. Doddie surprised himself by speaking first. "Let's pop back to the cash line-up, and I'll settle the bill for the groceries."

So, in they went. One hundred and fifty-five pounds and fifty-seven pence later, they were out of the store, and Doddie was loading the grocery bags into the back of his police car. He asked Colin to get in, asked him where they were going, and drove him off to beneath the Kessock Bridge, where Colin showed him his stinking old mattress, sleeping bag, and a short higgledy piggledy walled compound of corrugated iron. As soon as he was dropped off and Doddie started to leave, he noticed three other men appear from the shadows in his wing mirror, and Colin started to deal out the loot. For some reason, Doddie kept going back there when he was off duty, dropping off the occasional packet of cigarettes, Macdonald's burger and chips, and grocery shopping. Doddie warmed to Colin. The two men did not talk much; it was a silent transaction until one day, Colin grabbed Doddie by the elbow as he was leaving.

"Mr Macfarlane, I know things, I see things. I can help you."

He was right. As the weeks progressed, Doddie found himself cleaning up petty crimes in the area. Colin was his source.

So, here was Colin, unusually close to a police station with something to offer.

"Can we go somewhere else?" Colin was ill at ease. Doddie opened the passenger side door and indicated he should get in. They drove off and parked two hundred yards from a fish 'n chips shop. Doddie left Colin in the car while he went in and bought them a fish supper each. Colin complained about the lack of salt and vinegar as they tucked in, but Doddie ignored him.

"So, whit have ye got for me?"

"Strangest thing, Mr Macfarlane, I thocht it wis only Mozzie women who wore they long black blankets, but it seems that men do as well?"

Doddie looked puzzled.

"Tell me."

So, Colin launched into a long story about his return to his place under the bridge after he had been out begging for cigarettes, saying that a nice guy from England had given him a couple of packets.

"Get to the point," Doddie interrupted.

"Oooh, aye, weil, saw this guy creep under the bridge, take off his black stuff. He was a white guy. That was strange to me. As soon as he had taken it off, a white car pulled up, and he put his clothes in the boot, got in the passenger side, and they drove off as quick as they could."

"Describe him."

"He was in his late twenties or early thirties, slim built and athletic, tall with short fair hair, broken nose, blue eyes. He was wearing jeans and skateboard shoes. He wore a black hoodie with a badge on the front. Couldn't get a good look at the badge, but it seemed like there were three parallel green lines, with the one in the middle being shorter than the other two.

"No writing."

"Nah, naething else."

"I'll drop you hame."

"Thanks. AL, one, Under-the-Bridge Street," Colin grinned, revealing toothless gaps amidst yellowing teeth.

"Phew, where did you get that breath, Colin?"

"It's one of my most attractive features," he said as he slid down in his seat, luxuriating in the warmth of the car, knowing the journey would be short and sweet and that another cold night beckoned.

"A fish only recognises water when it discovers air." – Marshall McLuhan

Chapter 15: The Missing Link

Doddie and Pistol drove home in the dark. Autumn nights were upon them. The days were getting shorter. The silver birches were losing their leafy sheen. The slightest breath of wind was reducing their tenuous grip on the branches and the hillside colours were changing. It was a clear sky, so Doddie grabbed his torch and Pistol and set off for a short walk up a little footpath he knew well. Doddie was having a hard time giving priority and balancing his time between the secretive beatings and the fact that there was a murderer on the loose. He had wisely separated his resources so that one group could attend to solving the murder, and the other tried to get to the bottom of the assaults. It seemed like the latter were likely to be the easiest to solve because they were continuing. Somebody would eventually put a foot wrong, and the whole nasty little edifice would crumble. With the murder, nothing was happening to move it forward. He stopped by a gate and pondered for a moment. Actually, it was not true that they were falling short. The discoveries in the Cairngorms and the background and identity of the victim meant progress, albeit too slow for him. Doddie thought back to his team. Monica was the strength of the murder inquiry. She acted professionally, did things by the book, except when she didn't. When that happened, common sense took over, and her natural intelligence gave her the confidence to follow instincts that were invariably correct. Then there was Dermot, who had somehow made his way onto the murder inquiry from the locker watch. Apart from the identity contact mistake with Northern Ireland, it had been an upward trajectory since he came on board with the murder inquiry. This was a young man with great potential.

Pistol was ahead of him as he walked up the hill. There was a stone dyke to the left of him. On the right were some ferns with intermittent birch and the occasional patch of heather. He knew his dog would not wander too far; he would be too hungry for his evening meal. Doddie, too, was hungry and suffering pangs of hollowness. Lunchtime had been a hurried sandwich eaten at about 11.00 a.m. It was a long time ago now. He considered Colin's description. It would seem to be only a matter of time before they found the mystery Muslim "woman" and identified and interviewed him. He reminded himself that he needed to speak to Elsa Ross in the morning. They were still unable to release her husband's body, but she could do nothing more to help at this point and should go home. He would ask Monica to talk to her.

He rounded the next bend, and the white flash of his black and white dog caught his eye as he ran towards him. He was soon at his side, and the two of them turned and headed downhill to the house. They entered the back door, and Pistol lined up at his eating bowl expectantly. Doddie went to the cupboard, found a can of dog food, opened it, scraped it into his bowl, and gave it to him.

Pistol ate hungrily and with gusto. All Doddie could find for himself were Bran Flakes and Weetabix.

"Och, well, breakfast for supper, a two fer one deal, should save time in the morning," he chuntered to himself. He went into his lounge, grabbed the remote, and flicked on the local news. Picture of a wind-blown anoraked reporter at the crime scene in the Cairngorms. Picture of the Irish Sikh lad about to make his debut for Bruach Rangers on the weekend. Doddie was about to flick it off when a familiar face appeared on the screen. There was his bank manager, Mr Morgan Micklethwaite, who had been so helpful when Doddie had decided to buy his property. He was being interviewed in a park next to a playground.

"Yes, there's a lot of suspicious activity around here—sleazy looking guys walking past the playground, stopping to talk tae the kids. The police do nothing. I know they are overstretched and that, but I really do think that children at this playground in this park are particularly at risk."

"Thank you, Mr Micklethwaite. This is Colleen Ritchie reporting. Now back to the studio."

Doddie sat up; a light bulb turned on. He decided he would meet Morgan Micklethwaite the following day. Maybe, just maybe, he might have some insights into anything to do with child abuse and gangs beating up possible culprits.

"A secret radical who conceals himself
under a veil of discretion."
– Sarah Bakewell

Chapter 16: A Breakthrough

When Monica arrived the next morning, she was not surprised to find Doddie already in attendance. He was in the interview room, leaning back on his chair. In front of him were two shipwrecks, two sorry-looking examples of forlorn humanity with their heads bowed at the anticipated stormy blast. Their dishevelment was sartorial in name only, their shirts and trousers were a laundry pile, their hair was matted and could do with a brush, their faces were pale and unshaven, their eyes were red. Monica smiled and nodded, confident that if Davidson and Smith were not going to be shot at dawn, they were going to think they would be, and by the looks of them, such a fate would be a welcome release. She had seen it so many times before. She knew Doddie would say little, that he would allow a stream of consciousness defensive verbiage from the two sorrowful-looking constables. Monica was happy not to be a fly on the wall.

First thing when he had arrived, Doddie had phoned Morgan Micklethwaite's office and explained that he needed to see him at some point regarding police business. He left a message and asked that the office get back to him with a time. He then wandered down to reception and asked the night sergeant to take him to the cell where

Davidson and Smith had spent the night. On opening the door, he found them asleep on the floor, beatific expressions on their faces. Had Doddie been their mother, he would have been overcome at how sweet and innocent her two bairns looked. However, Doddie was not their mother. He smiled dreadfully, a grin like poison coming to supper.

"Sergeant, get me a bucket of cold water, please."

The night sergeant smiled with sadistic pleasure.

"May I get two, Sir?"

"Oh, aye, be my guest."

Within minutes, he was back at Doddie's side with two galvanized buckets full of ice-cold water.

"Emptied the water cooler. Thought it would be colder," he said, by way of explanation.

"New Olympic sport, Sergeant, synchronized constable soaking. Are you ready?"

They picked their targets and let loose. Shock and splutter, suddenly awake, definitely surprised and alarmed, the two miscreants came to life, although the sergeant, a gardener of some repute, wryly observed that he had seen "mair life in ma compost heap."

"Right, you two, upstairs right now."

Two pale ghosts of men staggered to their feet and followed the Pied Piper of Inverness upstairs to the interview room. Doddie sat down and ordered them to stand in front of the table.

"But nae too close; you're no exactly smellin' like roses, ye ken."

Davidson shuffled uneasily, but Smith looked distressed, spotted the waste paper basket, grabbed it, and promptly threw up in it. Davidson wavered as he stood there, looked uneasy but contented himself with letting out a long, lingering, noisy, smelly fart. Doddie covered his nose. He smiled and said, "Tell me about your day." He hesitated. "Yesterday, I mean. I know about today." He screwed up his nose.

Smith wiped his mouth on his sleeve.

"We were just trying to blend in. We didnae want to be scoped as plainclothes coppers."

Davidson butted in.

"Aye, aye, Sir, we just thought what could be more natural than a couple of young guys hivin' a puckle beers?"

Then between them followed a long explanation of how they had had a bite at the café, how they felt they might have been noticed as policemen, which would inevitably put any criminals off, and how they decided to up the ante and have a few beers. Still, nobody had appeared, so they carried on regardless and finally, things had gotten very silly.

"You're so fluent you're effluent. You two have a long shift waiting for you today. Go get your uniforms on, get out on the streets, and patrol and observe. Your day is starting now, and it will be a long double shift. I hope there is a lot of crime going on today, a lot of answering back and major problems to sort out. I hope those heids of yours throb and bang and batter and remind you of the evils of drink. Report to Constable Long. He has your assignment for the day. Get oot o' ma sight."

They moved quickly and left the office. Doddie got up and shouted after them.

"Afore you leave, I want this place cleaned and smellin' like roses, nae like the prop forwards crutch that is permeating it at the moment."

"Aye, Sir," they spoke in unison.

Doddie returned to his desk and checked his messages. Monica sauntered over.

"Bloody young coppers..."

Monica finished his sentence, "Hanging's too good for them."

Doddie changed the subject. He looked at his phone.

"Just got a message back. You and I are oot o' here. We're aff to see my bank manager." He grabbed his jacket. "I'll tell you on the way. Pistol, let's go." The dog got up from his blanket and came over eagerly.

As they pulled out of the car park, Doddie said, "Saw my bank manager on the News last night. Seems like he has made a bit of a plea to get rid of paedophiles from the streets. I wonder if this vendetta of his is something more than just words. I've known him for years. There's always been something about him I can't quite put my finger on."

"What do you mean?"

"I'm no saying, but you'll see." Doddie looked pensive.

They pulled up at the local branch of the Dingwall and District Bank, situated a little bit off the beaten track. It was an old building nestled between two corner stores. Monica screwed her nose up, pretending disdain.

"Richard Branson nae guid enough for ye then?"

"There speaks a woman from a county whare they winnae part wi' the dirt from under their nails. Aye, it's a wee bank, but it's no wee, if you get my drift. If ye need money, this wee gem will find it for you and at a goodly rate."

They entered through the swing doors rather like gunslingers entering a saloon. A set of tweeds and sensible shoes peered over the top of a pair of spectacles like an old-fashioned schoolmarm. Monica was tickled when she realised that the woman behind the desk had been typing on an old-fashioned typewriter. She smiled when she recognised Doddie.

"Aye, aye, Mary, how are ye daein'?"

"I'm well, thank you, Mr Macfarlane; I'll tell him you're here." Rather than pick up the phone, she went and knocked on an office door and entered without waiting for an answer.

"Send him in, send him in."

Monica and Doddie entered a room with clouds of smoke. Behind the desk sat a lit pipe attached to a diminutive man with a booming voice.

"Ach, Doddie, ye shud hae tellt me you were bringing company, I wud hae dressed better and tidied my desk more. Morgan Micklethwaite at your service," he said, and Monica introduced herself, but he barely heard her. "Been on many a safari in your neck of the words, don't you know. I love Africa, old girl. Do you get out to see the wildlife much when you're home? Which part do you come from?"

It was not difficult for Monica to muster up her broadest Doric; after all, it was her natural dialect.

"Fit like, Mr Micklethwaite? Aye, aye, plenty o' wildlife ye ken. I was aften awa' ben the back paddocks shootin' perdrix and corbies, masitly after ma morning jammy piece."

Morgan Micklethwaite was silent and confused. He was quiet for a short couple of seconds.

"Nae from Africa then?" He looked sheepish from behind his pipe.

"Nope, from Inverurie as near as dammit."

He recovered himself and indicated that they should sit. He noted Pistol sniffing something interesting in a corner.

"If that dug of yours takes a dump in my office, Doddie, I'm calling in your loan."

"No worries. He likes you."

Morgan Micklethwaite looked doubtful. "Aye. Well, let's get on with it then. Whit can I dae fur ye.?"

"I saw you on the idiot box last night talking about pervs henging aboot playgrounds."

"Aye, hanging's too good for them."

"That's my line; you keep away from it."

Monica dove in. "How do ye know whose a paedophile and who isn't?"

"I'm not at liberty to say, but I have my sources."

"Aye, aye. Now, you listen to me; any taking of the law into yer ain hands is going to result in trouble for you. You would hate to hear from me that hanging's too good for financial planners. You understand?"

Almost to the minute he was speaking, Dermot was chasing a Muslim "woman" through the streets. As a passing thought, he noted she ran nothing like a woman. The run-up to the Castle past Duncan Chisholm, the kiltmaker, almost did it for Dermot. He was not as fit as he thought, but the "lady" turned as "she" was passing the castle and flicked him a Vee sign. This spurred Dermot along. As "her" quarry was running down the hill on the other side, "she" caught the edge of "her" robes and came crashing down. Dermot was on "her" in a flash, had "her" hands behind "her" back and was reciting "her" rights. He reached down and pulled "her" niqab off and was surprised to see a familiar face.

"An extended horizon and a limited opportunity." – John Buchan

Chapter 17: Revelations

Stewart Innes Farquarson looked patently ridiculous as he sat unmasked in the interview room at the station in his black robes, trainers, and youthful appearance. The duty advocate had been called, and in had come "Legal" Lachlan Lambie, a man of huge intellect and larger naivete. Doddie had licked his lips when he heard who the legal representative was. Monica had bared her teeth, if that was possible. Doddie started the questioning.

"So, why are you dressed as a Muslim woman, Stewart? A bit different than stealing a bottle of vodka and a Mars bar."

His lawyer answered for him.

"Because that's what he is."

"Fuck off," thus spoke Monica. Doddie looked down at a typed sheet in front of him.

"It says here that you are a Catholic-Protestant, whatever that means. It also says that you are a male pupil at the Academy. I don't doubt the religious bit, son, but a female you ain't." Doddie sat back.

"It's no ma fawt."

"Whit's no your fault, Stewart? Stealing a bottle of vodka and a Mars bar frae a corner store, running away from a copper, being in possession of an envelope that is asking you to do things that are obviously illegal?"

"My client admits tae..."

"Fuck off," Monica interrupted Lambie before he could go any further. Lambie started to cry.

Doddie continued with nonchalance. "So, are you the ringleader of this wee enterprise?" He paused, awaiting an interruption from Lambie, but he remained silent, sobbing into a handkerchief he had produced from his jacket pocket.

"Naw, I get my information from a masked man in a white car."

Monica said, "Next time you get the call, we want the number and make of the car. Aw dun. Ye can awa hame and, Stewart," Monica stared at him, "you ca'canny."

Lambie was about to say something, but as if rehearsing for a concert and with perfect timing, Stewart, Doddie, and Monica chorused, "Fuck off."

So off did Lambie fuck.

"The ability to think around corners." – Sarah Bakewell

Chapter 18: The Thought

Dermot and Monica were still finding out about each other. The conversation that had been so stilted from Dermot when they first met now flowed with ease. Often they met for a hike on the weekends. Monica still wanted to keep their relationship a secret from work, a little private niche in their lives, which was their special place. Dermot was happy to go along with this. He still could not believe his luck. He was going out with a beautiful, confident, and competent woman who was also his boss. So, they often drove separately to a trailhead and hiked, most frequently a windswept beach that overlooked the Moray Firth. Dermot had come to love these moments of silent communion, strolling hand in hand with a woman he was falling in love with fast. However, he had never voiced that thought. He was frightened to do so, concerned that he would scare her away. Then where would he sit, a lovelorn policeman, looking across the room at the woman he loved, suddenly untouchable, forever out of reach? No, it didn't bear thinking about. He was smit and happy, and he must learn to live for the moments because they were to him magical. He only hoped that that was the case for her. She had revealed something about herself over the few weeks of their relationship. Her father had been Dr

Viv Richards. They had lived in the doctor's house in the village of Methlick about twenty miles from Aberdeen. He was the local GP who visited the farms in the area and held morning and evening surgeries from the annexe at the side of Springbank. The old stone house stood on a hill above the village just a short walk down the road to the River Ythan and the road bridge over to the main street. Springbank had been an idyllic setting for a wee lassie growing up. The old rowan tree in the back garden meant she could no longer look at a mountain-ash without being transported back to her childhood days. She remembered the day when she had been helping her dad shift a tree root on the bank before the road. They had worked at it with pick and shovel. She was too young to help but felt proud to be out there helping with this monumental task, a chunk of wood that was so large to somebody so small. When the earth finally gave up its last grip of the tree, she had been downhill from its quick release and could not avoid it as it rolled towards her. It hit her in the solar plexus. She remembered the struggle to breathe and eventually, the tears and finally, the big warm hug, telling her it would be all right.

Monica's Elysium came to a sudden end one summer Saturday when she was nine years old. She had been playing on her swing set on the front grass when her mother, Dr Veronica Richards, appeared at the door, shouting for her to come.

Together, they ran down the hill with an urgency Monica had never known before, her mother gripping her hand so tightly that it hurt. In her other hand, she carried her doctor's bag, so Monica knew it was a medical crisis. They crossed the river onto the flat stretch of road on the other side and saw the white shirts of the cricketers gathered around the wickets at one end. They ran right until they reached the entrance to the Methlick Cricket Club, the laird's ground. Her mother turned to her and asked her to stay where she was. She was immediately met by a couple of middle-aged ladies, who had been making the teas.

It had been a fast bowl, which had taken an awkward bounce. Her father had been batting and had not been quick enough to take evasive action. It had hit him on the skull just behind the ear. It was likely that he was dead before he hit the ground.

The ambulance pulled onto the field as Monica's mother reached him. Monica felt warm hands taking her into the pavilion. Her mother was with her father in the back of the ambulance. She did not realise at the time that she had come down the hill as part of a loving family and returned up the hill fatherless. Her father was dead, a victim of a freak accident, playing a game he loved. It was just her and her mother from then on, except that it wasn't. Both her mother and father were not simply much respected in this rural community but also loved. The farms and villages and small towns in the area wrapped themselves around them like a warm blanket.

Monica's sharing of confidences with Dermot and revelations about her early life experiences had knit the couple closer together. They had given Dermot the courage to share a little about what it had been like to grow up in a divided sectarian Belfast during the troubles. His last name told the story of his Protestant upbringing, although he would deny any religious belief when asked. That did not work in his home town, as he knew it wouldn't. Inevitably, he would be asked whether he was a Protestant atheist or a Catholic atheist, a superfluous question as his last name gave it away. Sitting on the fence had proved to be impossible. He remembered a friendly British soldier on patrol walking past his terraced house as he played in the garden. The young squaddie had smiled as he had retrieved Dermot's soccer ball, which he had kicked over the wall. The soldier had walked the short distance to the corner and turned left at the end of the street. Almost immediately, Dermot heard a shot followed by the sound of running boots. Dermot could not contain his curiosity and ran to see what had happened. There, beside a parked car, was the body of the young soldier, his head lying in a pool of thick blood, obviously dead. Dermot felt himself snatched up by strong arms and taken back around the corner, where he was almost flung into his mother's arms, who rushed him indoors. He can't remember much more of that fateful day other than his mother lecturing him about staying close to home, not giving in to his natural curiosity.

Dermot and Monica talked openly and honestly about their childhoods, issues, and problems but rarely about their work. They were still able to keep the professional and personal separate. So, when they came into work on the Monday after a weekend walking the Culbin Sands or hiking the wilds of Glen Affric, they were instantly Constable and Detective Sergeant again. They were compartmentalizing well.

At work, Elsa Ross had long since returned home. The search for her husband's murderer was three weeks old and was no nearer a solution. Doddie and Monica still held daily briefings with their team. The noble doctor still waited on ice in "Deadpan's Cheap Hotel," as McIvor himself called his row of iced drawers in the morgue. "The cheapest accommodation they've ever had," he would joust with whoever would listen. Some were outraged with his lack of respect, while others laughed nervously with him. Monica and Doddie gave as good as they got.

"Your attempt at wit is falling on dead ears, McIvor. If they called you a wit, they would be half right."

And Doddie had turned on his heel and left before the pathologist could have the last word because if there was anything that he loved more than his work, it was having the last word.

Fall was moving into Winter. It was the time of year that Doddie hosted a Christmas Party at his house for all who wanted to come. He provided the booze as long as his guests brought a selection of food. He had them sign up on a spreadsheet. Smith thought it would be funny if he put down "Smith's Crisps." Doddie noted this and showed him the roster for traffic duty partially filled in with only his name at unsocial hours.

"See, Smith, I can have my wee joke as weil. I like those strawberries dipped in chocolate. See what you can come up with, and I'll hiv another keek at this roster."

Davidson had put down Kendal Mint Cake. Doddie had asked him to rethink this, saying, "Kendal fuckin' Mint Cake, we're no goin' on a fucking hike. Awa and put some sausages on sticks and stopped being sic a bampot, or I'll have ye on points duty with Smith for the rest of yer days."

Rowlands always came with his wife, stayed for an hour, made his Mr Grace speech, "You've all done very well," and finished with his Windsor Davies imitation, "Shoulders back, boys and girls. Lovely pairs of shoulders, show 'em off then, show 'em off." This last delivered in what he thought was a wonderful Welsh accent, whereas the rest of the guests looked on him as if he was a white Pakistani. Nevertheless, they clapped and cheered in appreciation, and the "royal couple" shook hands and wished each one of them season's greetings. On one occasion, a drunken, kilted teuchter had taken the extended hand of Mrs Rowlands, bowed, and head-butted her on the nose. He was most apologetic and, in the process, grabbed her fine silk scarf from around her neck and proceeded to try to soak up the blood with it, at the same time adding two-fingered pressure to the bridge of her nose. He never appeared at the station again. It was suggested that he had been posted to St. Kilda to keep the peace. It would have been easy there because the last humans had been evacuated from that island at some point between the World Wars. He would not have found it easy to quieten the thousands of guillemots who squawked their nesting presence on the cliffs that were the island's battlements against the Atlantic storms that frequented the area.

The secret relationship between Monica and Dermot had become a well-practised act of adroit dissemination. So, at Doddie's get-together, a shrewd observer would have noted that each of them made their way around the room, drinking, chatting with many different groups but at no time with each other.

Indeed, a fly on the wall may well have surmised that they didn't like each other at all. That was just the way they wanted it.

When the night arrived, "Mine Host" had given Pistol some reindeer ears and a green and red scarf. He did not mind, for the night was full of scraps falling from the plates of the rich. The house was blessed with space, so those who drank had no need of a taxi or ride home; Doddie was happy for them to crash anywhere. McIvor was talking to anybody who would listen about the ten most interesting batches of stomach contents he had ever come across. A young computer technician reached over to put back the sausage on a stick he had just picked from the plate on the kitchen table. Mental Martin was expounding on the benefits of whisky as a panacea for all mental illnesses.

"Aye, aye, whisky it should be, it's nae ca'd 'the water of life' for nothing. You've all seen what real water does tae corrugated iron. Ye dinnae need that rust inducing, rot gut stuff flowing around yer body. Na, na, it's the whisky that fends off bad thoughts."

"But whit about the morning efter?" a young constable asked. Mental Martin dismissed him with a wave of his hand.

"We all hiv tae deal wi' mornings, son, but naebody has tae enjoy them."

Doddie had cranked up the music—always Bruce Springsteen. He was belting out "Darkness on the Edge of Town" at full bore. Monica had already run her fingers through his CD selection and was shouting above the din, trying to make herself heard to Doddie.

"Have ye no got anything mair lively, something to dance to?"

"Aye, aye, I might have ABBA in the shed," and he disappeared out of the back door accompanied by Pistol, who had now managed to discard his antlers.

Dermot was listening to a story about a fishing trip on Loch Ness. A couple of young constables were talking about a night out and how they had somehow found themselves in the village of Dores on the banks of the loch. They had seen the outline of a rowing boat on the water's edge and had taken themselves down there to have a wee look. To their surprise, they found oars and rowlocks in the bottom of the boat, so they had decided on a fishing trip on the spur of the moment. So, with drink enthused zealotry, they had grabbed an oar each, slotted in the rowlocks, and rowed a good way out onto the loch. They had rowed about four hundred yards off-shore, battling against the wind and the darkness when one had turned to the other and asked what they were going to fish with. There followed laughter and high jinks when they realised they had nothing—no rod, line or net. The wind took them back to the shore. They left things as they found them and somehow found their ways back to the town. Dermot reflected that this was a story where nothing happened—boring and inconclusive—but alcohol could make such things funny. Pity he was driving that night.

Doddie wandered around the room with an open bottle of Tutor's whisky, ready to top anybody up. To

Doddie, Tutor's was the worst brand of whisky ever to come out of his country, but he figured most of those around him were young and foolish. They couldn't care what they were drinking; indeed, at get-togethers at the pub, he had noted some of them drinking Jameson and Bushmills. Drinking Irish whisky was something worse than sacrilege. He had noted in a muttered moment that, "Hanging's too good for them," thus giving his opinion on Irish people, Irish whisky drinkers, policemen who drank Irish whisky, and capital punishment all in the same elongated breath. Alcohol, on this night, had not diminished his powers of observation. Throughout the evening, he noted the apparent aversion between Dermot and Monica, and resolved to dig deeper later. He could not have his team members showing such obvious dislike of each other. As he knew through experience, any antipathy jeopardized the outcome of any crime-solving. A happy team was a successful team, and they were amid a murder inquiry. It would not look good if it remained unsolved because of a childish refusal to share important information or some form of professional jealousy. He resolved to pull Monica to one side on Monday morning and see if all was okay. But for the moment, he was going to have to do something about Mental Martin, who had attached himself to a young second-year constable, far too young for him, and they were jigging along to "Dancing Queen" on his living room floor. "Shouldn't have found that ABBA tape," he muttered to himself. Mental Martin's flamboyance was in danger of endangering others who were jumping along with more gentle awareness, more consideration for all and sundry. Doddie felt a tap on his shoulder. It was Dermot. Doddie was taken aback by the look on his face, which was serious and indubitably sober.

"May I have a word in private with you, Sir?"

"This is a party. Don't call me 'Sir.'" But he could see that Dermot was not to be put off.

"Let's go outside. Pistol!" he shouted, and the dog, who was just finishing off a sausage Mental Martin had dropped as he twirled his dance partner over the floor, followed him out the door.

The moment they found themselves outside the back door, they were in a different world. The clear sky had starred away the warm blanket of clouds. A hoar frost had started to whiten the surrounds of the house. They shivered and walked a little way up the path behind the building, away from prying eyes, further from the boisterous bopping of indoors. They would not be disturbed.

Dermot laid his ideas before Doddie. "Mine host," who had been reluctant to leave his gathering before, was tolerant of the young man's whim and suddenly became all ears, all attention. His eyes opened wide. The respect and belief in the young man, absent since the photographic blunder, redeemed from his discovery in the mountains, was now at an all-time high. Doddie put an arm on the young fellow's back and ushered him back to the house.

"Let's get back to the warmth. You've opened this thing up. You just might have struck upon something, Dermot. First thing Monday morning, we'll have the team together, and you'll share your idea. Are you prepared to do that?"

"Aye, Sir, I am." Dermot reflected that this was probably the first time Doddie had called him something other than a bampot or something worse. He resolved to be well prepared for his Monday meeting. He would leave no stone unturned to get his point across with clarity. Before they reached the back door, Dermot said, "I'm not drinking because I'm driving, Sir. Thanks for inviting me. I've had a great time, but I'm going home now."

Doddie nodded, and Dermot veered away from the farmhouse door, made his way to his car, and pulled out of the yard and away home. Doddie re-entered the bacchanalia. Mental Martin was now slumped on an easy chair, pouring himself another dram. McIvor was about to slice the cake he had brought for the occasion, unfortunately, unable to do so without an explanation about the last thing he had cut open. More about the stomach contents of a dead drunk found up an alley, which had suddenly diminished the paper-plated line up for the delicious-looking cream gateau draped with strawberries and whipped cream with an inner of chocolate and apple. After about ten minutes, Doddie sensed a presence at his side. He turned, and there was Monica with an orange juice in one hand and a plate of cake in the other.

"McIvor's description didn't put you off his cake, I see."

"Nooo." She looked distracted. "If anything, it provoked me into eating it."

Doddie nodded. Monica was silent.

After about thirty seconds, Doddie said, "Are you having a good time?"

"Aye, aye." And she resumed her silence and stared around the room.

"Okay, okay, what is it, Richards?"

"Oh, nothing really. Just wondered where Constable Long was."

Doddie looked taken aback.

"He decided to go home."

"Oh, oh, I see." More silence.

"Look, if having him on the team is not working, if the two of you don't get along, I can have him transferred. I don't want to because he's becoming a fine copper, but I would rather keep you than him," Doddie said.

Monica looked aghast. "No, no, please don't do that."

Doddie looked quizzical and then resigned.

"Pistol!" The dog looked up from his corner of the kitchen. Doddie indicated to Monica that they should head outside. The chill hit them as they opened the back door, although they had both thought to put on a coat, hat, and gloves. They walked up as far as Doddie had travelled about thirty minutes earlier. They paused at the gateway to the path. Doddie explained Dermot's theory to Monica and what he had asked him to do on Monday morning. Monica's eyes lit up. There was no slow dawning there. She suddenly decided to leave. Doddie was surprised and a little disappointed.

"I promise that I'll explain sometime. I've had a great time. Thank you, thank you, thank you," Monica said, suddenly animated and brisk. She dashed to her car.

Doddie and Pistol stood confused and helpless as she pulled out of the driveway. Doddie looked down at Pistol.

"Way to shut down a party, eh, dug? Take them out for a walk, hae a short chat, and they cannae flee quick enough. Och, weil, time for anither dram," and they entered the ruckus yet again. Meanwhile, Monica had not been gone but a mile from the house when she pulled over and took out her phone.

"Are ye hame?"

The reply was in the affirmative.

Dermot was sat in his small flat, still dressed in his party clothes but in his stocking feet. He had poured himself a whisky and was sat at his laptop, focused on his presentation, when he received Monica's call. He was surprised but not unpleasantly so.

The buzzer rang about thirty minutes later, and he buzzed her in. He left the door off the latch and returned to his computer. He heard her come through and close it behind her. Within moments, she was in his arms and kissing him vigorously on the lips. Dermot held his arms in the air and started laughing.

"Whoa, whoa, to what do I owe this?"

"You're my fatal attraction, Dermot Long. I've wanted to do that all night."

After they had made love, Dermot walked naked across the room, poured Monica a dram, and grabbed his own glass from the lights of his computer from which the cursor still blinked its expectations. He climbed into bed beside her.

They propped themselves up on their pillows, and Dermot noted that, unlike Monica, he did not have the wherewithal to rest his whisky glass on his chest. He looked over at her and smiled.

"What prompted that?" Dermot asked.

Monica looked away, then said, "We're in the midst of a whirlwind romance, you and I. Things have happened so quickly. I guess I spent the time at Doddie's party making small talk, being bored, and looking for you, and I realized that the only person I wanted to be with there was you. Then Doddie takes me outside and tells me your theory, and it acts as an aphrodisiac, and I cannot wait to get my hands on you. And I am sorry, so sorry to interrupt your peace."

"Aye, well, you should feel guilty. I mean, I was busy, and the last thing I wanted was to be attacked in my own castle by some demented stranger." With that, she reached over and smacked him hard on the shoulder, spilling the whisky on her chest. Dermot looked aghast.

"Never waste good whisky," he said as he leaned over and licked the drops off her nipples. She laughed and pushed him away, but her efforts were helpless and not very forceful.

"Oh, dear, oh, dear, Dermot Long, what am I to do with you?" And with that, he set his glass down next to his alarm clock.

"The task of leadership is not to put greatness into humanity but to elicit it, for the greatness is already there." – John Buchan

Chapter 19: A Reflection

On Sunday after his party, Doddie had awoken surprisingly bright and fresh.

He had made it to his bed at about 2.00 a.m., leaving the last of the revellers sat around the kitchen table putting the world to rights. He had stepped over bodies in the lounge and knew others were already asleep in his spare rooms. He had taken Pistol out for his last call of the night, then taken himself off to his bedroom and flopped down fully clothed. He was almost instantly asleep.

On awakening, he had looked across at his radio alarm and found that the time had just nudged its way past 10.00 a.m., and it was uncharacteristically late for him. He was surprised at his lack of a hangover but reflected that, while he had seemed to consume a tremendous amount of "the creature," as his grandpa would have called it, he had always been moving, offering nibbles and drinks to his guests. He thought there was a lesson here for future reference and then rethought it as one probably too late to learn. Caring not for his dishevelment, he sat on the edge of his bed, sighed, and stood up. He put on his slippers and decided to go downstairs and deal with the detritus, the remnants of a night of fun. The house was ominously silent as the top step creaked beneath his weight, sending the message that after about fifty years or so, it could really do with a handyman to silence its groan.

As he entered the lounge, the expectant bodies were not there. Instead, the cushions were neatly placed at the corners of his couch, and the magazines were in a neat pile on his polished coffee table. Moving into the kitchen, he was "struck with wonder all too dread for words." Never had he seen it looking so clean. It was as if Mary Poppins had floated in on her umbrella, sprinkled her magic dust, and instantly turned Armageddon into Martha Stewart. Doddie surveyed the clean kitchen tops with not a pan or dirty dish in sight; indeed, not a clean dish in sight. The night's glasses were not there. He flicked open cupboards and found all washed and put away. He put the kettle on, put some Nescafé in his cup, a couple of sugars and a dribble of milk, and he was ready to pour. He sat down at the kitchen table to wait and muttered to himself.

"Those bastards. I'll never be able to find things now." He spied a handwritten note on the table and reached for it.

We took Pistol out to do his business this morning and fed him his breakfast. Thanks for a wonderful party. Signed: Smith and Davidson.

"Humph. Suppose I have to cut them a bit of slack now, the sneaky buggers."

Doddie could not bring himself to commit the sacrilege of making a mess with his breakfast. He poured his coffee into a thermos and grabbed a lead for Pistol. Together, they exited the building, locked the door, and headed for his car.

"Nairn beckons," he said by way of explanation to the ever-present dog.

Doddie had never regarded himself as particularly sensitive or nostalgic. Indeed, the bravado and carapace of the exterior he presented to his colleagues wasn't so much an act but more the man he became after his military experience. He had come from that cosseted only-child background, which only-children would ever understand. This merely meant he knew unconditional love and that his parents had confronted his faults. They only wanted him to be liked in society, accepted in society, and maybe even loved in society as they loved him at home. So, being so distant from his childhood in age, yet physically near to it in proximity, it seemed only natural to him to go "home" when he needed to think and get his perspective straight in his mind.

Doddie drove slowly out of his driveway, down the slight incline past the north end of the loch. He noted a northerly wind that had stirred a chop on the waters. The frost that had arrived the night before was still white on the ground, a deathly shroud that slowed the earth, preventing the burst of energy that would come in the Spring. He saw the one solitary bird watcher, wrapped against the cold, camera at the ready with a lens of giant dimensions. He noted the only car in the RSPB car park and headed slowly up the road to the A9. There was a Sunday stream of traffic heading into Inverness, nothing that jammed, nothing that hurried, just Sunday drivers out for a jaunt. The occasional car in both directions sported skis and snowboards on top, going up or coming down from Winter's playground on the Cairngorms. He decided he would not take the main Inverness/Aberdeen road. The A96 between Inverness and Nairn was once labelled the straightest road in the country, presumably before the first motorway made its appearance.

Being the day of rest, Doddie turned off onto a minor road at Culloden, slowed down, and took in the delights of the wee hamlets and villages on the way. He paused at Loch Flemington, a small row of houses that still looked out on the loch on the far side of the road. Memories of two unmarried great-aunties, a further two victims of war, came to him. They had seen their boyfriends—kilted and proud off to war in 1915—victims of man's inhumanity, dead far too young. Somewhere in a First World War trench, the boys had become men. Somewhere on July 1st 1916, the men had become spirits. They were lost deep in the mud of the Somme. The two women were never to know the men their boys had become. In their grief, they had remained loyal to the memories of what was and what could have been. Had Doddie known his own war traumas then, he would have taken them both by the shoulders and shaken them, telling them the loves of their lives would not have wanted this undying loyalty to an idea and an idol; that there were no idols; that they should meet someone else; that they should marry and have children and pursue their dreams at work and play, and that that was how they should honour their memories. The sacrifice of happiness to a ghost was not what any of those young men would have wanted. That was not what the message from the Somme, from D-Day, from the Falklands, from Iraq should have been. Soldiers were people in action who were a part of the world, who did not and could not step back from life. They fought for themselves, it is true, but also so that others could fulfil their futures as best they could.

Doddie's mind returned to the present. Pistol retrieved the stick that Doddie had hurled into the water for him. He was stirred from his reverie when the dog decided to shake himself all over him.

"Daft dug. Let's get going."

They drove down through Croy, slowed near the Castle at Cawdor, rejoined the main road, and entered the small town of Nairn. Before they reached the heart of the town, he turned left past the kirk where his mum and dad were married and wended his way to Viewfield Street. He parked the car opposite the old family home. Pistol and he peered over the old juniper hedge where the little hill down which he used to roll beckoned him back to a different time. He shrugged his shoulders at the changes that time and different ownership had brought to the house. He still remembered the unique sound each door made as it opened and closed as if it were yesterday. He turned his back, and he and Pistol walked westwards along the street where the sounds and smell of the sea were the same now as they were then. He felt his mind clear; the life clogging arteries of his being were suddenly searching for clarity, creating a space where might be found a solution.

They walked down the hill towards the old swimming pool, then turned right along the paved walkway just above the beach. The cold wind blustered over the firth. The distant peak of Ben Wyvis appeared in the distance over the Black Isle. It was a hill he had never climbed, yet he was as familiar with its presence as if they were old friends who played and were schooled together. Pistol hopped onto the sands and the flat slabs of red stone, which had been ever-present for thousands of years. Of course, they changed like everything else. All that was washed by the sea was never the same for long, but then everything sprang from the sea at some point, did it not? The German phrase, *"Alles ist aus dem wasser entsprungen"* came to Doddie as if from nowhere. "Everything comes from the water." Some long-dead German philosopher, Goethe, somehow, suddenly came to the mind of a Scottish policeman on a Scottish beach. Doddie smiled at the incongruity but then nodded wisely. Low life, crawling out of the mud and detritus of the ocean, dirtied creatures appearing from under a rock, that was what coppers dealt with daily, was it not? He suddenly saw the irony as well, and then he shook his head as if discarding surreal ideals for the more pending present. Slowly, Doddie's mind returned to the case and his conversations with Monica and Dermot the previous night.

Pistol and Doddie walked back up the beach and back onto the path. They walked east towards Nairn Harbour, past the windbreak that protected the putting green, then along past the paddling pool and the field with the Victorian bandstand resting on the green grassy knoll above it. This was where the annual Highland Games were held. The old stone buildings, houses built for fishermen and their families, signalled the old working part of the town. Doddie and Pistol reached the harbour, now a haven for leisure craft. He turned right and walked up towards the high street through the low stone houses, reaching and crossing the main road between Inverness and Aberdeen with the Asher's Bakery opposite. He turned left, and the two of them walked over the road bridge. They nipped down the river bank when they reached the other side and came upon the path alongside the River Nairn. Despite the vegetation and the tree cover being thick and dense as the autumn rains had done their work, they could still spot the occasional fisherman in the river, waders on and up to their thighs in water.

Doddie remembered coming to fish there as a child. He had had to cast his fly from the bank. It was some time before he had mastered the Spey cast and could fish without getting it caught on an overhanging branch. He could not remember ever catching a fish or ever even seeing one. His thoughts turned to Monday and the meeting, which he had handed over to Dermot.

As ever, Doddie's thoughts turned to leadership and his part in its downfall as he often self-deprecated. He liked his team, and he wanted the best for them. But more important than that, they had a murder to solve, a conclusion to reach to allow a wife—thank goodness, not a mother—to grieve her loss. Davidson and Smith were two young constables who had great potential but suffered from their youth. They did not know yet that consequences were often the result of a lack of forethought. They were a lot like he was when he was young, but he had had the army, which had mitigated his impulsiveness. Monica and Dermot were fast becoming an enigma. Monica had told him he was wrong to think they could not work together, that they were fine. But, two colleagues who work closely yet do not pass the time together at a party seemed unusual. He could understand it if he was telling one of his long-winded stories and holding his audience in thrall. But, no, there had been no cliques at his party. Everyone had mingled freely, rotated their way around the room, yet where Monica was, then Dermot was not. Strange indeed.

Doddie picked up Pistol's lead and walked back to the road and the bridge. This time, they walked up through the centre of the town. The businesses had changed over the years. There was no more Rose Brothers, the grocery store that had made home deliveries with boys on bikes. The red stone of the Highland Hotel was still there. He remembered the No Parking signs, which alternated; one side of the street was parking on a Monday, and the other was on a Tuesday. It had been somebody's job to flip them in an evening. He remembered his holiday job at the Nairnshire Laundry, the day he had been delegated to do a spot of painting and had walked home afterwards, noticing the stares of worried-looking people. His reflection in the mirror revealed that his head and face were covered in red paint. People must have thought he was bleeding terribly.

Pistol and Doddie walked past the now-defunct Odeon Cinema opposite the bus station and through the tarmac footpath that led to Viewfield Street. Nowadays, the area to the South was given over to a mass of tennis courts. Children and ambitious parents inspired by Andy Murray, pushing their protégés to a level most would never realize. They walked further along to the statue of Dr John Grigor, who stood before the Nairn Museum, majestic in his Victorian finery. Born in Elgin, he had been a physician in Nairn for many years and actively pushed the town forward as a tourist spot. He could legitimately have been called the father of the Nairn tourist industry. Some later promoter had coined it as the "Brighton of the North." Doddie would have preferred if Brighton had been given the moniker "The Nairn of the South," but England was the elephant with the way and the sway; Scotland was the mouse with the peek and the squeak.

It wasn't long before they had passed the Museum and were in a stretch of open green with a gap in the stone wall beyond where Viewfield Street became a road for vehicles. Soon, they were back at the car, and Pistol was taking his place in the passenger seat, luxuriating in the fresh air that was starting to move through the half-open window as Doddie drove off.

"Better to light a candle than curse the darkness." – Peter Benenson

Chapter 20: A Light Shines

Doddie was at work early on Monday morning, but he was not as early as Dermot. Doddie looked up from his desk to find a very nervous freckled-face pacing in front of him. He could not stop running his hands through his hair and jumping back and forth before him.

"Did ye enjoy the party?"

"What? Aye, aye, Sir. Great time. Thanks so much for inviting me." Dermot's distraction was all-consuming. His focus was elsewhere.

"What the fuck is wrang wi' ye?" Doddie was at his gruffest.

"What if I am wrong, Sir?" Doddie sat back in his chair, smiled, and opened his hands, palms up.

"Hiv your learnt nothing while you've been working here? We are all wrong every day, and occasionally, we are right. What if you are right and kept it tae yersel? Would you be able to look Mrs Ross in the eye?"

Behind them, people were starting to arrive; coffees were being carried in from the local Starbucks and Macdonald's, and chairs were being pulled forward to create an audience in front of the murder board. Doddie puffed his cheeks.

"In five minutes, you'll be on, son. I'll be there if ye need me. Take your time. Make your case."

Dermot returned to his desk, gathered up a sheaf of papers, and moved to the front of the room. He felt his right leg shaking uncontrollably, so he reached down and grasped his thigh with great force. He saw Monica out of the corner of his eye and wished so much she was close to him. She smiled across at him and noted he was in a nervous state. She stood up and went over to him. She said loudly so that all could hear, "Constable Long, I need a quick word in private." She ushered him outside the room and onto the fire exit stairs.

"Whit's a' this?"

"I've never spoken in public before. I'm shittin' a brick, Monica." The heel of his boot flicked back and forth, tap-tapping on a stair. She smiled at him.

"It's like losing your virginity. There are many nerves, and then there is great joy. You'll be fine. Get out there." She looked around to see if they were unobserved, then bent forward and kissed him on the cheek.

"Let's get in there. They're waiting for you, and they want you to succeed." They moved back onto the floor. Dermot moved to the front of the crowd. He was grateful for the table on which he had his papers.

"Thanks for coming," Dermot began.

Immediately, Doddie, who was sitting at the front next to Monica, interrupted, saying, "Like they had a choice."

There was a chuckle from the gathered throng.

"I have a theory," Dermot battled on.

Monica said, "Don't we all?" and smiled mischievously. Dermot felt the colour rising to his cheeks.

"I read a story in an English newspaper."

From the back, Davidson piped up. "You can read?"

There was laughter. Dermot felt his temper rise.

"I thought it might be relevant to our murder case."

"Can we have a translator here? Ah cannae understand him," Smith said, his arms folded, legs splayed apart, sitting next to his old mate, Davidson.

Dermot could control himself no longer.

"If you bastards don't want to listen to me, I can stop right here, get my notes together, write everything down, and you can sit and read it for yourselves if that's what you would prefer? Did nobody ever teach you manners?" He moved to sit down, but Doddie was up in a trice, grabbing his elbow and insisting he remain on his hind legs.

"Anger is a gift, Constable Long. Now you are ready to give it to us with no holds barred. Begin again. You have your audience."

Dermot began again, and this time, there was pin-dropping silence. People had reached down for note pads and pens.

"As I was saying, I read about an incident in a town in England where a paedophile, recently released from prison, lived. Of course, nobody wanted to be living next door to a convicted felon who preys on children. People, particularly those with children, were up in arms. On a Saturday night, after a lot of lagers and a lot of righteous indignation, a group of louts decided to take the law into their own hands. On the Sunday morning, Dr Iqbal Patel had a visit from the police. They asked him to accompany them to his place of work. When they got there, they showed the good doctor the mess that had been made of his office—graffiti everywhere in red paint, threats to kill him, violent suggestions about what ought to be done about perverts like him. Every window in the place had been broken, the front door was off its hinges, and the waiting room stank of urine and faeces. Dr Patel is a much-respected paediatrician. Here in Inverness, we know young people are being paid to beat up suspected paedophiles. We also know that the "pedos" don't report the attacks, suggesting there is no smoke without fire. If we look at the murder of Dr Ross in the Cairngorms, what if perchance some of this mob had been out for a weekend in the hills, come across Dr Ross, got talking to him, discovered he was a paediatrician, decided to teach him a lesson, and mistakenly killed him? A crime of passion, a homicide of opportunity, a case of Dr Ross being in the wrong place at the wrong time. Basically, a group of uneducated thugs who can't spell and worse. They didn't know the difference between a paedophile and a paediatrician. They grabbed the stick by the wrong end, reached a terrible conclusion, and killed a good man. That's my theory."

Dermot looked down at Doddie with a plea for him to now step into the breach. Doddie stood up.

"Constable Long shared his ideas with DS Richards and me on Saturday night. We think he may have something here. We may be clutching at straws, but I think we should move away from the murder case for the moment and focus our energies and resources on this gang of young thugs. We should find the source of their funding, seek out the puppet master, and follow up more rigorously. Smith and Davidson need to get out and bring in the known perpetrators of the attack at Bught Park. We're going to stake out that locker at the station again. We're going to get to the root of this issue. Well done, Constable Long. You did very well."

There were hoots and hollers and a round of clapping as Dermot found a seat.

"A river cuts through a rock not because of its power but because of its persistence." – James N. Watkins

Chapter 21: Back to School

Dermot and Monica were pulling out of the car park. After his presentation, they were ordered to go back to the school and pick up Stewart. The school had contacted the parents and asked them to come to the station with him. However, they refused, so Social Services were called, and a social worker was allocated to come along with him. They were to meet the pupil and his new social worker at the school.

Monica drove them both there. To Dermot, Monica seemed strangely out of sorts. Any attempt he made at conversation was met with a monosyllable. It was not exactly impolite, but the inference was that she would prefer not to talk. So, the short journey had morphed very quickly into an uneasy silence.

They were expected at reception and were quickly ushered into Sinclair's office. He craned his head around the two of them as they entered, breathing a sigh of relief when there was no Pistol to dump on his parade. Sat next to his desk was a middle-aged lady with purple hair, a nose ring, a double chin, and no front teeth. She was dressed in a smock-like frock with lime green leggings and Doc Martin boots. Sinclair introduced her.

"This is Summer Blossom-Rain, Stewart's social worker."

Dermot forced his face to remain blank. Monica reached forward, introduced herself, and shook her hand. Sinclair offered them seats in front of his desk. Monica spoke directly to the social worker.

"Has Stewart met you before, Ms Blossom-Rain?"

"No, he has not. But Mr Sinclair has told me about his previous experience with the police and the suspension of two of you. Any repeat, any humiliation of my new client, and there will be paperwork." She folded her arms aggressively.

Monica replied, "I was one of the two police suspended due to the actions of last time. Let me assure you that my boss, DI Macfarlane, never likes to have young offenders given a label. He prefers to allow them second chances without the burden of the law."

Dermot spoke, "May we get the young man in, Mr Sinclair?"

"I've sent for him. He should be here any minute." At that moment, there was a knock at the door. The secretary's head appeared, and she announced Stewart's arrival. Before he had appeared, Summer was out of her seat and standing to be the first to greet him. Stewart entered and was immediately stopped dead in his tracks by the apparition in front of him.

"Hi Stewart," Summer put her hand up for a high-five. "I'm your new social worker."

"Hiv my ma and da met ye?" he said, looking alarmed.

"Not yet, Stewart, but I can't wait to meet them."

"Aye, well," was all Stewart could say.

Dermot and Monica were out of their seats.

"Thanks, Mr Sinclair. We'll take it from here. We will make sure that Stewart's back in school by lunchtime."

They moved to leave. By the time they had reached the door, Sinclair had buried his head in some papers.

As they reached the car, Monica unlocked it automatically. She and Dermot opened the back doors so that Summer and Stewart could get in. As they pulled out of the car park, Summer spoke to Stewart as though she was speaking to a six-year-old.

"Now, you have nothing to worry about, love. If you don't feel like answering questions, you don't have to. Do you understand?"

A sullen "Aye" was all she got in return.

"Now, pet, do you have any questions for me?"

"Aye. How old are you?"

Summer looked taken aback.

"Why do you ask, my flower?"

"'Cos, you look older than my mother, and you've got purple hair." He looked at her in disgust.

"Well, now, my hair and my dress code is about who I am, my lovely boy."

Stewart nodded rapidly.

"That means you're a fuckin' eedjut then."

Summer looked perturbed at this but remained determined to be professional.

"Well, Stewart, I want my clients to feel at ease with me. My colours and how I look are non-threatening. Don't you find a certain peace and calm coming over you when you look and listen to me."

"Na, ah feel ah'd rather be banged up in jail, ah dinnae want onything to dae wi' you. Ah'll talk to these twa polis on ma ain, ye can fuck off and heng oot in a health food store. Daein' some yoga and findin' oot aboot yersel. Dae whit ye want, just stay awa frae me."

Dermot and Monica listened to all this on the drive back to the station and did their best not to smile and their better best not to laugh.

When they pulled up at the station, Stewart refused to walk across the car park with his social worker.

"If she comes wi' us, I'm nae daein' this."

"May I suggest you go for a wee dander, Ms Blossom-Rain, or I can have somebody run you back to your office?" Monica said.

The three of them left her standing there, turned on their heels, and headed into the station. Summer wisely said nothing but was at a loss for what to do for a moment. Eventually, she walked towards the car park exit with a view of doing something.

When they got into the Interview room, Monica offered Stewart a seat opposite herself and Dermot.

Dermot spoke first, "Stewart, you are entitled to legal representation if you wish, but you need to know that we are on your side, and we are not going to charge you with anything; we just want some information. Are you okay with that?"

Stewart nodded. "As lang as I dinnae hae to deal wi' yon fuckwit o' a social worker."

Monica tried not to smile.

Dermot said, "She's coming nowhere near you, son, I promise you that. What we need from you is any information regarding the source of the money you get paid to beat these guys up."

Stewart thought for a while, then said, "Well, I've never met him, but I think yon mannie must hae had a rough childhood—abused and that."

"Do you have any way of contacting him?" Monica asked.

Stewart hesitated.

"Ehhm no way of phoning him, but I could leave a message in the locker, I suppose."

Monica sat up. "If we wrote you a message, then would you do that?"

"Aye, aye, ah wud," Stewart was suddenly keen.

"Do you know any of the names of his crowd of thugs?"

"No, no, ah dinnae."

"Have you ever been to the Cairngorms?"

"Is that a band?" He looked confused.

"No, it's a national park."

"Whit mountains an' that? I have nae use for climbing mountains."

"So, you've never been there?" Dermot asked.

Stewart shook his head.

"If you are walking on thin ice,
you may as well dance."
– Movie: Men with Brooms

Chapter 22: Happy Hogmanay

It was untrue of the pessimists in the Inverness Constabulary to suggest that the murder investigation had stalled and was going nowhere. It was true that the investigating officers were pretty much on the same page in that they all believed that the murder of Dr Ross was somehow linked to the group that had taken it upon themselves to mastermind the beating up of suspected paedophiles. Doddie was frustrated because ever since the TV interview and subsequent chat with his bank manager, his instincts told him he was in some way linked to the beatings. But he had nothing to go on. Doddie was never happy with dead-ends, but he realised that his officers needed a break over the Christmas holidays. He actively encouraged Dermot and Monica to take time off over the New Year.

"Awa' ben and recreate and come back refreshed, ready to work like demons to catch these murderers. Where will ye go for your time off, Constable Long?"

"Back to Ulster to see my mates and my parents, Boss. How about you?"

"Och, I've work to do on the house. Walks and fixing the roof. What about you, Richards?"

"Off back to Methlick to see my mither."

Early in the morning of December 30th, a car slowly edged its way along a street and parked outside a detached house. The driver reached for her phone and texted quickly. The front door of the house opened, and a dark silhouette carrying a case exited the house, and with extra care and quiet, the man closed the front door and quietly made his way down the garden path. He opened the gate again, taking care to shut it with the latch silently. He moved to the car. The driver within waved a silent greeting. The man walked to the passenger side, opened the back door, dropped his case on the back seat, and moved to get into the passenger seat at the front. He settled himself quickly, reached over, gave the driver a quick kiss, put on his seat belt, and silently, they edged their way down the street and onto the main road.

Monica broke the silence as they were pulling out of Inverness on the Aberdeen road. "It seems that our secret is still safe after these few months, Derm."

Dermot sensed the grin.

"Aye, it does." He paused. "And if anybody should have seen us leaving, then you were dropping me at Dalcross for a flight to Belfast."

"Aye, and instead, we're off to see my mother in Methlick for the New Year. Last time I looked, Methlick was nowhere near Belfast." They both laughed.

"Let me know when you want me to drive, Mon. I've had a good night's sleep, and it will help to take my mind off meeting your mother for the first time."

"Och, awa', love, ye've naethin to worry about. My mum is a pussycat. She'll give you the warmest welcome."

"Hmm."

"Particularly when she hears our news."

"I thought she already knew about us?"

"Oh, aye, she does, but not the whole story."

Dermot did not answer for a moment. He was confused. Eventually, he asked.

"The whole story? Do I know the whole story?"

Monica changed the subject.

"I'm starving. Let's see if there's a place in Nairn where we can pick up some bacon and egg baps."

There was silence as they drove the rest of the sixteen miles to Nairn. Dermot knew better than to press her, but his agitation showed as he fidgeted in his seat. The morning dawn was revealing a frowning unease on a furrowed brow. Monica smiled to herself as she glanced across at him, milking every moment of his disconsolate unknowing. She pulled off the main road as they entered Nairn, turned right by the dilapidated Odeon Cinema opposite the bus station and found a place to park on the deserted high street. She pulled over, applied the hand-brake, switched off the engine, and released her seat belt. She reached over and placed her right hand on top of Dermot's left. She looked into his eyes, which were now racked with concern and extremely wide.

"Dermot, my darling, I'm pregnant."

His eyes opened further in astonishment; his mouth opened wider. But he did not speak.

Eventually, he said, "I'm to be a father?"

She nodded.

"A father? Me? How did that happen?"

She nodded again before screwing up her face at the last question.

"Of course, it's my decision. You don't have to commit to me. I'm fine with being a single mum. I've always wanted a child of my own. Don't worry. Believe me; I have no expectations of you, Derm. Let's walk down the street to Asher's and get some breakfast. I certainly need it, and you look as though you do as well."

She started to get out of the car. Dermot did the same. He didn't speak but turned to walk up the street.

"That's the wrong way, Dermot. Asher's is at the other end unless you plan on leaving me already."

"No, no, just wait here a minute; I'll be back."

She stood alone on the street and looked after him as he wandered towards the Highland Hotel, looking into shop fronts and coming out again. Suddenly, she saw him pause and linger, reach in his pocket for some change, fiddle with something in a shop doorway, and come away obviously triumphant. He returned to her side quickly and with a bounce in his step. He was standing before her. Suddenly, he knelt on one knee, fumbled in his pocket, and looked up at her.

"Monica Richards, will you marry me?" He took her by the hand.

She nodded. "Yes, yes, yes."

He reached up and placed a ring on her finger. It was plastic and gaudy, a massive pink heart.

He stood before her and sheepishly said, "It's from the bubble gum machine up the road. I'll get you something better later."

"Dermot, are you sure about this? You don't have to. I never expected it. It's what I wanted, I mean, a child. I'm an independent type."

"Shush, Detective; it's what I've wanted since I first saw you across our crowded place of work. C'mon, breakfast. We're eating for three. Unless, of course, there's an extra wee package in there that you're not telling me about."

"I'm not having twins, you daft apoth."

And she whacked him hard on the shoulder.

"Ow, that's assault."

He took her by the hand, and they walked towards the bakery. They could smell the fresh bread as they came closer to the shop. It was early, but it was open, and it looked like they were the first customers. A stout, flour-covered, middle-aged apron greeted them at the counter. Her cheery face was a pleasant welcome. Dermot spoke.

"Good morning. We would like four bacon and egg butties and two cups of coffee, please."

"Aye, looks like a fine day. Are you travelling far?"

"Yep," said Dermot. "May I tell you a secret?" He leaned across the counter. The server smiled.

"Monica here has just told me she's expecting our child, and I have just proposed to her, and she's accepted."

The lady beamed her pleasure.

"Well, that's a wonderful start to my day, young man. Better than the sun comin' up. Congratulations to you both."

Monica smiled and held up her plastic ring.

"Sort of a spur of the moment. From the Gobstopper machine in the high street."

The lady laughed. Dermot reached in his wallet to pay.

"Na, na, you may not remember yon trashy ring for long, but hopefully, you'll mind that you received a free breakfast frae Asher's Bakery on the day you made the most important decision of your lives. Awa and set yersels doon, and I'll bring it over to ye."

She waved them away and went back to pouring the coffee.

"A tunnel at the end of the light."
– Peter Davidson

Chapter 23: The Inkling

January 4th was the first full day after the holiday for the "murder morons," as Doddie had endearingly termed the unlikely cohort of coppers he had assembled to solve the killing of Dr Ross.

As he entered the fifth floor of the station, which was now dedicated to the issue, Doddie noticed that the pot plants at the entrance were wilting. He wasn't reassured when he looked around the room and saw the drooping heads of the likes of Smith and Davidson. Monica, at least, looked energised and ready for action, and Dermot had a beatific smile on his face.

Ever the pessimist, or was it the fatalist or simply the realist, Doddie felt he had seen more life on his two-week-old yoghurt. He then shook his head when he realised he hadn't got any yoghurt, that he hated the stuff.

"Must have lost the plot o'er the holiday," he reflected.

Davidson looked up from the sole of his shoe, which he had been studying with some intent.

"Happy New Year, Sir."

"Aye, well, same to you, son."

Doddie moved over to the whiteboard displaying the picture of the victim. There was a map of the Black Isle and an OS map of the Cairngorms with thumbtacks and tape indicating where the evidence had been found. Doddie pinned up a fresh photograph of a man. He looked at it closely, rubbed his chin, and ordered his team to pull up their chairs and gather around.

"Welcome back, all of you. Unlike you bastards, I have not been idle over the holidays. I have been doing some research."

Doddie paused and frowned, realising he had spilt some tomato seeds and coffee onto his neatly ironed shirt. He tried to brush away the stains without effect. He pursed his lips but did not share with his audience that his New Year's resolution had been to look smart, to be more neatly dressed. It was their first day back, and his old ways were already more prevalent.

He continued, "This is a picture of my bank manager, Morgan Micklethwaite. I have spent some of my holidays researching this esteemed gentleman's past. It seems that he was born in Peterhead. When he was two and a half years old, his parents were killed in a car crash. He survived unscathed. He had no other relatives, so social services stepped in, and he was taken into care. A string of foster parents came and went. Eventually, he was placed in a children's home in the coastal town of Cullen. For some reason unknown, despite many attempts, young Morgan Micklethwaite was never adopted, probably because he is as boring as fuck. That's an ice breaker of a joke; by the way, you have my permission to chuckle. He had a lively mind, was reasonably well-educated, and eventually found himself at Aberdeen University, where he took a degree in Classics. Now, here is the interesting bit. Some three years after he left The Bannister Children's Home, it closed on suspicion of child abuse from some staff. Nothing was ever proven, and many of the likely candidates had moved away by the time of its closure. What if Morgan Micklethwaite was a victim of sexual abuse and is now out for revenge?"

Smith put his hand up. Doddie indicated that he could speak.

"Are you saying that he is employing young lads to beat up suspected paedophiles?"

Doddie nodded.

"Where would he get his information, Sir?" Smith appeared to be more awake than he had seemed.

"Well, I've thought about this a great deal and am wondering if there is somebody on the force dropping hints to him."

He looked at the faces before him, but nobody gave anything away.

"In sterquilinis invenitur," meaning
"In filth, it will be found."
– Anonymous from the Middle Ages

Chapter 24: A Bad Atmosphere

It was not Doddie's usual MO to cause suspicion in the ranks of his team. He came back from his holiday, resolving to dig deeper into this case than they had hitherto gone. He certainly had come to believe that somebody within the station was releasing details about suspicious men, who may or may not be paedophiles. When he entered the meeting, he wanted to let the people know he believed there was a list out there, but he had no intention of casting aspersions in the direction of his fellow police officers. But something about the seeming apathy, the distracted fatalism that seemed to be in the room after their time off, had irritated him. He had looked around and seen a group of very talented crime solvers, but they were short on energy. They seemed to have about as much drive as a Datsun going uphill when Lewis Hamilton was needed in his Formula One. So, he resorted to creating a seed of doubt but realized that superstition did no good, knowing it would stifle and prevent cooperation. But he had mitigated his accusations and ended the meeting by suggesting that the leak was not coming from the inquiry team; none of them would be that stupid, and they had moved the case into a pretty good position. No, he suspected that another resource within the station brought the information. He explained that when he found the perpetrator, there would be hell to pay. When Monica asked if hanging would be too good for them, he answered with emphasis, "Aye."

And the meeting broke up.

Dermot sought out Monica at her desk.

"What is it, Constable?" she asked formally.

"I think that I know where the leak might be coming from. Don't tell DI Macfarlane because I need my suspicions to be confirmed."

Monica looked at him questioningly but said nothing.

Dermot worked at his desk most of the day. Occasionally, Monica looked over at him. She was determined not to ask him about his suspicions, but she could not hide her intrigue. As the day neared its end, she looked up from her desk at Dermot's workstation, but he had gone. Monica frowned but resolved not to act.

Dermot was sat in his car in the car park outside the police station. There were private vehicles dotted here and there between the police cars. He looked at his watch, noting it nudge closer and closer to 5.30 p.m. At about 5.31 p.m., a person emerged from the entranceway. Dermot muttered, "Like clockwork."

He moved quickly from his car, ensuring he was a reasonable distance from the person and proceeded to follow him. Dermot realised that the civilian suit in front of him was unlikely to notice him. His steps were brisk and obviously on a mission. He was a dog on a bone, eagerly driving towards a destination. In about twenty minutes, Dermot watched his quarry stop outside a business front, pause briefly to look around, and disappear through the front door of the premises. Dermot resolved to wait.

Thirty minutes later, his prey emerged, but this time, in the company of another suit. They both looked about them, shook hands, and separated. He decided to continue to follow his original target. About thirty minutes later, they approached a block of flats, and the man disappeared inside.

That night, sitting around at his flat, sharing a cup of tea with Monica, Dermot shared his interesting after-work adventure with her. As soon as Monica had heard whom he was tailing, she had lost interest in his adventures. Mustering her ailing focus from a tiring day at work, she yawned and asked, "So what was the name of the business that he visited?"

"Oh, the Dingwall and District Bank. Funny little building, sandwiched between..."

But Monica, suddenly alert and tense, wouldn't let him finish.

"What did you say?"

"The Dingwall and District Bank. Why?"

She stood up and grabbed his phone, sitting on the coffee table, brushed off the crumbs from the digestive biscuit he had been eating, and said with some urgency, "You have to phone Doddie. And I mean, right now."

She thrust the phone into his hand.

At this very moment, Doddie was sat savouring the smells of his favourite Indian takeaway as he waited for his chicken vindaloo and biryani rice with poppadoms and onion bhaji to appear from the kitchen behind. Doddie had been a patron of this shop for years. Its name first attracted him—the "Delhi Belhi" appealed to his sense of humour. He had never been to the subcontinent but had heard from those who had that inevitably a visit would result in a case of Delhi belly, which could result in hours sat on the toilet whilst the world fell out of one's bottom. He chuckled then because he knew that visitors from India suffered similarly when they first visited Scotland. The restaurant owner, Bishan Bedi, had smiled when Doddie had asked about the name.

"You British are not the only ones with a self-deprecating sense of humour." He had wiggled his head like a nodding dog in the back of a car.

Doddie's phone rang, and he noted Dermot's name. He frowned and picked it up.

"Aye, what is it? This had better be fuckin' guid. Ahm jist aboot to sample a morsel of Indian heaven."

"Sorry, Sir, I didn't mean to interfere with your sex life."

Doddie held the phone away from him with disgust.

"Sex life? What are you talking aboot? I'm buyin' a wee' Ruby Murray tae hae fur ma supper. Do ye no hiv Indian restaurants in bloody Belfast, ye Bampot?"

Silence.

"Constable Long, whit dae you want?"

"Ohhh, aye, Sir, I have some information for you."

And Dermot proceeded to tell him about the Dingwall and District Bank connection.

"How did ye know about my connection to the Dingwall and District, Constable Long?"

"Monica, err DS Richards told me, Sir. I thought you ought to know."

Doddie sighed at the other end of the line.

"You did right to tell me, son. Now fuck off and let me get my supper home before it gets cold."

"There is no loyalty without betrayal." – John Le Carre

Chapter 25: Digging

Doddie awoke the following morning, relieved that he had remembered to put the toilet roll in the freezer the night before. He hastily retrieved it from amongst the frozen fish and pre-made pizzas. He retreated to his toilet, pushing a hungry Pistol to one side in the process. He reached behind himself as he sat down to find *The Daily Telegraph Book of Crosswords*, which was always there for him when he needed to do his business. To Doddie, sitting on the toilet without something to read or a problem to solve was anathema. His time perched on the porcelain were moments of creative problem-solving. As the remnants of the previous night's curry left his body, he muttered sotto voce, "Better than sex."

While toiling with a particularly difficult cryptic clue, his mind wandered to the upcoming day. He was rehearsing how he was going to approach Dermot's revelations from the previous day. He did not want to frighten off his target. He needed all his diplomacy and subtlety. He had explained by text to Dermot and Monica that the secret of their discovery must be kept, that any revealing of the names of the persons concerned would mean execution by him with the rider that "hanging would be too good."

A passing thought occurred to him. How could it be that Monica and Dermot, who seemed to have little time for each other, communicate such vital information? After all, he had seen how they avoided each other at his Christmas party and had sensed their unease when he had paired them up to do police work together. When all was said and done in the present inquiry, he resolved to sit down with them and have a heart to heart. Doddie understood that a display of empathy from him was as rare as rocking horse shite, but he had worked on managing his team more effectively over the years. He shook his head as, having finished his business, he stood up.

"No, I haven't," he said aloud. This produced a frantic scratching at the toilet door from the hungry Pistol.

Having washed his hands, he exited and smiled at his waiting dog.

"Breakfast for you, old son."

He walked towards the kitchen, opened a cupboard, and found some dried food for man's best friend. The bowl rattled and banged as the dog set aside any niceties during the important business of consumption.

As Doddie drove into Inverness that morning, he mulled over his plan. He had been taught in the military that no plan survives the first contact, but he was instructed that this was never a reason not to plan. Indeed, he reflected, as he reached over to the passenger seat to pat Pistol on the head, he had also been taught to adapt. Doing things on the fly had been a recognised strength of Doddie's then and now. On the other hand, flying by the seat of his pants had often caused him more trouble than he cared to remember. His mind wandered back to when he had given chase to a small-time burglar and petty thief, "Finger" Forbes, around the town. Doddie had been in a police Land Rover; Forbes had been in a battered old Mini. Eventually, Forbes abandoned the car and fled across the local allotments. Doddie gave chase using all his off-road skills and the vehicle's four-wheel drive to plough through the crop of vegetables that the allotment holders had lovingly and tenderly nurtured. George Smith had let it be known in no uncertain terms that his prize marrows were not going to win any prizes in their flattened, sorry state. There was no point in Doddie denying his part in their downfall when the Land Rover's tyre marks were there for all to see. The fact that the masticated mess had somehow made it from the desk sergeant's counter to Rowlands's desk was a fact that proved Doddie was not universally popular amongst his colleagues. Rowlands had warned him that such behaviour was not designed to maintain the good name of the force, but he could hardly blame him for doing his best to catch the thief. Having escaped through the other side of the allotment, Davidson was sat on a park bench, having his lunchtime piece. Recognising the flustered Forbes, the policeman had stuck out his size thirteen boots as he was running past, and within moments, the villain was cuffed and ready to be escorted to the station.

Doddie didn't stop on his floor on arrival at work but headed upstairs to Mental Martin's office. His personal assistant, Umbago, asked if he had an appointment, which, of course, Doddie didn't. But, at that moment, Mental Martin appeared at his door wearing a pink leather suit with a waistcoat, a woman's wig of fiery red hair, and a spray of flowers above his right ear.

"It's for my next client," Mental Martin said by way of explanation.

"Whit's wrang wi' him?" a gobsmacked Doddie asked.

"Her? Oh, she's fuckin' nuts," he said as though that was explanation enough. "What can I do for you?"

"A moment of your valuable?" And Doddie indicated that he would like to enter the privacy of his office.

Mental Martin stepped back and allowed him through.

Doddie didn't beat about the bush.

"Do you have any knowledge or access to any information regarding possible paedophiles in the town?"

Mental Martin looked pensive, scratched his right ear lobe, and adjusted the flowers in his hair.

"Aye, I do. I keep rough unofficial notes through clients and write down their suspicions about possible local deviants. Because of privacy concerns, I keep them locked away in a lower drawer of my filing cabinet."

"Does anybody else have access to these?"

"No, not really, although I suppose my assistant could access them if he even knew they existed."

Doddie nodded. Mental Martin looked unusually serious.

"I need to borrow your assistant for an hour or so."

"Be my guest. Grab him on your way out."

Leaving the office, Doddie approached Umbago's desk. Umbago was so absorbed in his work that he did not notice Doddie looming over him. Eventually, Doddie leaned across the desk so that he was literally in his face. Umbago jerked back in his chair, startled by the intrusion.

"I need to talk to you. Yer boss in there said I could borrow you for an hour or so."

Umbago looked confused.

"Beautiful day. Let's go for a walk."

Doddie beckoned him up and out. Umbago seemed to move from bafflement to fear. Nevertheless, he shut down his computer, stood up, grabbed his coat from the back of his chair, and moved towards the door, where Doddie was now waiting for him.

The ride down to the front of the building in the elevator was an awkward silence from Umbago and a smiling whistling from the relaxed detective. Umbago noted to himself that the tune was a hymn. He couldn't help feeling that "For Those in Peril on the Sea" was a dirge directed in his direction. He had been nervous before, but now his inner trepidation was about to burst out.

"I thought we would take a wee dander around the shopping area of the town." Doddie smiled with what he thought was ingratiating impishness, but it seemed more of an evil, twisted demonstration of devilishness to Umbago.

They emerged from the front door of the police station into bright sunlight. Doddie led off briskly.

"Umm, where are we going?" Umbago prodded uselessly.

"You'll see. Just try to keep up."

They meandered a mazy way with seemingly little purpose until they eventually found themselves in front of the Dingwall and District Bank. Umbago was brought up short and took several deep breaths.

"You look a bit peaky. Let's go in, and I'll see if they can get you a drink of water."

"No, no, it's okay." But Doddie had his arm in the small of his back and was pushing him through the open doors. Inside, they found the small waiting room. The secretary looked up from her work.

"Mr Macfarlane, I don't have you down for an appointment."

Doddie was already moving for the office door. He was in the process of opening it but suddenly realised that Umbago was no longer with him. He had left the building. Undaunted, Doddie presented himself to his bank manager, Morgan Micklethwaite.

Morgan Micklethwaite looked nonplussed but quickly reasserted his welcoming smile, which he gave everybody he met.

"This is an unexpected pleasure. What can I do you for?"

Always the same little joke, always the creepily false bonhomie. Doddie sat down in front of his desk before he was bidden. Morgan Micklethwaite retracted his extended hand and quickly sat down.

"Aye, well, I didnae come here alone, but funnily, the fellow I was with took panic when we entered your bank here and ran off. Must owe you a lot of money, yon mannie." And he chuckled.

Morgan Micklethwaite had recovered his cool. He smiled.

"Who was the man you were with?"

"Oh, just a friend of yours. A guy called Umbago Lombard." Morgan Micklethwaite blinked and reddened briefly but quickly reasserted himself.

"Hmmm, unusual name, but I'm afraid I've never heard of him." He sat back in his chair a little more confidently, although hardly brazenly. Doddie stood up.

"Och, well, maybe you know him by another name, but you were seen leaving the bank after hours one evening last week with him."

Morgan Micklethwaite shook his head and smiled.

"Sorry, you've had a wasted journey."

"Oh, aye, well, it's far from being wasted, isn't it? I will be making sure that you and Lombard get a chance to meet because he ran off rather than see you. Suspicious that, don't you think? And the young constable who followed him here the other night definitely saw the two of you leaving together. Of course, no photographic evidence as such, just the word of one young fellow with sharp eyes and Lombard's sudden absence now. It's time I left; after all, 'time and tide' and all that. You know where to find me if you should want a chat."

Doddie turned on his heel and briskly left the office. He nodded, smiled at the secretary, and exited the bank's main doors.

"I saw what I saw, and I saw what I didn't." – J.R.R. Tolkien

Chapter 26: Roosting Chickens

As Doddie walked back to the office, he phoned Mental Martin's mobile phone and was not surprised when he didn't pick up. He was probably with a client. However, Doddie was surprised by the message:

"Mental madness rules. Leave a message after the shriek." A shrill scream and laugh followed, which probably emanated from an old black and white horror movie.

"When you get this message, let me know if Lombard has made it back into the office or not."

He decided to take the long way back to the station and found himself walking along the banks of the River Ness again. The blue sky gave forth hope of warmth, but being January, it was only a faint hope. Doddie shivered as a cold gust of wind blew off the top of the water. He was not ready to deal with the hustle and bustle of the station yet, so he found a public bench slightly sheltered from the breeze. He sat down and tried to gather his thoughts.

There was a link between Umbago and Morgan Micklethwaite. He was certain that if there was a leak from the station, it had emanated from Umbago. He had known Morgan Micklethwaite for many years, but he now realised he did not really know him at all. He believed that he was married but did not know whether he had any children. Certainly, he hadn't noted any family photos on his desk. His dealings with him had all been professional. When he applied for his mortgage, there had been no small talk aside from the weather and if the salmon were going to return to the Ness in good numbers. He had asked Monica to do some digging to find out a bit more about this man's background. As this thought crossed his mind, Monica phoned as if on cue.

"Aye, whit is it?"

"Oh, yeah, Boss, good morning to you too. How's your day going, Monica? Did you have a good weekend? Did ye niver attend yin o' they professional development courses to show ye how to lead and get along with your workforce? How about a bit of fuckin' politeness?" Monica said.

"Have you onything useful to tell me or no? If no, fuck off and dae somthin' useful."

"As a matter of fact, I do have something useful for ye, so listen up, o peerless and inspiring leader."

Monica went on to say that Morgan Micklethwaite had been brought up in an orphanage just outside Auldearn. At the time, there had been unsubstantiated rumours of sexual misconduct amongst some of the staff. Nothing was ever proven, but as Monica said, "Have you ever noticed, Boss, that if you pick up shit with gloves, the gloves get shittier, and the shit doesn't get glovier?"

"It's ma job to come up with the pithy sayings, Richards, but here's my leadership training coming out. Well done, Richards. And that's about as good as it gets."

With that, Doddie hung up.

"A sea change of 'see change.'" – Anonymous

Chapter 27: A Pregnant Pause

It was early February. Dermot and Monica had wanted to keep their relationship a secret from work. The ever-practical, always realistic Monica realised that even if they had wanted to distance themselves from their professional life, it would soon become evident that Monica was "with child" as Monica's mother had quaintly called her condition. So, after some discussion on the weekend, the two lovers agreed to let the cat out of the bag on the following Monday morning. Monica was going to approach Doddie and tell him. She was not looking forward to his reaction. For all her relationship with her boss, she knew he was so focused on whatever inquiry he was working on that he would brook no diversion. His was a one-track train, careering along a non-stop line without pausing at stations en route.

Dermot and Monica were at their desks early, both pretending to be focused on work at their stations. Monica kept making surreptitious glances at the door, awaiting Doddie's entrance. He was uncharacteristically late. Twenty-five minutes into the working day, Pistol appeared around the corner wagging his tail, and thirty seconds later, Doddie appeared, looking more dishevelled than usual. He was carrying a cup of store-bought coffee, which he had spilt on his clean white shirt. He was looking at his shirt with disgust and his cup with disdain. It looked likely that he would fling the cup into his waste paper bin, angry at the mischief it had perpetrated on his person. Monica and Dermot watched as he settled into his office chair, took a sip of his diminished drink, caught Monica's eye, and beckoned her in. Monica was surprised because she had been planning how she would make that move towards him, but he had let her off that particular hook by making the first move.

She moved across the room to his office, catching Dermot's eye in the process. He tried to give a reassuring look, but he failed miserably and returned to his work.

"Grab a seat, Monica. Err, good morning, hope you had a good weekend." He smiled sheepishly, displaying something green stuck between his teeth. "Thought I'd show you my empathetic side, get all of my flannel out of the way, make you feel good and important before we got down to business. Good, now that that's done, what do you think about my theory that Umbago and Morgan Micklethwaite are in cahoots, working against a group of paedophiles? What should we do next, Richards?"

"Before we do that, I have some news of a personal nature that I need to share with you."

"Aye, aye," Doddie waved her news to one side. "Do you think Umbago is acting on his own or is Mental Martin in on it with him?"

"Er, no, I think Dr Nunn has too much to lose. I think he's acting alone. Now, about my news." But Doddie cut her off.

"You know that Umbago has not been seen since he ran off yesterday?"

"He won't be far away. Now, may I talk to you on a personal matter?"

Doddie looked distracted.

"Aye, aye, what is it?"

"I'm pregnant, Sir."

Doddie scratched his old scar above his left eye.

"Doesn't Umbago have a relative living in Bruach?"

Monica puffed out her cheeks with an obvious fluster.

"Er, yes, I think he does."

Doddie scratched his chin.

"Hmm, you're pregnant, you say?"

"Aye, aye, about eleven weeks gone."

Suddenly, Doddie jumped up as if he had been stung from below.

"Pregnant, Monica, pregnant! Why the hell didn't you tell me?"

"Err, I just did."

By this time, he was around the desk with arms outstretched and resting on her shoulders, face aghast.

"Pregnant? How the fuck did that happen? Who the fuck did this to you, Monica? I'll kill the bastard."

By this time, Monica's nostrils were flaring, and her temper was rising. She reached up and swept Doddie's arms from her shoulders.

"Whatever happened to the empathy?" She reached forward with both hands and pushed him forcibly on the chest so that he toppled backwards, made a grab for the chair, seized one of its arms, and pulled it over onto the floor on top of him. Monica was now standing over him, hands on her hips, jaw thrust aggressively forward. Doddie caught a glimpse of the murder squad staring through the windows of his office in amazement. Dermot was now at the door, but a daggered glance from the now-flushed Monica told him to back off.

"Don't you dare move, ye thrawn, cantankerous old bastard. Stay there and hear me out."

So, Doddie sat on his backside, his arms supporting his weight behind him and his legs splayed awkwardly in front of him.

"See this?" She flaunted her new sparkling engagement ring in front of him.

"I'm going to get married. If I ever let you up off the floor, you are going to give this blushing bride away if I have anything to do with it. Have you anything to say?"

Doddie opened his mouth to speak, but nothing came. Monica turned on her heel and walked out of the office, slamming the door behind her. All eyes, so intently fixed on the scene in the office moments before, were now very intent on any other task. Monica continued walking, buzzed the elevator, descended the building, walked over to the local café, and ordered herself a cup of coffee.

Fifteen minutes later, a smiling Dermot was standing over her. He touched her affectionately on the shoulder before sitting down opposite her. She looked up sulkily.

"That bastard Macfarlane, that one-eyed, narrow-minded, one track Neanderthal of a man! Aaaargh! Hanging's too good for him! Yaaaaa!"

Dermot reached across the table and placed his hand over hers.

"What the fuck are ye smilin' at? You saw how he treated me."

"Actually, I saw—we all saw—how *you* treated him!"

Monica looked up and suddenly grinned.

Dermot told Monica how Doddie had slowly stood up, picked up the chair, made another attempt at the coffee stain on his shirt, sat down at his desk, put his head in his hands, rubbed his temple, sat up in his chair, smiled, and walked out of his office. He looked around at his team, who gave him their fullest attention and said, "Right, you bastards. I have just been asked to give DS Richards away at her wedding. I am delighted to do so. What you saw happening in my office was just DS Richards and I fine-tuning the arrangements. Any questions?" He glared at them, challenging them. Dermot put his hand up.

"Aye. What is it?"

"I'm the bridegroom."

The room went silent at his announcement. He stood up and departed, saying, "I'm going to find my fiancé."

"Show me the company a man keeps,
and I will show you his character."
– Admiral Horatio Nelson

Chapter 28: A Bruach Connection

Umbago had disappeared. It had been four days since he had run from the Dingwall and District Bank. Morgan Micklethwaite had come in to be interviewed but would not admit to knowing him despite evidence to the contrary. Monica questioned him about his time in the Children's Home in Cullen, but all he said was that those were among the happiest days of his life. Doddie asked Davidson and Smith to take a drive up to Bruach to meet and chat with Iona Lombard, who turned out to be a first cousin of Umbago's with whom he was very close. She had seen or heard nothing from him but promised to get in touch if he turned up.

Meanwhile back in the café, Dermot reached his hand across the table and placed Monica's hand gently in his palm. He tried to soothe her fervent venting. He smiled his most winning smile. Eventually she mustered a rueful grin. He rose from the table and made his way to the door. He waved at her as he made his way back to the Station. As he reached the station car park, a car door was suddenly opened in front of him, barring his way.

"Get in," Doddie was at his endearing best and Dermot cringed.

Dermot silently climbed into the passenger's seat of Doddie's car. They drove off to an unknown destination. Dermot stared determinedly ahead at the road. They climbed up the hill, past the hospital, and eventually turned off at the Culloden Battlefield at the Visitor's Centre. They parked, and Doddie walked silently towards the burial mounds. Dermot followed, all the time wondering when the blast would come, what would his reaction be. Eventually, he could hold his silence no longer.

"Am I to be another victim of this ancient battlefield, Sir?"

Doddie reached up with his right hand and started to play with his right ear lobe, reached down with his left, and affectionately stroked Pistol on the head. He looked across at Dermot with piercing eyes that he had used so often to intimidate and interrogate.

"I thought that you and DS Richards couldna stand each other. You played a masterly game there, son. Just when I thought I had melded a talented team of individuals, some Irish Valentino comes along and fucks it up."

"Aye, well, Sir, I am sure Monica will return to work after her maternity leave."

"Aye, maybe, but I suppose you'll be wanting a honeymoon and all the disruptions of a wedding when we are in the middle of a murder inquiry."

Dermot put his hand up and shook his head.

"No, Sir. Monica and I have discussed it; we will wait until we've solved this before asking for time off. We're getting close, don't you think?"

"Aye. Maybe." Doddie seemed doubtful. He sighed and shook his head, then took a deep breath.

"Radio in. You and I are off the Bruach to follow up on Umbago."

Dermot did as he was bid.

There was a longish delay getting through the town. Not designed for heavy road traffic, the town planners had done their best to adapt, but it was a good forty-five minutes before they entered the south side of the Kessock Bridge and made progress through the Black Isle. The blue sky reflected off the snow-capped Ben Wyvis. Soon, they were meandering further up the A9, past the Dornoch Firth, and closing on the village of Bruach.

"I heard that you had ordered Davidson and Smith to Bruach to interview Iona Lombard," remembered Dermot as they drove across a low river estuary.

"Aye, I did, but Monica had already promised them to the local secondary school to give a talk to the teenagers."

"Davidson and Smith? The pupils will murder them."

Doddie grinned his most malicious of grins.

"Exactly."

As they pulled into the village of Bruach, Dermot noted the golf course and the directions to the football stadium.

"Do you play golf, Sir?"

"Naw. A good walk spoiled."

Sat-nav found them the address of Iona Lombard, and they parked the car. They opened the gate on a very well-kept garden that looked like it would be replete with flowers and gentle growth in the Spring but was asleep in frosty hibernation now. The door knocker was an ugly-looking gargoyle. Doddie used it with vigour.

There was a little dog's yap from the other side of the door and a voice that said, "Haud on, I'll be there in a wee minutey."

They heard doors closing and comforting words, presumably to the dog, who was now likely a prisoner in another room.

The door opened. Iona greeted the two policemen with a welcoming smile, waving away their proffered IDs with the inference that they were not necessary. She trusted them. Whatever Doddie and Dermot expected to find in the house, neither of them had thought of the well-manicured elegance they saw before them.

Iona Lombard was probably just scraping the underside of forty years of age. She was tall and thin, dark-haired with an aquiline nose. Intelligence danced from her grey eyes, and confidence accompanied every movement. As in every Highland home Dermot had ever entered, the kettle was soon on, and they were perched on the edge of some comfortable chairs before a peat fire, glowing in the hearth. It gave off that wonderful aroma that only peat can give. Doddie had long ago instructed Dermot that if food was offered, it was not to be turned down, particularly if it was home-baking. Scones, butter and raspberry jam appeared on the neat tray with the best tea service that arrived on the coffee table in front of them. Tea was poured, scones were soon being munched, and Doddie and Dermot found that the questions they had prepared were absolutely unnecessary. Iona launched into the tale of her cousin's visit.

Yes, he had been there. She had never seen him in such a terrible state—he was uncharacteristically unshaven, his eyes were red with lack of sleep, and he could not sit still but paced back and forth as he told his tale of woe. He had panicked when he realised he was being led to meet Morgan Mickelthwaite. He admitted that he had been working for him for a few months now. Yes, he had been supplying him with a list of possible and known paedophiles in the Inverness area. He had been paid well for his trouble. The officers let her talk, but Dermot sensed that Doddie was getting a little agitated. Eventually, Doddie asked the question.

"Where can we find him, Iona?"

"Oh, he left a couple of days ago and didn't say where he was going."

"Did he give any hint that he might be staying in the area? Anything at all?" Dermot asked.

Iona was quick to respond.

"I'm afraid not, Constable."

Doddie and Dermot thanked Iona for her time and help. Doddie left her his card and asked that if she found or heard any news of her cousin, she was to let them know no matter how unimportant it seemed. As they walked down the driveway, Dermot said, "What do we do now, Boss?"

"We go to the pub."

So, they walked towards the high street, found a pleasant-looking hostelry, walked into the public bar, ordered a couple of orange juices, and sat on two spare bar stools. Dermot had already been warned not to speak but to watch, listen, and learn.

The pub was not quite deserted. A couple of council workers in high visibility vests sat in the corner, eating pies and drinking coffees. At the end of the bar sat what looked to be a regular. There was an imperious ownership about him that suggested he was a local character. Eventually, Doddie signalled to Dermot that they should approach him. They walked over, and Doddie introduced himself and Dermot. Without blinking, the local said, "What are a couple of coppers from the Big Smoke doing in sleepy old Bruach?"

Doddie smiled and complimented the man's perception.

"Youse twa may as weil be sporting a flashing blue licht on yer heids. Policemen all look and sound the same to me. How come you've nae introduced yerselves to MacNeish yet? He'll no take kindly to you wandering on to his patch without letting him know."

Doddie explained that they had been in touch with the village bobby, and they were going to drop in on him later.

Dermot spoke up. "We're looking for Umbago Lombard, Iona's cousin. He visited her a few days ago, but she doesn't know where he is now."

"Findlay Calder is my name." He smiled a broad beam. "Let me finish ma pint, and I'll take ye to him."

The three men left the pub. Findlay climbed into the front of Doddie's car, and Dermot scrambled into the back behind the passenger seat. They drove off with Findlay giving them directions. Soon, they found themselves at the Bruach Rangers Football ground.

"I'm one of the groundsmen here," Findlay announced proudly. "Let me show you around."

"We hivna got time to visit the tourist spots," a frustrated Doddie exclaimed.

"Bear with me," and Findlay tapped the side of his nose and winked.

They parked and got out of the car. Findlay led them across the pitch in the direction of the stand. They reached the changing room door, and Findlay reached in his pocket for his keys, opening the door. Inside the "Away" side changing room, they found a mattress lying on the floor, a camping stove, and the detritus of dirty dishes and opened cans. It was obvious that somebody had been sleeping here. Dermot turned to Findlay.

"How did he get in?"

Findlay pointed to a window that was half-open above a toilet cubicle.

"I guess, if you are prepared to wait long enough, yer man here shall return."

Doddie turned to Dermot.

"I'll leave you here to keep watch, Constable Long, while I head out to meet Constable Sandy Macnish. If he returns, don't confront him; just radio in, and we'll come running."

Doddie walked back into the village and found the small house that doubled as the police station. The place seemed to be deserted, but Doddie knocked on the door nevertheless. There was no reply, so Doddie went around the back. There, he heard the faint strains of music emanating from within; it sounded like classical music from a ballet. Further reaction produced nothing. So, he reached for his phone and called Sandy. Immediately, the phone was answered.

"Constable Sandy Macnish here. How may I help?"

Doddie could hear the same music playing in the background, so he knew he was in there.

"DI Doddie Macfarlane here. I'm outside, so let me in."

"Be right there," and he hung up.

Doddie heard the bolts being pulled back, and suddenly, there was Sandy. Doddie stepped back. Standing before him was a monstrous brute of a man, approximately six feet eight inches tall, athletic in build, solidly muscled, red hair, and a long red beard. But it was not his physical presence that startled Doddie. Sandy was dressed in a full white tutu and ballet shoes. The delicate leotard and frilly ballerina's dress looked totally out of place on the man. The ballet shoes were as delicately laced as far as possible on size thirteen feet and calves like an elephant on steroids.

"Welcome to the village of Bruach, Detective Inspector. Come away in, and I'll put the kettle on." He offered no explanation regarding his outlandish get-up. He smiled an open-faced greeting. He led Doddie to the back of the building to an office, where stood a desk filled with dirty teacups and multiple carelessly opened files, most of which had spilt onto the floor. Sandy busied himself filling the tea-pot with loose leafed Barry's tea.

"What can I do you for?"

"Err, we're looking for a man named Umbago Lombard, whom we know has been in the area visiting his cousin. He works as a civilian employee in our station in Inverness."

Sandy turned away and reached down to grab the teapot on the bottom of a row of shelves. In the process, he revealed an immense set of buttocks, which had somehow managed to find room in his ballet gear. Doddie averted his eyes as the two ferrets battled to escape the sack. As if on cue, Doddie's phone buzzed. He picked up to find a breathless Dermot on the other end. Now thicker with the effort, his Irish brogue conveyed that he had found Umbago and was giving chase.

"Where's he headed?"

"To the golf course."

Doddie got off the line.

"Nae time for tea, Macnish. Get the car out; we're headed for the golf course."

Sandy didn't hesitate. He grabbed the keys, flicked off the kettle, and they ran to the front door. With sirens blaring and blue lights flashing, they headed for the golf links.

Doddie phoned Dermot back.

"I'm on the beach. I'm afraid I've lost him. He's somewhere up in the dunes."

"Keep yer eyes peeled and stay on the beach. We'll come from the golf course side."

Sandy dropped Doddie at the far end of the course, explaining that he would park at the clubhouse and walk towards Doddie along the dunes. The course was flat, so the rise of the dunes would give them a good view of the surrounding holes.

As Doddie heaved himself, sweating and puffing, up over the slipping sands, he cursed himself that he had left Pistol asleep at the station under the caring eye of Monica.

"Where's my daft dog when I need him?" he muttered under his breath. He reached the top of a particularly steep dune and paused to catch his breath and scan the horizon. There was a foursome of middle-aged men on the course, putting out on a green just over a fairway and a lower level of sand about five hundred yards away. Apart from them, there seemed to be nobody else on the course. There was no sign of "Margot Fonteyn;" the local bobby was out there somewhere. Doddie suddenly wondered whether any locals would find anything strange in Sandy's dress. Maybe they were so used to the bizarre and eccentric in this close-knit community that very little surprised them.

The wind was beginning to get up. Doddie noted that the waves off the coast were starting to become edged with white as the gathering bluster mustered increasingly white-capped surf. He looked to see if he could spot Dermot, but there was no sign. The grass was coming alive in the increasing gale, and black clouds were drifting ever closer. A rainy squall looked inevitable. Suddenly, he spotted a figure waving on the beach. It was Dermot. Doddie called him.

"I see ye, what is it?"

"It's Umbago. He's out at sea in a rowing boat. It's getting rougher. It doesn't look safe. There is nowhere for him to go."

Doddie noted that Sandy was with the foursome, about to drive off on the next hole. He phoned him.

"Get back to the car. Come and pick me up. He's out at sea in a rowing boat. We need water transport."

He phoned Dermot and asked him to stay on the beach and keep an eye in case he tried to get back ashore. It took Sandy a good fifteen minutes to return to his car and drive around to pick Doddie up. They raced off to the harbourside, where Sandy had already phoned a boat-owning friend of his. They parked up and ran towards a boat that boasted the name "Bruach Brain" on its hull; the owner, Brian, had dyslexia. Already in the wheelhouse with the engine running, the two men dashed across the gangplank, and Sandy hastily unroped the boat and introduced Doddie to Brian. Then they were off and beyond the shelter of the harbour and out amidst the surf. Briskly, Sandy directed Brian to head for the surf opposite the golf course. As they approached, Doddie spotted Dermot pacing up and down the beach. Dermot phoned him.

"Can you still see him?"

Dermot confessed that he had lost sight of him.

"Stay there just in case he comes back."

Doddie felt something land on his head. He reached up and found it was a buoyancy aid. He looked to one side and saw that the "ballerina" had discarded his shoes and was sporting his own buoyancy aid in a pair of rubber boots. It was possible Sandy now looked more incongruous than ever, a bearded bear of a man.

The sea and the wind were now significantly stronger. Brian headed out towards the links of the golf course. Eventually, they could see Dermot walking up and down the beach, waving his arms vigorously to keep warm.

Doddie asked Brian to pattern his search back and forth along the strand parallel to the golf course. They began about one hundred yards offshore, moving out about fifty metres each time. Eventually, Brian shouted and pointed, quickly changing direction and heading North further away from the shore. Doddie and Sandy strained their eyes to see but could not spot anything. Soon, however, they caught sight of an empty rowing boat as it crested a wave. They pulled alongside. Sandy grabbed the painter trailing in the water as it bobbed upwards and closer. He moved it to the stern and tied the loose end to the gunnel. Doddie was immediately on the phone to the coastguard, having concluded that they were now seeking the body of Umbago.

They spent the next hour conducting a search pattern, trying to understand how the current and winds would impact the movement of a body. They had no luck. Eventually, they returned to the dock. They drove back to Sandy's small station, and he put the kettle on while Doddie spoke on the phone to the coastguard and the Inverness station, which was faxing a picture of Umbago to them. Having checked off all that needed to be done, Sandy produced a packet of jammy dodgers with the tea, and the two of them proceeded to dunk them and savour the contradictory flavours of the tea and biscuits. At a quiet moment, Doddie had to ask, "So why are you dressed like you are? Have you some sexual fetish I should know about? Perhaps this is the new uniform for Police Scotland, in which case, I need to retire."

Sandy laughed and produced a glossy-looking programme for an upcoming play going to be performed in the village hall to raise funds for charity.

"Retired Scottish rugby player Doddie Weir is suffering from Motor Neurone Disease. We decided his charity "My Name's Doddie" would be the one to benefit from our skit night at the village hall. As you can see, my skit involves me being a ballerina. I'll pop away and get changed into something more appropriate for police work if you don't mind. Err, would you mind if I slipped into my civvies as I am officially off-duty?"

"Be my guest, but be aware that we will have to go along if a body is found."

Doddie resisted saying that anything was better than how hc was already attired.

Sandy nodded and disappeared. During his absence, Doddie, who knew nothing of Umbago's character, speculated whether the man had committed suicide or simply fallen overboard. Of one thing, he was sure: Umbago was dead.

Sandy returned and said, "Hope you don't mind, but I've just phoned my mate at the Fish and Chippie, and he's dropping us around a couple of fish suppers. Hope you like fish?"

Doddie nodded, suddenly realizing that he was hungry. At the same time, he was concerned because he felt there was something he had forgotten to do.

However, within fifteen minutes, there was a knock at the door, and Sandy appeared with the fish suppers. They were salted and vinegared to perfection in keeping with maintaining Scotland's world-class status as a mecca for clogged arteries and heart attacks.

Sandy offered Doddie the two containers of mushy peas and curry sauce, "Help yersel; a've got plenty."

Doddie could only acknowledge with a nod as his mouth was so full.

After they had finished, Doddie felt the excitement of the day wash over him. He could easily have nodded off. Sandy was talking, but Doddie was only half paying attention. Then suddenly, he sat up, eyes wide.

"Constable Long. He's still on the beach! I told him to stay there and wait for instructions."

He reached for his phone and immediately, there was an answer.

"Yooo hooo, what to do, and the cow jumped over the moon. Ha-ha!"

"Dermot, it's Doddie. Are ye still on the beach?"

"Doddie, Doddie, two by four, can't get through the bathroom door."

Doddie held the phone away from his ear as a maniacal laugh shocked his eardrums.

"Whit are ye talking aboot, ye daft bampot? Are ye still on the beach?"

"I'm forever blowing bubbles, pretty bubbles in the air. They look so fine; they reach the sky," he sang on obliviously.

"Stay where ye are. We're comin' to pick ye up."

"Look at me, Mammie, I'm dancin'. It's lovely here on the beach. I might go for a swim," and Dermot laughed hysterically. He hung up.

"Macnish, grab blankets and heat a thermos; we're going back to the golf course. I had forgotten about Constable Long."

For all that Doddie's first impressions of Sandy were not good, Doddie was impressed with how quickly he sprang into action now that there was a problem to solve, a crisis to avert. Within minutes, they were in the car and heading for the golf club and the dunes beyond it. Doddie pulled into the car park, narrowly missing the Lancia, which was hogging too much of the driveway as it pulled through the gates.

"Which way to the beach, Macnish?" Doddie was already running. Sandy pointed at a gate that led onto the first tee. They were quickly through it and on a sandy path leading to a grassy rise, which they both knew was a precursor to the shoreline beyond. They ran as quickly as they could, but Doddie found the sliding sands agony on his legs. Sandy was at the top of the rise before him and immediately shouted back down to Doddie.

"I see him," he said and disappeared over the lip of the hill while Doddie gasped and wheezed his way to the top. When eventually he made the viewpoint, he saw Sandy running towards a naked man, paddling and skipping in the surf. Sandy reached him and pulled him out of the shallows onto the shore, hauling him up the beach to the shelter of the dunes. Dermot was singing.

"Raindrops on roses and whisky in kittens."

Sandy looked at Doddie.

"Hypothermia. Let's get him into the warm."

"Everything in life is somewhere else." – E.B. White

Chapter 29: Missing

Doddie had not intended to spend the night in Bruach, but Dermot's delirium and hypothermia left him with no alternative. They wrapped him up in blankets, turned up the heater in the car, and laid Dermot out on the back seat. The good news was that the young man was continuing to shiver; the bad news was that he was attempting to sing "Danny Boy" in a voice that was reminiscent to Doddie of his six-year-old mate, Dawson Henderson, setting alight to a local cat on their way back from school in Nairn.

They managed to get Dermot into the police house, cranked up the electric heater, and Sandy conjured up some hot soup, which they forced down a reluctant throat. Doddie phoned Monica and told her the situation, assuring her that Dermot was in "good hands" but omitting to say that those "good hands" were Doddie's and Sandy's.

"And by the way, Richards, can you look after Pistol for the night? I'm sure he won't be any trouble."

Doddie held the phone away from his ear as a load of invective was let loose upon him. Doddie silently mouthed the words "pregnant" and "hormones" to Sandy, who nodded wisely, suggesting that he knew all about such things, which, of course, he didn't. After they had hung up and checked on a sleeping Dermot, Doddie phoned the coastguard to find they had not found Umbago—not a sign of him, dead or alive.

The following morning, a confused but healthy-looking Dermot woke from his rest on the sofa to total confusion about his surroundings. It wasn't until he had had a cup of hot, sweet tea thrust into his hand by an irritated Doddie that the situation was explained to him.

"And I thocht ye had brains, and instead, I discover that if your brains were dynamite, they wudna blow the tap o'yer heid aff. Did ye no think to get yourself aff the beach into something warm?"

Dermot's blood was up.

"We were in the midst of a manhunt. You told me to stay there. Did you want me to disobey you?"

"Aye, weil, that's not the point," Doddie said sheepishly, turning away and pretending there was something of great interest above the kitchen sink.

Replete with Sandy's bacon and eggs, they hauled themselves into Doddie's car and settled in for the thirty-nine-mile drive back to Inverness. On the drive, Dermot took the opportunity to phone Monica to reassure her. He explained that he was in the car and that Doddie was driving in hopes that she wouldn't say anything untoward.

"Put me on speakerphone," she insisted.

"Fit like," said Doddie in his best Doric.

"Ye can shove yer 'fit likes' where the sun don't shine. You put my man through anything like that again, and I'll be using yer scrotum as a door knocker. Understand?"

"How's Pistol?"

"He sure as hell isn't missing you, ye old bastard." And Monica rang off.

"Shame, I wanted her to go upstairs and interview Mental Martin about Lombard. Call her back and ask her, Dermot." Dermot's eyes widened, and he let out a gasp.

"Go on. Are you a man or a mouse?"

Dermot did as he was bid and was amazed at the equanimity and willingness at the other end of the line.

"Can't believe it. She must love you more than she loves me," Doddie said with a mischievous twinkle in his eye.

They were approaching Dornoch now. The sun reflected off frosty banks, bits of ice showing up sharp on the rivers and lochs. The car was silent.

Monica was sat at her desk. Some of her colleagues had heard the fraught phone call and grinned as they reached for a pencil, a cuppa tea or anything else that might provide an excuse not to give too much of their glee away. They loved it when Monica berated Doddie. It was not that they didn't like him; mostly, they did, but a part of them wished they could speak the truth to power as Monica inevitably did. It was her strength and her weakness. It was this lack of diplomacy that could stand in the way of her career. Saying it how it is maybe wasn't the way to progress up the career ladder, particularly as Monica sported her minority status on two counts. For her part, she often thought about this forthright aspect of her character and then reasoned that it had worked well for Doddie, but on the other hand, it hadn't. He was likely never going to make Chief Constable, but then, she reflected, he wouldn't have wanted it. She would then sigh and reflect that there were not two but three counts against her. Not the least of which she was from Aberdeenshire. She reached over and patted Pistol on the head. He wagged his tail and stood up.

"Let's you and I head upstairs to see Mental Martin and nae shitting in his office." The dog grinned as if that was exactly what he intended to do. Monica headed off to the elevator with Pistol close behind.

They reached the outside of Mental Martin's office to be confronted by a strange-looking woman sitting at Umbago's desk. She was large and muscled. Her floral dress was sleeveless, which meant that the many tattoos on her arms were visible. Her neck was ox-like, and her long blonde hair stopped somewhere about her knees. Strength and athleticism oozed from every pore. As they entered the office anteroom, she stood up to greet them.

"Hi, I'm Anthea Nunn, Dr Martin Nunn's better half. I'm standing in whilst Umbago is away. What can I do you for?"

Monica explained the urgency of seeing him, so Mrs Nunn picked up her phone and explained they were there on urgent business. Within seconds, a flustered Mental Martin appeared at his office door.

"You've found Umbago. Is he okay?"

Monica put her hands up and shook her head.

"I'm afraid not, Dr Nunn, but we are sure that you can help us." And all three of them entered the office.

"Have you had any contact since he left?" Monica asked.

"Not a thing. It's very worrying."

"What do you know about Umbago? Any background would be useful."

Mental Martin rubbed his chin, wrinkled his brow, played with an ear lobe.

"Well, I know that he's from Edinburgh. He often talks about his mother but never his father."

"Do you have a contact number for his mother?"

"Mental went to his filing cabinet, dug out Umbago's file from the personnel section and handed it over to Monica.

She noted that Umbago had a degree in criminology from Edinburgh University. There seemed to be no reason for him to have moved to Inverness other than the job. His mother lived in a second-floor flat off Royal Park Terrace, opposite the green swarded gnoll, which was nestled beneath Arthur's Seat and the Salisbury Crags. His mother's name was Samantha. Monica noted down her email and mobile number for future use. As soon as she finished the meeting, she would phone and ask one of her colleagues in Edinburgh to pay her a visit.

"Wood on fire is fuel, knowledge on fire is power." – Henry Mackenzie

Chapter 30: Calling in Loans

The next morning, Doddie was early at the office. He was pacing about, chomping at the bit, wondering where his day shift was. Of course, he was an hour early, and there need be no sign of them. Doddie felt that his bank manager was heavily involved in the beating up of suspected paedophiles, suspicious men lurking around playgrounds. So, he grabbed Smith and Davidson as soon as they arrived, beckoned them with his finger, and as they approached with some trepidation, said, "Come with me."

Davidson was the first to speak.

"Are ye taking us oot fur breakfast, Boss?" Smith licked his lips.

"Away tae fuck. We're aff to ma bank. I want you two in there and looking menacing. On no account are ye tae say onything. That's ma job. We're going to invite Morgan Mickelthwaite down to the station to answer a few questions. Understand, we're not arresting him, but I want people to notice the uniforms and him getting in the car. Got it?"

"Aye, Boss," Smith spoke. "Do ye want us to have our truncheons out, smacking them in the palm of oor hands?"

"Naw, I just want ye to look like hard men, nae the saft blobs of jello that I see hanging around here."

Davidson looked offended at this, and Doddie grinned.

"That's exactly what I want, Constable Davidson."

Doddie drove his own car to the Dingwall and District Bank. Morgan Micklethwaite and his PA were just opening when the three cops arrived. Doddie noted that the surprise the bank manager showed also contained a tinge of nervousness. This was a healthy sign and boded well for the interview.

Doddie began, "This can go two ways, Mr Mickelthwaite, you can tell us the truth here, or you can tell it to us down at the station. Either way, we will get to it. It would be easier for you if we did so with honesty and cooperation. Firstly, you know Umbago Lombard, do ye no?"

The bank manager looked down at the hands in his lap.

"Aye, well, we've met a couple of times."

"In what context?"

"Och, I cannae remember. Maybe to do with a loan."

At this point, Davidson farted long and loud. It wasn't long before the acrid, rotten-egged stink of it permeated the office. Smith looked serious and expressionless. Davidson looked like he was straining to produce another one. Doddie tried not to look aghast but turned to frown at Davidson with menace. Davidson chewed imaginary gum, put his left hand on his hip, and looked across at Morgan Mickelthwaite, which he thought was a "don't mess wi' me" sardonic, tough-guy look, but it was far from looking minatory. Davidson was like a lost teenager trying to fit in with the crowd. His face strained, and he let out another loud and smelly fart. Doddie looked away in disgust.

"So, Mr Mickelthwaite, Lombard disappeared when we brought him here last time, and we haven't seen him since. Can you explain that?"

"No, I'm afraid not. As I said, I don't know the man."

Suddenly, there was a shout from behind him, and Doddie felt himself pushed out of the way. The swivel chair slipped from under him, and he found himself falling to the floor. Davidson had leaned over the desk, grabbed Morgan Mickelthwaite by the collar, and brought his head down towards the top of the desk before reaching with his other hand, grabbing a handful of hair and crashing his nose to the desktop with violent force. Blood spurted from Morgan Mickelthwaite's nose, and Doddie, from his position on the floor, could tell instantly that his nose was broken. Davidson sat the dazed bank manager back up in his chair, held onto his collar, and spoke inches away from his face.

"You speak now, you lying bastard, or I'll be selling your balls for earrings." He reached under the table with his other hand, grabbed between Morgan Mickelthwaite's legs, and squeezed. Doddie recovered himself, stood up, tapped Davidson on the shoulder, told him to let go, and ushered him out of the room.

"You go with him," Doddie said, and a startled Smith needed no second chance. He grabbed Davidson by the arm and wrenched him out of the room. Doddie reached for his handkerchief and handed it to Morgan

Mickelthwaite, who was now recovered from the surprise of the onslaught and ready to mount the high horse of litigation.

"Okay, I'll talk but keep yon nutter away from me." And he opened up like a keg at Hogmanay.

"I think I'll go out on a whim."

– Supermarket customer

Chapter 31: The Mickelthwaite Tale

While fleeing from Doddie and company on the Bruach beach, Umbago had hesitated. People who knew him had always thought of him as mild-mannered. Saying "boo" to a goose was not in his make-up. His co-workers always looked upon him as the line of least resistance. It wasn't that they did not respect him. He was always punctual and efficient at work. He went about his business if not with nonchalance or aplomb, then at least with tranquil testimony. It would be praiseworthy if his employer were to write him a reference, but it would never be an effervescent description of his character. So, friends and family would have been surprised not only that he fled from the long arms of the law but also that he did so with such athletic and unforeseen determination.

The ebbing tide had left him firm sand to run along. The rowing boat was not a chance encounter; it was one he had planned for. So, when he finally reached the boat, it was true that he was sweating and out of breath but also true that a calmness had descended over him. He knew that the beach pursuit was over and that it would take them some time to organize a boat chase. So, he took his time and skilfully negotiated the breaking surf. He edged into the easing swell and headed out to sea, frequently turning to scan the horizon. He had travelled about three-quarters of a mile offshore when he heard the thrumming tones of a powerful engine. White breaks in the swell revealed the hull of an approaching pleasure boat. That it was seagoing was obvious, that it was well-handled was clear. Soon it was alongside. A boathook was thrust toward him, and hands reached down and helped him aboard. A brief discussion followed, and the rowing boat was pushed out of reach. Then they were off, heading north. Umbago was ushered towards the man who was steering the boat.

A hard tanned, harder calloused right hand was thrust into his. A smile appeared from behind a bushy white-streaked beard. Weather-beaten features, wrinkled with wisdom and lore, reassured him that he was in good hands.

"Lachlan McBride at your service."

Umbago nodded.

"Where are you taking me?"

"Och, a long way frae here. Get yourself below decks. We don't want you seen when the coastguard come snoopin.'"

He was ushered below by the taciturn sailor who had helped him aboard. A door at the ship's bow revealed a small room with a bed. It was a tight fit, but Umbago made it in as the sailor shut the door. Umbago took a couple of deep breaths as he felt a wave of claustrophobia sweep over him. He was not reassured by the motion of the ship, which was now a vigorous up and down. But he gritted his teeth and sought oblivion in sleep.

Umbago awoke sometime later. There was no longer the buffet of the waves nor the roar of the engine. Now, there was only a gentle motion. Soon, the engine came to a complete stop, and Umbago felt the gentle rock as the boat came to a halt at what he imagined was a pier or dock. He heard footsteps approaching, the door was opened, and he was ushered up on deck.

"Where are we?" he asked Lachlan. The darkness gave no clue of his whereabouts. He saw the outline of moor and hill as a half-moon shone out on a crisp starry night.

"We'll get you snug and safe before dawn comes. Morning light comes late in these parts at this time of year. Geordie here," he nodded in the direction of his crewman, "will take you up to the house, and you can settle in. You need to hide up during the day and be inconspicuous at night."

Geordie appeared with two torches. They disembarked and walked up the length of a wooden jetty, jumped off the end onto a peaty, heather covering. Silently, they edged up a gentle hill towards what looked like the silhouette of a substantial house. No lights appeared as they approached. It looked to Umbago that the place was deserted. As they came closer, he realised that it was also a ruin. Geordie finally spoke, "Don't worry; the roof doesn't leak."

Umbago tried to sound light-hearted. "Phew, that's a relief."

"There is no roof."

Umbago sensed the smile rather than saw it. However, the front door was big and solid, and Geordie grabbed the handle and wrenched it open. It creaked and growled its opening on its rusted hinges, and the two men were inside.

Inside, the torches revealed a tarpaulin of substantial size expertly slung between the four corners of what would have been a substantial sized room, now open to the elements. Stone and wood lay scattered underneath. Set amongst the dilapidation, Umbago spotted a Coleman's cooking stove, a supply of gas canisters, packages of dehydrated food, and large containers of water. He also saw a sleeping bag and air mattress already blown up. Geordie disappeared behind a wall and returned with a couple of fold-up chairs and a small folded table. With deft hands, he flicked them open and indicated that the two of them should sit.

There followed the details of what Umbago was to do. He was to lay low during the day. There was plenty of food and water for him to last at least a week. An omnibus edition of George Macdonald Fraser's Macauslan stories had been provided for his entertainment. If he wanted, he could go into Kirkwall or Stromness at night as long as he didn't make it obvious from whence he came. The boat would return with instructions from the "boss" in a few days, and apart from that, he was on his own and was to sit tight. Geordie shook him by the hand, wished him "good luck," and headed off in the direction of the pier. Umbago still did not understand exactly where he was except that he knew he was on the Island of Orkney, given the two towns mentioned.

After Geordie had gone, Umbago rummaged through the food and utensils, found a kettle, cranked up the Coleman's, and began to brew a pot of tea.

The greying of the darkness suggested that dawn was not far off. He looked at his watch and noted that it was already 8.30 a.m. The winter darkness was deeper and longer up here than on the mainland. As he sat down to enjoy his brew, he noted that the sun was beginning to rise in the east, and slowly, his new home was being revealed to him. This was indeed an old building. Umbago was no expert but guessed that it was at least two hundred years old. Except for the roof, it was solidly built with old thick stone, an ancient wide chimney, and a front door with steps leading down from two solid-looking portals. He suddenly remembered his phone and hoped that he had enough charge left to seek out and confirm his location once and for all.

The Hall of Clestrain came up. He did not waste time on its history but found that he was not far from a main road that would take him the eleven or so miles to Kirkwall or the two miles to the small village of Stennes. Having established this, he quickly flicked off his phone to conserve the battery. He resolved to lay low for the day and, if the weather stayed dry, venture a walk into Kirkwall or Stennes. He figured there could be no harm in that as nobody knew him in the area at all. He suddenly felt very hungry, found some oatmeal, and heated more water for a bit of breakfast.

The day was a winter bright, the blue allowed sunlight, but a chill breeze came off the water. Umbago found out quickly where it was relatively warm and where it wasn't. The knocked-out windows and the absence of a back door allowed cold air to seek him out. He moved his cooker to a sheltered corner. He sought the most protected area under the tarp for his bed, ensuring he had the best chance of staying dry if the rain did come. Having eaten well, he had nothing else to do but to curl up in his sleeping bag and read George Macdonald Fraser's *The Complete MacAuslan*. He had just settled himself in, found himself surprisingly warm, and was hoping that his day was not going to be too boring when he found his eyelids drooping. He was surprised as his head nodded, and he shook himself to stay awake but found that he could fight it no longer. Sleep took him, and his book flopped to one side.

Umbago awoke and took a few moments to comprehend his whereabouts. When it dawned on him where he was, and he remembered what had happened to him, he realised that it was dark. He glanced at his watch and realised that it was just shy of 5.00 p.m. He had slept the whole day. That was a shock to him, but he then realised he had been through an ordeal of large proportions, and the worry and adrenaline had drained his being. Sleep had been needed, rest had been a necessity, but so too was food, so he grabbed his torch, rummaged through his supplies, and found chilli con carne and rice. All he had to do was add boiling water and let the soppy mess sit. He lit the Coleman's and boiled up the kettle, ensuring there was enough for a cup of tea as well. As he ate, he knew he would not be ready to sleep for a long time that evening. He also realised that his legs were stiff from the run along the beach, the cramped night on the boat, and the long dormancy of the day.

"What the hell?" he voiced aloud.

He packed up the detritus of his meal, put on his walking boots, grabbed his coat, his wallet, phone, and torch, and he headed out of the gap that was the back door. The moon was not quite full, but its brightness gave him enough light to see where he was stepping and gave him the direction along which lay the road. He felt the spongy give of the peat underfoot and the scuff of the heather on his boots. He made good progress so that soon, he came close to the ribband that was the tarmac. There was no traffic for the ten minutes it took him when the main road between Kirkwall and Stromness was visible. Umbago had already decided that he was quite happy to make the brisk two-hour walk to Kirkwall if necessary but hoped that if a vehicle passed, it might offer him a lift. After all, this was the countryside of an island, not the brisk bustle of a southern motorway. He felt his feet hit the tarmac. Immediately, his pace quickened. The day of rest and the motion of freedom suddenly lightened his step. He felt an irrational uplifting of his spirits.

He had been striding forth for about fifteen minutes when he heard the unmistakable sound of a car engine approaching from behind. He took a moment to turn and flash his torch at the oncoming vehicle, more as an attempt to make the driver aware of his presence than as a plea for a lift. But the van, for such it was, overtook him at a cautious rate, and, as if the driver had second thoughts, he saw the brake lights come on, and it pulled over about one hundred yards in front of him. The van reversed at a goodly rate of acceleration, and as it pulled level with him, Umbago realised that it was a Royal Mail delivery van. The passenger side window came down, and a friendly face came out of the dark.

"Going to Kirkwall. Can I offer you a lift?" The accent was English; the tone was young; the gender was female. Umbago accepted and got in.

The young postie explained that she had had a busy day doing her rounds and was returning home to Kirkwall later than usual. She was keen to chat, and Umbago was keen to listen. He was determined not to give too much of himself away, so if there was a lull in the conversation, he resolved to fill it with a question. He didn't think he needed to worry because the solitary post person was all too happy to talk, having had too much of her own company throughout the day.

"My name is Penny. I came up here from my native Somerset a few years ago on holiday. As soon as I went home to Clevedon, I pulled as many strings as possible with my local GPO employers to get myself transferred up here. It took something over eighteen months, and I'm never going back," she said with slow, emphatic conviction and a determined nodding of the head.

"I love the wind and the weather here. I love the people. I love the culture. I love the history. Have you seen the Italian Chapel, the village of Skara Brae, Scapa Flow?"

Umbago shook his head. She then went into a rapturous explanation of the various historical sights and their significance, not just to local history but also to world history.

"Have you heard of Dr John Rae?"

Umbago shook his head.

"Great man. Much maligned Arctic explorer. Discovered the fate of the Franklin Expedition in its quest to conquer the North-West Passage, the sea route across the top of North America. If Charles Dickens or Lady Franklin were to visit here today, we'd throw them off the islands."

"Why's that?"

"Oh, you don't know? Rae accused the Franklin sailors of being cannibals, eating the flesh of their dead comrades to survive after the ice had claimed their ships. Dickens wouldn't have it. No civilized Britisher would stoop to such savagery. Of course, they did, flesh and blood like the rest of us. No pun intended, ha! Because of this, Rae was never given the credit or knighthood he deserved. Victorian society was pretty narrow and cruel for those who did not tow the party line and were not sons of the Empire. Of course, now he is honoured, and there is a magnificent statue of him in the cathedral at Kirkwall. When I picked you up, you were near to where the great man was born at Clestrain."

Penny the postie was eager to get home; her driving was not exactly breakneck speed, but it was undoubtedly a swerve-like meander on a road that was not a motorway, albeit not exactly a dirt track. She continued to talk as she drove. Umbago wished she would talk less and focus more on her driving.

"Tell you what; I'll drop you at the pub, pop home and get changed, and maybe come back and join you."

The lights of the town were beginning to appear before them. Umbago took an inner sigh of relief as they slowed at the edge of the town.

"In the firm's vehicle. Not great for my career if I career!" Umbago sensed the smile at her little joke as she slowed to the required 30 mph. The narrow streets brought them to the harbour, and the welcoming lights of a pub beckoned. Penny pulled over, stopped, and let Umbago out.

"Maybe see you later." She leaned out the window as Umbago made his way to the entrance.

There was a turning of eyes as Umbago entered the public bar. This town was well used to the tourist industry and workers off the oil rigs, but a visitor in wintertime was unusual enough to spark interest.

A large-bellied, middle-aged barman with a balding head of fair hair nodded as he approached the bar. His florid complexion suggested he was not averse to a wee drink himself.

"What can I do you for?"

"A pint of heavy, please."

The barman said nothing but opened his hands towards the bar taps, showing the selection. Umbago pointed at a brand called "Norse Numb Nuts" for no other reason than he liked the name.

"Pint of NNN coming up." He reached for a pint glass and began to pull the amber liquid expertly into the glass.

"Stranger in these parts. Where are you from?" Umbago saw no reason to lie entirely, so he went back to his origins.

"Edinburgh."

"What brings you to our neck of the woods?"

"A winter escape."

Umbago noticed a free chair and a table at the end of the bar and moved his ready pint onto it to claim as his own. He then saw the menu on a chalkboard at the side of the bar.

"Are you serving food?"

"Aye"

"May I have cod and chips with a side of mushy peas?"

"With the pint, that will be 12 pounds 50."

Umbago paid and moved to sit at the table. He had just taken the first sip of his pint when the door opened, and in came a policeman.

"Aye, aye, Archie," the policeman addresses the barman with an easy familiarity.

"On duty, I see, Shug. What can I do for you?"

"Can you post this picture around the premises? This just came in from Edinburgh."

Umbago blinked as he caught a glimpse of a picture on an official piece of paper and took a sharp intake of breath when he realised it was him. He took a couple of sips of his pint, stood up, pretended to make a move to the toilet, and left the pub. As he found himself on the street, he bowed his head as he recognised Penny, the postie, now clad in jeans and a knee-length winter coat heading down the street towards him. As she approached, Umbago ducked into an alley. The steps passed, and he heard her enter. He walked back to the street and hastily and briskly walked towards what he thought was the road by which he entered the town. He managed to resist the temptation to run.

Penny was standing at the bar, bantering with the locals as she awaited her drink.

"If you've post for me, ensure it's no bills."

"Where's ma tax rebate?"

"How come my mail disnae arrive in the morning anymore?"

Penny smiled and looked around as her pint arrived. As she reached for her wallet, she saw the picture of Umbago lying on the bar, waiting to be pinned on the wall. She stepped back with surprise.

"Hey, Archie. I gave this man a ride here this evening."

Archie looked at the picture and immediately turned his attention to where Umbago had been sitting. All that remained was his half-emptied pint mug and the receipt with the number for his food order. Archie reached for his back pocket, pulled out his phone, and dialled the police. Within minutes, Shug was back in the bar, asking questions. He approached Penny, and they sat down where Umbago had been. Penny told her story.

"He can't have got far." Shug radioed in and explained the situation. The sound of a siren was soon heard.

Umbago found his way to the town limits. The street lights came to an end. He confirmed that he was on the main road to Stromness and headed out into the darkness. He stopped and listened often but all he heard was the slight breeze, and all he saw was the moonlit road before him. He realised that it would not be long before they came looking and understood that every vehicle that passed was likely to be more of a threat than a help. He saw that it would be relatively easy to step off the road and hide in the heathery moor. There were no bushes or trees to aid his concealment, but he felt that it would be relatively easy to avoid detection if he lay flat on his face and embraced the earth as low as possible.

The first car he heard was coming from the town. Its slow pace gave him plenty of time. He leapt off the road at a point where there was a convenient bank. He lay down between the hollowed undulation between him and the road. The car passed without pausing. As soon as it was gone, Umbago was on his feet, brushing himself off and back on the road.

He saw the blue flashing light before he heard the approach of the police car and yet again jumped off the road and concealed himself. The car piled past him, going far too fast to see him lying there. He resumed his walk.

Practised as he now was, several times during his long trek, now weary and footsore and increasingly hungry, he dove onto the moor as police cars plied back and forth along the road. As the hours grew later, it became increasingly likely that they were the only cars out and about. Finally, he came to the bend and saw the outline of the building he knew to be his refuge in the distance. He was now off the main road but dared not risk using his torch. The moon was high in the sky and provided enough light to prevent all but the occasional stumble. Soon, the house loomed larger. Despite its menacing bleakness, Umbago was relieved as he edged around the outside wall and inside via the back entrance, where the back door should have been. Risking his torch, he found two packets of dehydrated food, fired up the Coleman's, and waited for the water to boil. When the two packets of dehydrated food were ready, Umbago dug into his repast with all the gusto of a hungry man. Finishing up, he shivered and dove into his sleeping bag, and he quickly fell asleep.

Daylight came late the following morning. The wind was blowing from the north; the dark clouds produced light flecks of snow. They were not settling on the ground yet, but Umbago knew that the chill would soon change that situation. Having plenty of time to think, Umbago reflected on his stupidity, which had risked everything simply because he was bored, lonely, and fancied a pint. He was more annoyed about his weakness than fearful of being caught. After all, he thought, according to his morality, he had done nothing wrong; rather, he had done so much right. Sure, he had broken the law and what had happened was unfortunate. However, reflecting more on the unfortunate chain of events, he realised that it was not the cause that was wrong but the way he had gone about it. He raised his chin and muttered to himself, "If I'm caught, I shall have my day in court, and I will get my message across because it is a good message."

With that, the wind grew stronger, and the snowflakes grew bigger and more numerous. He huddled in his sleeping bag and opened his book.

All day, he dozed, brewed tea, and read his book. When the darkness came at about 4.30 p.m., he heard cars pull up on the road. He peered around the corner of the building to see about a dozen uniformed policemen running in his direction.

"Edinburgh is a mad dog's dream." – Hugh MacDiarmid

Chapter 32: Auld Reekie

The woman sat at the small dining table of her second-floor flat and looked out over the park on the other side of the old stone wall. The road beneath her was far too narrow for the number of cars parked there. Some were close against the old stone wall, forbidding exit except for the driver's side. On the other side, cars had edged themselves onto the pavement. Conscientious drivers had ensured that their wing mirrors were flicked inwards, hugging the side of the car tightly so as not to risk almost inevitable destruction as vehicles passed up the street.

On the other side of the wall, dog walkers strolled, threw their balls, and picked up after their deposits. In the distance lay the peaks of Salisbury Crags and Arthur's Seat. It was hard to imagine that the scene was in the heart of a city, only minutes from Holyrood House, where royalty occasionally rested its head opposite the Scottish Parliament Building.

The woman reached for the milk jug and poured a small measure into a matching cup and saucer. She then picked up the teapot and poured the tea into her cup. A raisin scone tempted her, so she sliced it open on the matching tea service plate, spreading a sparing amount of butter and jam onto it. She brought it towards her, picked it up, and was about to take her first bite when she stopped and put it down. She opened the window, reached under the table, and pulled out a gas-powered horn. She pointed it towards the park and squeezed the rubber at the top. A deafening noise was emitted so much so that a middle-aged dog walker leapt startled into the air. Down went the horn, and from beneath the table came a mega horn. Aiming it through the window, she intoned, "Pick up efter yer shitey arsed dog, ye selfish cow."

So shocked was the woman that she reached into her back pocket, pulled out a poop bag, and tidied up the mess. The woman in the window reached again for her treat, took a bite, followed by a slurp of tea. She was about to take a second bite when her buzzer went off. Reluctantly, she stood up, abandoning her tea and muttered all the way towards answering the intercom.

"If yon's that woman to complain tae me, she'll git anither piece o' my mind, so she will. A've got plenty o't to spare."

She pressed the answering buzzer.

"Aye."

"Police, Mrs Lombard, may we come up?"

"If you must."

And she buzzed them in.

She answered the door with the catch on the chain. The ID revealed the plainclothes officer as DS Morag Macrae with the uniformed Constable Brian Urquhart accompanying her. Before she opened the door, she said, "She had it coming; her dug always haes the shits, and she niver picks up efter the beast."

Macrae looked puzzled.

"We're here about your son, Mrs Lombard."

Mrs Lombard's mouth dropped open.

"He's no deid, is he?"

"No, no, nothing like that. May we come in?"

She removed the catch and let them in. There was an immaculate front hall, a welcoming mat and hats and coats hanging neatly on pegs for every occasion. She ushered them to the front room, which doubled as the dining room, the table from which she had been watching before. She indicated that the two officers should sit down. Macrae got straight to the point.

"Have you heard from your son recently, Mrs Lombard?"

"Naw, ah dinnae hear from him unless it's Christmas or my birthday. What's he done?"

"He's disappeared."

The woman laughed incongruously.

"He's been doing that his whole life. Hiding away somewhere in Inverness, no doubt. He'll surface when he's a mind to. He always does."

"Mrs Lombard, where's his faither?"

The lady flung back her head and laughed.

"That bastard's long gone. Alive or deid, ah dinnae ken."

"You don't seem overly concerned, Mrs Lombard."

"Why should I be? That fucker treated Umbago and me like a piece of shite on the end of his shoe."

Macrae leaned forward, suddenly intent.

"Tell me how he treated you and Umbago, Mrs Lombard. While you do so, maybe Constable Urquhart could put the kettle on?" She nodded meaningfully to her colleague, who removed his cap and stood up. For the briefest of moments, Mrs Lombard looked unsettled.

"Er aye aright, son, you'll find all you need in the kitchen and some jammy dodgers in an unopened packet in the cupboard."

Urquhart walked past the front door and into the back, where he found himself in a kitchen with a view of the old Meadowbank Stadium out back. There was a wooden pull-up drying rack with laundry newly washed drying above him. He rummaged in the cupboards and easily found a tea caddy with loose leaves in it. On a small mantel above the kitchen table, he spotted a family picture with a younger Mrs Lombard and a toddler happily smiling as he struggled along beside her on some sandduned beach. Next to her was a man whom he presumed to be her husband. He had his head tilted to one side, his face creased by a sardonic grin as if the photographer had had to coax some inclination of niceness from him. His nose was curled. He was looking sideways at his wife with a look that suggested more hatred than love, more disgust than admiration. Urquhart thought to himself that if he had been the woman in the picture, there was no way he was going home with this man, let alone let him anyway near her son. This was sheer violent evil. Urquhart was determined he would take as long as possible making the tea and allow Macrae to work her magic.

"Umbago was the only good thing to come out of that relationship. I don't know why I stayed with him."

"Did he beat you up?"

Mrs Lombard flung back her head and laughed.

"Beat me up, lassie? Na, he didnae beat me up. A beating is what happens outside a pub on a Saturday nicht. What he did to me was far, far worse than that. I could have handled it if he had slapped and kicked me. Naw, that bastard did far worse. He played mind games. Ye niver knew where he stood. He would cuddle up to you on the sofa and smooth talk and charm, and you just sat there and waited for the moment he would turn, wait for the charm to become sheer evil, wait for the names, the devastating, shattering things he would call you. Then he would beat me; then he would rape me; then he would humiliate me completely. But ye ken, lass, I could have dealt wi' all o' that. It was when he'd slip out of bed in the night and turn his attentions to Umbago that I knew I had to do something. I noticed and heard nothing until my lad was eleven years old. Even then, I denied it, but one night, when Jim Lombard was not home, I heard my boy's screams in his sleep. I went to him and held him, and he told me all. And at that moment, I dressed him and packed him up, and we fled. We came here. You understand that we were living in Hawick at the time."

Macrae leaned forward in the chair and took Mrs Lombard by the hand.

"Did he follow you, Mrs Lombard? Did he find you?"

A tear rolled down her cheek, and she snatched the proffered tissue from the police woman's hand.

"Naw, he never did. I was too clever for him. Umbago and I beat the bastard." Defiance crept back to her face. A light glinted behind her eyes, but then she lowered them.

"Naw, I beat the bastard. Umbago never did."

The rattle of teacups could be heard as Urquhart appeared from behind the door. He entered the room and placed them on the small coffee table in front of them.

"Sorry, I took so long. I took the liberty of picking up this in the kitchen. Is this your husband, Mrs Lombard?"

He pointed to the family portrait.

"That's him."

"And you've no idea where he is now?" Macrae asked.

Macrae leaned forward into Mrs Lombard. She held her eyes with hers.

"Mrs Lombard, we're really worried about Umbago. You can trust us. We want what's best for him. Will you phone this number if he gets in touch?" She handed Mrs Lombard her card.

Mrs Lombard nodded but said nothing. Macrae and Urquhart stood to go, having left the tea untouched. She walked them to the door, and they exited the ancient stone steps down to the entrance and out. As they were about to get into their vehicle, the peace was shattered as Mrs Lombard blew her horn. Three teenagers on the other side of the wall jumped.

"You three wee fuckers, pick up yer dug's shite afore I set the pawlice onto youses."

Urquhart saw them flicking the V signs at the old lady and the abuse being hurled back and forth but pretended he hadn't, and he hurriedly got into the driver's seat. Macrae was already belted.

"Let's get oot o' here before we get involved in more than we came for."

"There's the way it ought to be; there's the way it is." – from the movie Platoon

Chapter 33: The Arrest

Umbago saw the police coming across the moor towards him and smiled. He felt relief. He now understood why he had ventured everything in a risky trip into the town the night before. The ride with the postie, the drink at the pub, the hasty escape; all were tokenism. In his heart of hearts, he wanted his life exposed; he sought solace and release, and he wanted to be caught. As they approached, he noted that some of the police were armed. He raised his arms above his head and walked out the back door and towards the line. When they saw him, they called out and demanded that he lie down. He did as he was bid, and they were quickly upon him.

Roughly handcuffed and marched back to the road, he was bundled into the police car and driven back to Kirkwall. He was processed at the police station and thrown into a police holding cell. He noted that he had not been charged with anything and knew, therefore, that he could only be held in custody for a limited amount of time. Indeed, he was impressed when the desk sergeant appeared with a cup of tea and a digestive.

Doddie and Monica were on their way back to talk to Morgan Mickelthwaite again when the call came in that Umbago had been arrested in Orkney. Rowlands had organized a helicopter flight for them to fly up there and be the first to interview him. They had a couple of hours to wait before they had to be at Dalcross, so they decided to go ahead with the interview at the bank.

"Don't tell him we have Lombard, okay?"

Richards nodded in agreement.

They were shown into his office. The bank manager looked tired and not his usual self. Without invitation, Doddie and Monica grabbed a couple of chairs and sat down opposite him on the other side of his desk.

"So, tell us about your friendship with Umbago Lombard." Doddie got straight to the point.

"Aye, well, you see, a couple of years ago, I was seeking counselling, and the man who was giving it to me was Dr Nunn. Yes, you probably didn't know that your police shrink did a bit of fireside chatting outside hours at his house. I told him the story of my young life in the orphanage, where I was abused by many care workers there. As I was walking down his garden path to leave, a young man stepped shyly back to let me through; he didn't acknowledge me but moved to the front door after I had left. For some reason, I waited for him while sat in my car. When he came out, I was there to greet him. I invited him for a pint, and he came along. During what turned out to be a long, bibulous evening, he opened up about his life with an abusive father, and I told him about my time in the children's home. We hatched a plan to get our own back on known paedophiles on police files and men who had all the behaviours and actions suggestive of paedophilia. Accordingly, we trawled the secondary schools and approached likely-looking teenagers. We would pay them to get after some of these guys and give them appropriate warning, more a "what would happen if" than preliminary hiding just in case. Wrong of me, I know, but we only picked on adolescents whom we knew were having a hard time at home and would welcome the chance to make a bit of money and, better, get a bit of their own back."

"So that's how you recruited Stewart Farquarson and his mates."

Morgan Mickelthwaite nodded.

"Everything was going along very well until you guys got an inkling of what we were doing and, indeed, the lead into the murder. The paediatrician's death was the worst thing that could happen to our organization."

"The good doctor's wife wisnae too happy aboot it either."

Doddie could not resist a timely reminder that his bank manager was not the only person who had suffered in this.

"I ken, I ken, but my boys didnae kill him. Somebody like that would be a hero to them. All they wanted to do was to frighten off potential abusers. They were sure they were doing the right thing. Umbago is a gentle soul. When he realised you were bringing him in here to meet me, he panicked and ran away. I managed to trace him to his cousin's place in Bruach. I own a boat, so with the help of a couple of boating friends with similarly rough childhoods, I arranged to have him picked up and dropped in Orkney, thinking that he would be safe there. The trouble is, I had forgotten that it is easier to hide in the city than in the countryside. So, isolated Orkney was the natural solution for somebody like me. Now, I don't care. I had that feeling about Umbago, that instinct he wanted it all to be over, that really he would be happy to be caught."

Doddie nodded. "I have to tell you that the local police in Kirkwall raided Umbago's refuge, and he gave himself up without a fight."

"But none of us had anything to do with the murder of Dr Ross. I swear it," Morgan Mickelthwaite said.

"Aye, well, but you're coming wi'us. Read him his rights, Richards."

Monica did as she was bid. They cuffed Morgan Mickelthwaite and dropped him off at the station before heading for Dalcross and North.

"Are you really bringing Pistol with us all the way to the Orkneys?" Monica asked as they made their way out of the station car park.

"Of course, who else would recognise guilt when he saw it?"

But Pistol's presence was not a foregone conclusion. As they made their way over to the "paraffin mosquito," as Doddie called it, the pilot leaned out and said, "Macfarlane, ah'm no takin' yon manky mongrel of a pooch aboard ma nice clean helicopter."

"Fleein" Finn Forbes was famous for speaking his mind. He shook his head and waved his fist at Pistol, who mustered an ominous grin of intent.

"Away tae fuck, Forbes. Rowlands's okayed it."

Forbes frowned at that and turned his nose up as Pistol jumped into the cockpit next to him. The pilot pushed him towards the back unceremoniously. Doddie and Monica strapped themselves in. They put on their earmuffs, and

Doddie, who had brought along his headphones from home, slipped them over Pistol's head. The noise of the engine was frightening to anybody who hadn't been in a chopper before. Quickly, they were up and soon over the Moray Firth heading north to the Black Isle. Monica never tired of admiring the scenery of her native land, so for once, she forgot about the case, ceased to think about her impending wedding, and let her eyes savour the views of the North East of the country. She had never been to Orkney, so she didn't know what to expect. Doddie had told her he had honeymooned up there despite his bride wanting to travel somewhere hot. The marriage had started its descent from that point, according to Doddie. It hadn't helped that he had produced the poem "Bloody Orkney" and read it to her on their wedding night. He told Monica about it wryly and ashamedly.

"Och, there's probably very little romance in the words: 'This bloody town's a bloody cuss, no bloody trains, no bloody bus, and no one cares for bloody us, in Orkney,' but I thought it was funny at the time. But Sheena was cold, and the toilet was an outhouse. I should hae kenned better."

Monica smiled as she recalled it. The sea and cliffs flowed by beneath them. She thought that maybe it was better than what her own honeymoon would look like. It would be too close to the baby's birth for Dermot and her to have much time away, but she didn't care. She was excited about her new life with him and with their child. Occasionally, she wondered what she had seen in him, what had attracted her to him. Intuitively, underneath it all, she had recognised steel and courage, she had seen intelligence and perceptiveness, but most of all, she had come to love his stumbling and often bumbling honesty, his attempts always to do the right thing by herself and his mates. Besides whatever it meant, she was deeply in love with Dermot. And if he did not say so enough to her, she nevertheless knew that he felt the same way.

All too soon, she spotted the few buildings and flags that signified the last point of land on the mainland of the UK; the far north-easternmost point called John O'Groats. There was nothing there but a goal for long-distance runners and cyclists, eccentrics who determined to use their athleticism to trek from Land's End in Cornwall the nearly nine hundred miles from tip to tip. Two iconic points at the tips of two beautiful countries, one trashy, gaudy spoiler on the English bottom, one mildewed white hotel on its Scottish equivalent, these two destinations stood as tatty bookends, a sharp contrast to the magnificent countryside in between. Monica had read that somebody had actually swum between the two places and then laughed when she read further. They had done so in a tank on a trailer pulled by a truck! There were weird eccentrics in the world, and there were bloody nutters. She grinned as she thought she worked for the former and hoped he did not become the latter. She stroked the ever-alert Pistol as they came into land at Kirkwall.

As the blades came to a halt and the silence became a very pleasant contrast, the pilot shouted after the three of them as they walked across the tarmac to the waiting police car.

"Oi, yon bloody dug has had a shite at the back of ma nice clean bird. It stinks in here. Git back here and clean up yer mess, Macfarlane."

"Awa ye go, Forbes. Ye spend yer waking hours in the shite and your sleeping hours dreaming of it. Ye shoulnae hiv insulted him as ye did. Ma dug knows how to make friends and influence people," and Doddie turned back towards the police car. Forbes flung his hands in the air and waved his fist in their direction. Pistol turned, and Forbes later swore blind that the dog smiled at him.

The police station at Kirkwall wasn't exactly state of the art, but then Kirkwall itself wasn't exactly the Big Smoke. Monica took in the narrow streets, the wee shops, the quaintness of it all. She had to keep reminding herself that they were not here on some police junket but to interview a man who may be a murderer.

They were shown to an interview room. Soon in walked the pale figure of the suspect flanked by his solicitor and a middle-aged plump-looking sergeant. The solicitor reached over the table to the seated officers and introduced himself.

"Lawson Lambert, here to see justice done." Monica reached over and shook the proffered hand. Doddie pretended to be studying something on the ceiling while keeping his arms folded determinedly. Monica looked sideways at Doddie, expecting him to take the lead. Nothing happened; silence ensued. Umbago gazed straight ahead; his solicitor looked expectant. Eventually, Doddie unfolded his arms, placed his hands shoulder-width apart on the table and fixed Umbago with a steely stare. He was about to speak when Lambert leaned across the table and grabbed Doddie's nearest wrist.

"Whit's that dog doing in here?"

Pistol was stretched in the corner of the room, sound asleep. Doddie pulled his hand away and addressed Umbago.

"Why did you run away? You've cost the taxpayer a heap of money."

"You don't have to ans—"

Doddie cut him off. "Aye, he does."

Then he proceeded to go through a litany of taxpayer expenses. Travel costs to Bruach, calling out of the coast guard, the helicopter flight and so forth, ending with, "Only the guilty run, Lombard."

Umbago looked uneasy, squirming in his seat, fiddling with his hands. Monica opened up.

"We've talked to your mum. We know about your childhood."

Umbago looked surprised. He looked across at his solicitor, who met his eyes but said nothing. Monica continued.

"Whatever you've done, there will be mitigation."

Doddie leaned forward and asked, "Did you kill Dr Ross?"

Lambert, operating in what he thought was his client's best interest, started to protest, but Umbago put his hand on his arm and stopped him.

"No, I didn't." Then he was the slow train leaving the station; eventually, there was faster gaining momentum, and there was no stopping him. Umbago told his story.

"Viewed from a distance, everything is beautiful." – Tacitus

Chapter 34: Nest Building

Dermot had a reputation for being an amiable buffoon, somebody who did his job but was not destined to set the River Ness alight with drive, intelligence, and panache. He was, everybody thought, slow and steady, never likely to win the race. If somebody had said this to Monica, she would have produced that winning smile of hers, and the dimples would have appeared, she would have patted them on the back and tried not to be patronizing, and she would have condescendingly explained to them that they were so very, very wrong. She might have explained to them that here was a man who could think outside of the box. He could read between the lines, even when they were very close together. He could sense nuance, naivety, false nonchalance, and nonsense when it was presented to him. She could have explained that growing up on the hard streets of trouble-torn Belfast, one had to learn very quickly whom one could or could not trust. She had seen physical and moral courage in him. She smiled when she thought about their first date and how awkward it had been. It had taken her input to put him at ease, her direction to lead him towards comfortable conversation, her determination before the first seduction. She instinctively knew that he would be a wonderful husband and father. She was at peace with their relationship and relaxed in her pregnancy, but she was determined to be married before the baby arrived. So, she flicked through her calendar, looking at dates.

On some days, Dermot did not know what side was up. He was on cloud nine most of the time about the prospect of marriage and a child, but occasionally, he was overwhelmed with the responsibility. He had, however, accepted that Monica would make the dates and arrangements for the wedding and that it was his job to simply fit in. After all, as he explained to her with a wide, mischievous grin on his freckled face, she was technically his boss. She had reached out to cuff him on the back of his head for that, but he had been too quick for her and grabbed her around the waist. After that, they had set dates and timings on the back burner whilst they made vigorous love on the floor of Dermot's digs.

"Do you have a best man in mind?" Monica asked him as they lay propped up in front of the fire.

"Hmmm, nobody from back home, that's for sure. I'd thought about Davidson, but he'd be sure to lose the ring or spill his pint down your dress. I don't know many people here in Inverness other than through work. You've snapped up Macfarlane to give you away. There's Mental Martin upstairs, McIvor downstairs. Rowlands is too long in the tooth; besides, he'd have us doing yoga during the speeches. Do you think Pistol could organize a great stag night, supply a great speech?"

They had both laughed at that. He had stroked her growing belly, marvelling at what was happening just inches away. He was serious for a moment.

"I'll think about it. I promise you it will be somebody who won't let you or me down."

On the following day, a Saturday, Monica phoned Doddie.

"Aye, what is it?"

"That's pretty polite for you."

"Aye, well?"

"May I come over and see ye?"

"Is it about work?"

"Naw, it's about the wedding."

"You've had second thoughts and want to marry me?"

Monica laughed.

"Och, aye an' ah've got Davidson standing in to push ye up the aisle in yer wheelchair. 'Do you Monica Richards take this bampot and so on and so on?' What time can I come over?"

"Come over in an hour. Should give ye enough time to pick up some fish n' chips. I'll have a steak and kidney pie and curry sauce."

"You're on. I'll see you then." And she rang off.

Monica stopped at her local chippee, turned her nose up at the kidney and couldn't understand why it was married to the steak. What did she know? She grew up at a different time when kidneys were beans.

The sun shone as she drove out of Inverness. She always enjoyed the drive up beyond Culloden Moor and onwards to Doddie's place by the loch. She arrived, and Doddie and Pistol were waiting outside the house.

"Let's take a dander down to the birdwatcher's car park." He thanked her for the chips, and they walked down the road, turned left, and walked up the lane where they came on the car park. The banks of the loch whispered with the breeze in the trees. It was too early in the season for midgies. They found a rock on the shore and watched and listened as the waters lapped. The occasional bird tweeted, the birches quivered, and the chips and contents were consumed. They sat down. Monica started to speak, but Doddie put his hand up to stop her.

"Ye ken, Monica, my dad, my twa cousins, and I fished this loch many times as children. We took it all for granted. We thought that the days would never end, that eternity beckoned, and we would still be casting our lines from the boat. The waters would lap, the reels would creak, our lines would whisper as they gently laid the flies on the water. Occasionally, one of us would reach for the oars and gently manoeuvre; sometimes, we would have a fish on the line, then we would go from steadiness to excitement. We would net our brown trout, try to imagine its weight, and believe that it was heavier than it was. But, you know, Monica, we never managed to get to this end of the loch. These northern shores are a world away from the boat mooring, a lifetime removed from what was. Now what is, is here." He looked at her and smiled. "You don't really know what an honour it is to be asked to give you away on your big day. It means a great deal to me. And if I seem ungrateful, well, then you need to know that I'm not. It's just life, Monica. Life got in the way of the gentle, kind, sensitive, wee boy who grew up in Nairn. On the day, I will make your faither proud, but he shall understand that I will be equally as proud. What can I do for you the day, lassie?"

Monica put her arm around his shoulders and hugged him tightly.

"Can we settle a wedding date now that will allow time for Dermot's folks to get to Inverness and my mother to make the leap from Methlick? After all, I would kinda like her to be there. I want to be married afore my wean arrives."

"Aye, aye, lassie, I've come prepared." And he reached in his pocket and brought out a diary.

Meanwhile, Dermot was to the east of Inverness on the Ardersier road. Not having satellite navigation, he had a road map open on the passenger seat of his car. He found the church he was looking for and drove up a side road. Around a bend in the road, he came across a wooded area beyond which was the entrance to a lovely garden and a quaint little cottage. He parked his car and walked to the lych-gate. As he approached, he noted that the cottage was set on a hill overlooking a bay where a large boat was wrecked and rotting. He knocked on the door and waited. Soon, he heard a shuffle beyond and a wrinkled old lady opened the door. Her smile and eyes were wise and strong as she greeted him.

"You'll be the young Irishman looking for a place to lay your head and, likely, the head of somebody else. Come away in and see what you're letting yourself in for."

She led him through the house, the large dining room with the view over the garden and beyond, the warm kitchen and the purposeful bedrooms. Everything smacked of cosiness and intimacy. Dermot signed a rental agreement there and then, agreeing to a six-month stay.

"Where are you and your husband going to live?" Dermot asked.

"Och, nae problem; we'll go and live wi' ma brither in Nairn."

He shook her hand and took his leave. As he made his way to his car, he supposed that he should have talked to Monica first, but whatever, he wanted to prove that he could make a decision as well.

"Wisdom is oftentimes nearer when we stoop than when we soar."
– William Wordsworth

Chapter 35: Monday Morning

Dermot arrived at work, parked his car, and was eager to get to his tasks. He had not seen Monica over the weekend and was keen to tell her his news. As he locked his car doors, he saw her pull in at the other side of the car park. She saw him and waved. She smiled, and Dermot went weak at the knees as he spotted the familiar dimples. They walked quickly towards each other. Dermot said, "I have news."

"So have I." They hugged and gave each other a peck on the cheek.

"Right, you two lovebirds, I need you inside pronto for a briefing, so get yer lovey-dovey stuff out of the way quickly, and let's get going," Doddie said, appearing with Pistol.

Monica noticed the one pink and one blue sock, winced as she saw he had not done his shirt buttons correctly, and shook her head at the remnants of tomato on his check jacket.

Monica smiled at Dermot.

"It'll keep."

The murder squad gathered before the whiteboard smothered in photographs and arrows of suspects and, of course, Dr Ross, the victim. Doddie stood up to speak.

"Firstly, Richards and I are convinced that Lombard is incapable of murder. He is allied to Morgan Mickelthwaite and his little group of teenage pedo beaters. They will be charged as such, but we have pieced together the movements of both suspects. We believe that Lombard ran because he panicked. Morgan Mickelthwaite's boat and mates plucked him off the rowing boat and ferried him to Orkney. Both guys were childhood victims of abuse. There are very good reasons, albeit illegal ones, why they are both conducting a private vendetta against people they think are kiddie fiddlers. Indeed, if I wasn't a dyed in the wool copper, I might be looking in the other direction at their nefarious activities. Aye, what is it, Davidson?"

Davidson had his hand raised.

"What does 'nefarious' mean, Boss?"

"It means 'fuckin' wicked and bloody crooked,' Davidson. It's what you and I are paid to stop. Next time ye dinnae ken, then Google it."

Doddie continued.

"We know that Dr Ross was killed in the Cairngorms, and the body was dumped in Munlochy. We seem to be coming around to the belief that this was a crime of opportunity rather than one of malice aforethought. It would also seem like the perpetrators panicked and dumped the body without any real attempt at concealment. They knew it would be found. Aye, what is it now, Davidson?"

Doddie was exasperated.

"What does 'per—per— mean?"

"Constable Smith," Doddie said.

Smith, who was sat at the back next to his mate, Davidson, looked up from his reverie.

"Aye, Sir."

"You keep your truncheon handy, son. See when yon bampot mate of yours puts his hand up again, whack him firmly on the shins."

Davidson looked crestfallen, and Smith grinned.

Doddie continued.

"I think that we've all been guilty of straight-line thinking. We need to move away from the beaten track. I don't believe Morgan Mickelthwaite, Lombard, and the kids working for him are guilty of murder. However, I believe there was a third party in the Cairngorms where the good doctor was killed. And let's not forget that Dr Ross was good. He was popular amongst his patients and well-loved by all accounts. Sure and all, I do subscribe to the belief that he could have been beaten up because teenagers don't know the difference between a paedophile and a paediatrician. I believe a group gave him a hiding, but I now think that somebody came along and finished him off. Any questions?"

Davidson slowly raised his hand, and Smith quickly reached for his truncheon. Rapidly, he spoke.

"This is no a question, Sir. I have been looking at some known visitors to the Cairngorms then or thereabouts when Dr Ross was killed. Obviously, the names are meaningless without context, but I came across some of the receipts that I checked from the offices in the car park. One man stood out. His name is Fred Purbright. He purchased a book about the geology and flora and fauna of the region before taking the funicular up the hill. It may mean nothing, Sir, but I Googled the name and discovered there is a man by that name who is the chairman of a birdwatching society, which, of course, means nothing again alone except that this twitcher group happens to be based in Dr Ross's hometown. This may mean nothing as well, but I don't really believe in coincidences. It seems to me that this may be a tree up which we should bark."

Davidson's explanation was met with stunned silence. Doddie screwed up his face, reached up, and started playing with his right ear lobe. Monica put two fingers of her right hand above and below her mouth and began to nod gently. Dermot smiled across at Davidson and gave him a silent round of applause.

Doddie spoke.

"Well, of course, I knew when I put this outstanding team together, encouraged them to express themselves, and gave them scope for a free flow of original ideas that officers like Davidson would thrive. You may have something here, laddie. Get together with your mate, Smith, and leave no stone unturned in seeing what you can discover about Mr Purbright. Well done, son."

"Constable Long and DS Richards, I want you to head back to the school and sit down with Sinclair and talk to him about what he knows about the pedo bashers. Pistol and I will get together with Lombard and Morgan Mickelthwaite in a room and talk about who and what they are doing. Aye, Davidson, what is it?"

Davidson was no longer sat attentively but had his computer open at his station.

"I have just found out that Mr Purbright of Welwyn Garden City is a missing person and has been for the last few months," he announced with a grin, which was as near an extravagant bow at the end of a performance as was possible. If he expected a standing ovation and encore, he was to be grossly disappointed. Monica was already on the phone with the local police in Welwyn Garden City. Doddie was looking at flights to London from Dalcross with a view to sending somebody down there. He looked up from his computer.

"Right, Davidson and Smith, you're on a flight to London this afternoon. I want you to get yourself to Welwyn Garden City and liaise with the local police. Any information you can get on this character will be useful. Never thought I would say this but, well done, Davidson."

There was a brief round of applause, and Doddie spoke again.

"Aye, weil, flattery is nice to hear as long as you don't inhale. Now, your work begins. Awa; hame and pack some essentials, both of ye. I'll get somebody to pick ye up and take you to Dalcross. Any questions?"

"You can't mend bridges when the opposite bank is sinking." – Anonymous

Chapter 36: Cross Border Ties

Davidson and Smith had not only never flown before, but neither of them had ever been to England. Monica, who had been put in charge of their travel arrangements, was surprised when Smith approached and told her he couldn't go because he did not have a passport. She looked aghast at him, complete and utter surprise covering her face. She asked their friend, Constable Catherine Cattanach, to drop them off at the airport. She arranged to meet them at the train station in plenty of time for the journey to the airport.

"Cat the Cat," as the constable was affectionately known, had been like a big sister to the two young constables since they had joined the force on the same day a couple of years previously. She had often despaired at what she had taken on. Dishevelment, disorder, and dilapidation were frequently in evidence where the two constables were concerned. But Cat persisted despite pressure from friends and colleagues to abandon a couple of losing causes and let them sink or swim on their own. Her only retort where the two constables were concerned was a "wait and see" smile, an unshakeable belief that the best of them would eventually come out. But for the moment, the world was still waiting for the sunrise.

"There's good stuff in those guys."

This had been greeted with a shrug of the shoulders and a belief that if she wanted to interfere with natural selection, then that was her business.

At the airport, Cat was a witness to Smith's repeated failure to get through the metal detector. Eventually, it was revealed that Smith kept a spare key for his house and car clipped to the back of his underpants. Cat had tried not to shake her head at that, but her face must have betrayed her confusion because Smith smiled back at her reassuringly and tripped over Davidson's suitcase, which he was dragging along behind him. It was just as well that she had not been on the plane with them.

Davidson was happy that he had a window seat that looked across the wings. Smith sat down next to him. Both had their small suitcases on their knees. On the other side of the aisle sat a young woman who averted her eyes when Smith beamed a morning greeting. Before take-off, the steward came along and asked them to put their cases in the luggage rack above. Davidson could not find room enough in the nearest rack, so he went to the middle one. In the process, he accidentally caught the latch on his case so that it opened, spilling all its contents on the young woman below. She was shocked, especially when Davidson did his best to retrieve the situation by attempting to pull his various shirts and raiment off her, mistakenly grabbing her left breast in the process. He apologized profusely. The young woman reddened but said nothing. When all was eventually tidied away, she reached down in front of her and retrieved some Y-fronts with the thistle logo of the Scottish rugby team and the title "Baw Bag." Davidson thanked her and hurriedly stuffed them in his pocket. The situation worsened when they were asked to fasten their seat belts. Neither Smith nor Davidson could find half of their belts, so they knotted the long ends over themselves. It took the steward to fix the situation. Both took out their notepads when the health and safety talk was given. The demonstration was finished when Smith put up his hand to ask a question. The steward was taken aback by this but indulged him.

"What happens when we get to London?"

"Then you disembark the plane."

"Will you tell us when to undo our seat belts?"

"No, a light will come on revealing that."

Smith nodded wisely, and the steward moved away to her seat.

After they had taken off, Davidson tried to retrieve his book from his case. He achieved this but not without it falling on the head of the young woman beneath. Just as well, it was the slim volume of *The Old Man and the Sea* and not *War and Peace*.

Davidson and Smith were both surprised when all too quickly, they were asked to belt up again because they were about to land at Heathrow. The disembarkation was also not incident-free. Now twice the victim of unfortunate spillages, the young lady wisely decided to remain seated and allow the two policemen to go first. On the way out, Davidson tripped over the step and spilt his luggage again on the floor of the tunnel. She was now stuck behind him yet again as he desperately tried to stuff his belongings back in his case while turning around and grinning at her sheepishly in the process.

"I guess that a date is out of the question?" he asked with a wink.

She frowned, raised her eyes to the heavens and shook her head.

Somehow, the two constables found themselves on the tube heading towards central London, still with little idea of getting to Welwyn Garden City. Piccadilly Circus seemed a good place to get off. Having done so, they went and sat by the waterfall and statue of Eros to take stock and plan their next move. They were both hungry, so they decided to find an Indian restaurant to set them up for the next stage of their journey. Having had a couple of beers and overdone the vindaloo, they finally decided to suss out where and when to get a train to Welwyn Garden City. They had missed the last one and had nowhere to spend the night. As they wandered out onto the street, Davidson spotted a sign showing accommodation for medical staff at a local hospital. The two of them decided to pretend they were residents there, entered through the front door with more aplomb than they felt and found their way to an unoccupied TV lounge as it was getting late at night. They found a row of comfy chairs and decided to spend the night there, trying to avoid detection. At about 3.00 a.m., Davidson shook Smith awake and explained that they would have to leave because he believed that the security guard had heard something and was headed in their direction. Sure enough, a flashlight could be seen beaming its way down the corridor. Somehow, they escaped and found themselves out on a deserted street.

After a few aimless wanderings, they found themselves on a street with many foreign embassies. Now, feeling the effects of the curry, Davidson was becoming desperate to find a toilet. They spotted a policeman on duty and asked him where they could find one. He pointed them in the direction of Regents Park, explaining to them that it would not be open for a few hours.

Having no alternative, they decided to climb the fence, which proved too much for Davidson and his vindaloo, and the world suddenly fell out of his bottom. Smith was more fortunate. Now that they were in the park, they did succeed in finding an open toilet. Davidson did the best he could to clean himself up, and Smith beamed his relief when he emerged from the cubicle. Davidson sought the privacy of some vegetation, stripped off and decided to burn his soiled trousers and pants. The cold air bit at his bare knees as he did so, but they both huddled around the fire for morning warmth. After this, Davidson rummaged in his case for a clean pair of trousers only to discover that he didn't have any. But all was not lost because he had a pair of Stewart tartan pyjamas, bright red but better than getting arrested. So, they waited in the cold for the park to open at 9.00 a.m. and snuck past the gatekeeper when he wasn't looking.

They were making their way to the station when Davidson's phone rang.

"Where the fuck are you two? You were expected yesterday!"

Doddie was not happy. Smith grabbed the phone.

"Sorry, Boss, missed the last train. On the way to the station now." And he hung up.

Somehow, Smith and Davidson made it to Kings Cross and on the train to Welwyn Garden City. More by luck than good management, they had got in touch with the desk sergeant at the police station and arranged a pick up at the railway station. Walking out onto the platform and into the waiting car park, they spotted the police car and headed towards it. A uniformed policewoman was leaning against it, sipping a Starbucks and looking at her phone. Davidson introduced himself.

"Are ye here tae pick up Constables Davidson and Smith?" The constable looked away from her phone.

"Yes, who's asking?"

"We are they." Smith produced his most ingratiating smile.

She looked on with an expression of total disgust. There was one policeman in red pyjamas, and both had a day's growth of beard; their hair was matted and greasy, and there was an unpleasant odour about them but of one in particular.

"ID?"

They both produced their IDs.

"Okay, get in." Smith moved to open the passenger door.

"Nope, in the back, both of you. My name is Constable Edith Chambers. We'll head straight to the station." Before setting off, she reached in the glove compartment and produced a bottle of Febreze, which she sprayed liberally around the car, particularly in the back. This produced a coughing fit from the two constables. There was no conversation between the railway station and the police station. She pulled up at the front of the building and signalled that they should get out and report to the desk sergeant. She left them and went off to park the patrol car.

The desk sergeant wasted no time but ushered them into an office where a slim Chinese woman in her late forties sat behind the desk. Her black hair was in a tightly pinched bun. Her slim build, immaculate uniform, tidy desk, her 5ft 4 inches of height rather enhanced her air of authority than diminished it. She introduced herself as Chief Superintendent Grace Lu, late of the Hong Kong Police, but since 1997, a part of the local police here in Hertfordshire. Her precise English confirmed her birthright.

"So, Police Scotland has a murder victim and a missing person who were in the same place at the same time and are both from here. You are here for background. I will give you my Coles Notes on the case, and you are going to your hotel to get cleaned up and, errr, dressed properly and read them and come back here. I was going to ask how you had gotten into this sorry-looking state, but Macfarlane told me not to bother, that it would likely be a sorry tale and that I would not understand it anyway." With that, she handed them a file and signalled that they should leave.

The Premier Inn was just a stone's throw from the police station. On the way there, Smith spotted a British Home Stores and directed Davidson in there to buy some new trousers and underpants. He went to the hotel and checked in. He had the file with him, so he flopped onto the bed and started to read.

"The field cannot be well seen from within the field." – Ralph Waldo Emerson

Chapter 37: Links and More Links

There was a detailed file marked "Confidential" that contained two things; one was a potted history of Dr Ross's life, the other was much larger and contained a list of Dr Ross's patients for the last five years or so. There was a less detailed file on Fred Purbright, which Smith set to one side.

George Ross was born and bred in the border town of Peebles. He was the only child of Dr Patricia Ross, a local GP, and James Ross, a local farmer. Because of his upbringing, natural intelligence and love of the land, it was thought that young George would grow up and become a country vet. But he had always wanted to have brothers and sisters and heard when he was old enough that he was always destined to be the only one. Complications during his mother's pregnancy meant there would be no more natural-born progeny. Therefore, it did not come as a massive leap of imagination to find him studying medicine at Edinburgh University. It was there in his first year that he met the love of his life, Elsa Summerton.

George had been persuaded reluctantly to attend a rugby game at Murrayfield. It was not just any game; it was the annual Calcutta Cup match between Scotland and England. He was decked out in his kilt and face paint with two medical student mates. They had found their seats, and he was in the middle. Next to them arrived a young English woman with her Scottish boyfriend. She was sat next to one of George's mates, who, in typical style, began an anti-English rant, much to the embarrassment of George and to the annoyance of the Scottish boyfriend. George stood up and insisted with unaccustomed vehemence that he swop seats. From that moment, Elsa and George were smit. It became a standing joke between them that they didn't remember the score, let alone who won. Elsa attained her degree some years before George and returned to her native town of Welwyn Garden City. George promised that he would follow as soon as he had qualified. Elsa held out little hope that that would happen, so she was surprised one day when he turned up at her flat, explaining that he had just attained a post as a fully-fledged paediatrician for the NHS in the city. Engagement and marriage followed. They both seemed immensely happy.

Why Smith found all this superfluous information in this police file, he did not know, but he recognised that any background was good background.

Davidson walked through the door in a new pair of Levi's jeans and a crisp new white shirt. He flopped his case down on the fold-up single and said, "I suppose you got here first, so you get the double." Smith reached over to the bedside table and hurled the other file over to him.

"Wrap yer peepers around that."

Inside was a veritable pantheon of Dr Ross's patients. The list was in alphabetical order, so he immediately searched out the letter "P" in hopes of finding Purbright, but no such luck.

"So, our missing person was never a patient in any way," he muttered to himself.

Davidson flicked through the file absent-mindedly and continued chuntering away to himself all the way through, becoming increasingly irritating to his mate lying stretched out on the other bed.

Then suddenly, he sat up and said loudly, "Suppose, just suppose?"

"Suppose what, ye daft apoth? Can ye no keep yer theories tae yersel? I'm trying to focus here."

But Davidson was not to be stopped.

"Some people are very private, are they no? Often they're not at all keen to give away personal secrets. Do you think it might be possible for Fred Purbright to have gone along to see a paediatrician using a false name? Maybe he didn't want it to be known that he was seeking medical advice on his children and such like. You know that what we should be looking for is not the name but something that went wrong in Dr Ross's treatment so that a parent or a potential parent might hold a murderous grudge. What do you think?"

Davidson was excited now and unwilling to allow his enthusiasm to be diminished by anything his mate might say or do.

"I think," said Smith with an air of tired tolerance, "that you need to keep your crackpot theories to yourself and let me get on with what I am trying to do. In short, shut the fuck up."

Davidson barely heard the insult; he was dividing the files into those with no bad outcomes and those with some bad ones. So, he cast to one side those cases where the child had obviously recovered from a childhood illness or injury and started to get into the sad tales of childhood leukaemia and heart defects and encephalitis and any other issues that would so obviously devastate a parent. Then he separated them into cases where the treatment seemed to fail. He then decided to limit his choice to the ten worst outcomes. He filtered through tragic cases of children for whom life had been far too short and was just about to toss aside a case of a ruptured appendix, which would have been likely routine to any surgeon but had resulted in death, and something stopped him. The parents were Leo and Dariol Lamplight. Their daughter was Georgina, who sadly had not made it beyond two years. It seems that on an early visit to Dr Ross, he had misdiagnosed the child. They had gone home only to have to rush off to the emergency in the wee small hours and be a witness to their dying daughter's last breath.

"I have found something." Davidson stood up and began to pace.

"I think that Leo Lamplight and Fred Purbright are the same person."

"Why do you say that?"

"Because Leo is a lion that purrs and a Lamplight shines bright, thus Purbright."

Smith screwed his face up in disbelief.

"Sounds tenuous to me."

"Maybe so, but I'm going to try to find out if there is really a Leo and Dariol Lamplight living in the Welwyn

Garden City area." With that, Davidson reached for his laptop and signed in.

Meanwhile, Smith phoned the Welwyn Garden City police station and managed to get through to Chief Superintendent Lu.

"Hmm, what do you two want?" Smith could hear the disdain and lack of respect in her voice. Smith was determined to make the most of a second chance to make a first impression.

"Hi, ma'am, Davidson and I believe we are onto something here. We are trying to trace Leo and Dariol Lamplight, who had a child who was a patient of Dr Ross. Unfortunately, the child died. Davidson believes there are no such people and that Fred Purbright is the real name. We really need to interview Purbright's wife. Can you send us a car so that we can visit her?" Reluctantly, Chief Superintendent Lu agreed, and Constable Edith Chambers was dispatched to pick them up and take them to Purbright's address.

Chambers was waiting at reception when the two Scottish policemen appeared out of the elevator. She looked relieved that the two were now reasonably presentable and very relieved that they no longer stank. As they walked through the hotel car park to the waiting vehicle, Chambers told them that she had been instructed to attend the interview with them but had been told to let them do the leg work.

As they walked up the garden path of this neat area of suburbia, Davidson noted the newly painted red front door, the bay windows, and the well cared for aura of the home that suggested an "everything in its place and a place for everything" neatness. They rang the doorbell and heard movement on the other side as somebody walked briskly down the hallway.

Edwina Purbright was a slender, dark-haired beauty of athletic build. Her narrow face was thin to the extent that her features were now gaunt, her eyes were red, and she looked as though she hadn't slept for days. They were ushered into an equally neat front room, and Smith and Davidson sat next to each other on the sofa while Chambers took a seat next to the fireplace. Mrs Purbright offered them tea and biscuits. While she was away in the kitchen, Chambers silently directed Davidson and Smith's attention to the family photo above the fireplace. There was Mrs Purbright and her husband, and sat between them was a child no more than eighteen months old. As she entered with a large and heavy tray, Smith stood up to help her. As they settled before the tea, Mrs Purbright said, "Have you any news about my Freddie?"

"Only that we traced him to the Cairngorms National Park, and he hasn't been seen since."

Mrs Purbright reached into the sleeve of her cardigan and pulled out a handkerchief, which she proceeded to nervously twist and untwist as she twitched and twisted in her seat.

"Is that your husband and child in the photograph, Mrs Purbright?"

"Yes, it is. That was taken a couple of years ago now?"

She looked down at her hands, which continued to tighten and squeeze the handkerchief. Smith noted the tension and the whiteness of her knuckles as she tried ever harder to choke the life out of the cotton comfort. Smith reflected that if it had been soaked through, it would likely now have been bone dry.

Davidson continued his questioning.

"Mrs Purbright, where is your baby?"

She looked up. "Georgina died a couple of years ago now." She said matter-of-factly.

Smith took over.

"May I ask how she died?"

Mrs Purbright took a deep breath. "She had acute appendicitis, which the paediatrician failed to diagnose properly."

"Mrs Purbright, who was your child's paediatrician?"

"Dr Ross." She curled her lip as she spat her answer.

Davidson said, "We have no record of you in his files."

"Fred insisted that we use a false name. To this day, I don't know why."

"Did you go under the names of Leo and Dariol Lamplight?"

"Yes, we did." Davidson sighed. Smith took in a sharp intake of breath. Chambers stood up and moved towards the tray.

"Shall I be mother?" And she began to pour the tea.

Davidson leaned forward in his chair and gazed directly into Mrs Purbright's eyes.

"Think very carefully before you answer this, Mrs Purbright. Is your husband capable of murder?" He reached for his cup of tea, sat back in the chair, and the room took on a silence that hung in the air. Mrs Purbright spoke.

"My Freddie is the kindest of men. When we first met, it was love at first sight. He doted on me. Nothing was too good for me. Then Georgina arrived, and I knew that I had to take up a secondary position in his life." She smiled wanly. "When she was taken from us, Freddie never talked about her again. He took down all her pictures and put them in boxes in our attic. It only is since he has been missing that I have put up this solitary picture of us as a family. Still waters run deep, Constables, so, yes, my Freddie is capable of murder. And you are investigating the murder of Dr Ross, and I think he could have done it. I never blamed the good doctor for what happened. I did not need to blame or punish him; nobody could punish him more than he did himself. Yet, my Freddie dove so deep that I could no longer reach him. He disappeared from my life even though we still shared the same bed. Yes, my Freddie could have killed Dr Ross."

"Mrs Purbright, where do you think he is?"

"The secret calmness of emergency." – John Le Carre

Chapter 38: Home Again

Davidson and Smith caught their flight back to Inverness, having departed Welwyn Garden City, saying farewell to a very confused Chambers and a totally baffled Chief Superintendent Lu. Neither of them could understand how a couple of teuchter coppers from the back of the beyond—a couple of gullibles, causing chaos and calamities in a variety of ways—could somehow stumble on what looked to be the truth in the Dr Ross murder case.

There was relief around the station when they had gone, but at the same time, those who had met them had to admit to a certain admiration. They hadn't exactly come, saw and conquered, but they had blundered, stumbled, and shocked.

The flight was uneventful. They both buckled their seatbelts properly. There was no embarrassing spillage from either case. They knew not to expect crowds of welcome and flags and bunting when they entered the terminal but had expected a little bit more than simply Dermot to see them home.

Dermot had welcomed the chance to get out of the office on his own. On the previous day, instead of driving Monica home as she expected, he had driven her out of

Inverness to their new accommodation at Petty. Monica had been stunned that he had made such a decision without consulting her. After her initial shock, she said nothing as he drove her home, slamming the door with vehemence when he dropped her off. The silence had continued the following morning. Dermot was becoming increasingly frustrated and was having trouble keeping his fiery Irishness under wraps, mainly as they were due to take possession on the upcoming weekend. So, when Davidson and Smith smiled and ran up to him at the terminal, full of the joys of Spring and happy to be home, expecting slapping and hoopla in return, he had been subdued. He muttered a distracted thanks as they bestowed a bottle of duty-free Laphroiag on him as a gift. He was silent on the way back to Inverness and noted the two constables sleeping soundly on the back seat, a couple of latter-day cherubs, their heads resting each upon the other, babes in arms.

They walked across the parking lot to the station, and Dermot delivered them to Doddie as expected. Doddie had torn into them about not arriving on time and turning up as a mess and letting Police Scotland down and, worse, letting Scotland down. They presented him with a bottle of twelve-year-old duty-free Glenfiddich, and he remonstrated with them about bribing a senior officer. Davidson explained that they had also given a bottle to Dermot, and he was the same rank as them. At that, Doddie called Dermot into the office and asked him to explain to them the wherewithal of travel within the United Kingdom.

"Explain to them what, Sir?" Dermot looked confused.

"Tell Gullibles's Travels here that there is no such thing as duty-free on domestic flights."

"Oh, aye, there is no such thing as duty-free on domestic flights." He shrugged his shoulders and grinned.

"And?" Doddie looked flustered.

"Oh, aye, so, I guess you were conned and paid above the odds for our whisky. Thanks very much. You can go now."

Their shoulders slumped, their heads went down, and they opened the door. Doddie shouted after them so that everyone in the office could hear.

"Ach, youse twa maddies hae done a job fer us, which is mair than ah coulda expected. Awa and find some cups, and we'll start abody's day wi' a dram." He looked across at Monica and grinned. "No fer you, lassie. Reach for the water cooler."

There were smiles all around as Davidson and Smith regaled them of what and how they had found what looked to be the truth.

Doddie stood up.

"Maybe when we've solved this murder, you can tell us all what happened when you first arrived in London." He grinned. "Innocents abroad, eh?"

"The otherness of the other." – Porter

Chapter 39: Forgiveness

Dermot had a couple of days of silence from Monica. He had sat at his desk, texted her, and watched her at the other end of the room hear the buzz on her phone, check who it was, and ignore it. He had phoned and left messages, but no reply had come. He was becoming cognizant that he had made a mistake, realised in his foolishness that he had made a big decision without consulting her and wondered how he could find his way back into her good graces. He thought about flowers delivered to her desk in the early morning, but she was too down to earth and practical to succumb to that ploy. He was in abject misery and beating himself up. He had tried the brave face and the cavalier attitude, but it was no use. Everybody on the floor knew that things were not right between the two love birds. "Hell hath no fury like a woman scorned," Dermot muttered except, he thought, *I did the opposite of scorn, whatever that is.* It was Doddie who came to the rescue. He called them into his office and indicated that they should sit.

Monica flared. "I'm busy. What do ye want?"

Dermot said, "My lunch is in the microwave. Can this not wait, Boss?"

Doddie smiled beatifically, his perceived guise as the marriage counsellor. The two officers waited for the shoe to drop.

"Fuck 'busy' and 'lunch.' Pistol needs a walk and a dump, and I need you to take him out."

Monica rose from her seat.

"Awright, lunch can wait. I'll take him to the park," Dermot muttered.

"Aye aff ye go, ye Irish bastard."

Doddie was grinning, shaking his head, and waving his finger by this point.

"Na, na, na, ye dinnae understand. You are baith takin' Pistol to dae his business. Not Dermot Long on his own, not Monica Richards solo, both of you. Aff ye go and take yer time."

They shook their heads but stood up.

"Gie us his lead then, ye auld bastard."

"Och, he winnae need that; he'll not leave your sides."

Monica and Dermot reached the door together, and there was an awkward moment when Dermot had to step back to allow his very pregnant fiancé to go through the door first. There was silence between them as they left, with Pistol walking like a referee at a boxing bout, silence in the elevator, silence as they walked across the car park to the green football pitches beyond. Pistol did his business. Monica was the first to speak.

"Did Macfarlane gie ye the shite bag?"

"Naw."

"One of us will have to go back in and get one."

Dermot said, "I'll go."

"Aff ye go then."

Dermot shook his head.

"Not yet." And it all poured out of him, how he was unthinking, how he should have talked to her, how he was the stupidest Irish bastard, and how he would do anything to make it up to her.

Monica frowned. She looked at him and shook her head.

"You and I are a team, Dermot. You need to stop being so grateful for this relationship. You seem to think that I have taken pity on you, that I am superior to you in rank even in our bed. It is not true, Dermot. You mean as much to me and more in this relationship. I want this marriage, this baby, this relationship. I want us to share. I loved the place you have rented for us at Petty, and I can't wait to move in there on Saturday with you. But, Dermot, you should have discussed it beforehand." She reached over and gave him a quick peck on the lips, but Dermot was a drowning man, and he reached over and embraced her, his life raft, his float, his rescuer. Monica extricated herself and reached for her phone.

"Ye'd better get down here wi' a shite bag right now. Pistol here has got a severe dose of the die-holyia-hi-hey, and you're his master, and you need to clean it up."

The dimples appeared, and Dermot hugged her again.

When they returned to the station with a bag full of Pistol's deposits, Doddie signalled the team to come together for a briefing. They gathered before the board, some still at their desks, some had pulled up chairs closer. Everyone noted that Dermot and Monica were back on speaking terms. Doddie stood before them, ready to begin.

"Before we discuss the case, I want you to understand that as your boss if there are any problems between you and your team members, you need to talk to me. As you see," and he pointed to Dermot and Monica, who were now sitting together, "I am also a bit of a star at helping to patch up differences." Dermot shuffled in his seat, his colour rising, and Monica turned her nose up in disdain. Doddie moved on to the business of the day.

"Since Davidson and Smith went down South, we have had a change of priorities. Our chief suspect in this case is now Fred Purbright. Finding him is a priority. We can deal with Lombard and Morgan Mickelthwaite later, and the teenage vandals can also wait. We've posted Purbright's Missing Persons picture locally. In fact, we've flooded the market in Speyside. If he is there, he cannot remain hidden for long."

"There is a definite possibility of a firm maybe." – MASH

Chapter 40: Spring

Spring was approaching on the plateau of the Cairngorms. There were still the cold breezes, the nights were getting shorter, but the burns were starting to fill up as the snow began its daily melt. There was an unmistakable stirring amongst the fauna. So quiet for so long, the birdlife was beginning the joyous movement to find a mate. The Arctic hare was shedding its winter white, and the ground-hugging ptarmigan could be seen flying low over the receding snows and settling in the tufts of heather, which were rising above, seeking anew a growth that had lain dormant for so many months.

In Tomintoul, Wullie and Martha went about their business of maintenance and upkeep. Their lives didn't change much as far as routine was concerned. Wullie would spend most of his days out on the hill, keeping an eye on the changes, talking to his many local friends and helping to fix a fence here and rescue an ewe there.

One evening, Wullie was sat in his shed having a pre-prandial dram when his fax machine began to rattle and roll. Wullie reached over to grab the paper that quickly appeared. He looked at the picture of Fred Purbright and the accompanying message from Doddie, requesting he keep an eye open and ask around. Wullie smiled, finished the last of his dram, and returned to the house to show Martha the picture and, in doing so, failed miserably to conceal his excitement. This was just the sort of challenge he relished. A manhunt in the wilds, nosing around the National Park, questions, and, hopefully, answers from his neighbours and friends was food and drink to an outdoorsman like him. A long marriage meant that Martha knew her man well. He was a dog on a bone when such a challenge presented itself to him. He would work day and night tirelessly. He would leave no stone unturned; indeed, if it were necessary, he would leave no tern unstoned. He would get his man.

After eating his supper and washing the dishes, Wullie opened his maps on the table and pored over them. Since he was a boy, he had always loved maps. Even the added easiness of Google Maps and the innovation of satellite navigation could not diminish his love of the detail of the Ordnance Survey. The colour, texture, folds, and creases were always a massage to his senses.

"The priority, Martha, is to get around all the hunting lodges that are shut for the season but, of course, have caretakers on site. Ask them if they have seen anything suspicious and so forth. I will need you with me." His eyebrows were raised questioningly.

"Of course, I widnae miss it for the world. Let's get a good nicht's sleep and set off early in the morning."

Martha was brushing her teeth when the phone went. She heard Wullie pick it up and noted the excitement in his voice as he answered the simple affirmatives. She climbed into bed but left the light on. She saw the sparkle in her husband's eyes as he came into the room.

"That was Doddie. It is believed that the missing man in the picture has been seen grocery shopping in Aviemore. It is not known whether or no he has a vehicle."

In the morning, Martha packed sandwiches while Wullie brewed some tea and poured it into two large thermoses, adding some heaped teaspoonfuls of sugar for good measure. He justified this to Martha as she gave this gesture a disapproving stare.

"Well, lass, we may need the energy if we are to be out all day. There is a chill, and snow is still possible, so just in case, eh? A bit of the sweet stuff to give us a boost?"

Wullie and Martha talked about going to Aviemore to see if they could spot the man, but Wullie figured that Fred Purbright would have left quickly after picking up his groceries. Besides, neither Wullie nor Martha were conducting a search in a built-up area at home.

"Let's start at the hunting lodge at Lochindorb." He placed his finger on the map. "After all, Jimmy Turner will have been hunkered down there looking after the place in the winter. He grew up in Grantown-on-Spey but has spent most of his life in and around the loch. If a fish farts in the loch, he sees the bubbles."

So, husband and wife loaded up the Land Rover with warm clothing, wellie boots, backpacks, and lunch baskets. Martha drove out of the town on the A939 to Grantown road. They wended their way down the hill. The patches of snow lay along the side; the trees were still leafless, although Wullie noted that some early buds were making a tentative entrance. While Martha drove and Wullie mulled over his ideas, he thought that maybe he should have phoned Jimmy before they left. After all, there was no guarantee that they would find him at home, but then Wullie knew that Jimmy rarely picked up the phone. Wullie knew Jimmy well. He spent his mornings checking the buildings and doing maintenance work. If visits to a village were necessary, then to Jimmy, they were necessary evils and could be left to the afternoons or evenings.

Coming through Grantown, they continued on the same road onto the moors, passing the small settlement at Auchnagallen. Martha knew to look for the left turn onto the "B" road at Dava and down to the loch.

As they turned the final bend, the loch glittered before them and floes of very thin ice dazzled in the sun, which was guaranteed to melt them away before the day became much older. The island on which the castle's ruins, which used to be one of the seats of Red Comyn, the Wolf of Badenoch, was situated, was deceptively close to the shore. It was he who had sacked Elgin Cathedral and most of the rest of the town in the 1300s.

They drew parallel with the castle and came to the wood plantation that housed the hunting lodge. They turned right onto the driveway, made their way through the woods, and came to a gravelled area in front of the building. Martha parked, and they both hopped out of the vehicle. They began to walk towards the front, but a voice from behind caused them to pause.

"Martha and Wullie Macpherson, as I live and breathe. This is a pleasant surprise."

Jimmy, resplendent in his tweed suit and deerstalker, marched across the gravel towards them. He was a big man with a balding head, possibly in his fifties. His complexion was weathered. He had a bit of a paunch, but his stride showed energy, strength, and athleticism. He matched his surroundings, solidly built but had seen better times, although the old lodge boasted new beginnings, a testament to the money made during the hunting and fishing season.

"What can I do for you both? Martha, still as bonny as ever, whatever did ye see in this skeletal waif of a man? Where was I when you were seeking?"

"Och, away wi' yer silver-tongued flannel, Jimmy Turner, are ye know going to show off your hosting skills and make us a brew?"

He reached across, put his arm around her shoulders, and marched towards the front door.

He called over his shoulder.

"You can come along too, Wullie, if you really want."

Over tea and scones, Wullie produced the picture of the missing man. Jimmy studied the features with some intensity, knowing he had not seen him but ensuring he would recognise him if he did.

Nothing comes quickly in the Highlands regarding comings and goings. Wullie and Martha stood up to take their leave. Thirty minutes after their fond farewell, they were still passing the time of day with Jimmy. As they opened the doors of the Land Rover, Martha said, "It's been grand seein' ye, Jimmy. You keep those grey eyes of yours peeled, and ye see anything suspicious, give Wullie and I a bell."

Jimmy nodded, "Nae problemo, Martha."

They drove out of the gravelled area onto the rutted entry road, and Martha suggested before they pulled onto the main road that they drop in on Carrbridge and distribute the picture in the lovely wee village. So, they took the road back to Grantown and followed a different route out of the town. Soon, they were by the golf course outside the village. The silver birches at the side of the road shimmered in a slight breeze, seemingly anxious as they passed. They came to the left turn into the village where the Carrbridge Hotel was situated. They parked in the hotel car park. Wullie looked over the road at the old, humped bridge and marvelled that it was still standing. Nobody was at the desk as they entered the lobby, so Martha pressed the bell. A tall, middle-aged woman appeared out of the back office in an immaculate white shirt and a thick tweed skirt with sensible shoes. She beamed a welcome as she recognised Wullie and Martha.

"Och, and I thought I had a couple of customers." She reached across the counter and grasped Martha by the hand, after which she moved to the other side and gave Wullie a big hug.

"And what brings you two hicks into the big city?"

Wullie laughed.

"Do we need an excuse to visit our favourite hotel owner, Morag? Martha just wanted an excuse to reminisce about your school days."

Morag Menzies had already linked her arm with Martha and was making her way to the seating area in the front hall.

Wullie said, "I'll head off into the village about my business. Martha will get you up to speed about why we are here." With that, Wullie returned to the vehicle and picked up about ten pictures of Purbright lying on the back seat.

Wullie walked up and down the high street, dropping the photographs at various businesses along the way, noting that the post office already had a picture of Purbright in its window. He dropped a couple of pictures in at the Landmark Centre and noted that the porridge competition was being advertised along with one for chainsaw art. He wandered back on the other side of the street and leaned on the road bridge, admiring the old drovers' bridge built in 1717 and was now too unstable to support the adventurers who used to love jumping off it into the pools below. It was built two years after the first Jacobite rebellion and many years before the Battle of Culloden in the eighteenth century. Wullie marvelled at how structures back then were built to last. He marvelled at the passing of time, at what the bridge had seen. The waters had passed beneath—the flow of history, the comings and goings of generations—the timelessness of waters apart from what was, yet still a part of what is. There was a constancy and consistency there that Wullie envied. He sighed at the thought, crossed the road, and entered the hotel.

Martha and Morag were still at the chairs in the front foyer but were joined by a high tea. A rack of scones, sandwiches, jam, butter, and cream had taken a hammering, but there was sufficient left for Wullie to reach across to grab a raisin scone and pop it into his mouth.

"There's a reason for raisins," he quipped before taking himself off to look out of a window and allowing the conversation to continue. The two old friends barely acknowledged his presence as they continued to talk about old times.

Eventually, Martha stood up to take her leave. Morag hugged her, and together they walked to the front of the hotel to join Wullie. Promises were made to meet again soon, and Martha found herself in the passenger seat of the Land Rover as Wullie was ready to take his turn driving. Without preamble, Martha said, "One of the hotel guests swears she saw our man hitching along the road by the golf course two days ago. It was raining, so she only caught a brief glimpse of a face under a hooded parka, so she could not swear to it. He was headed towards Grantown."

When they arrived in Tomintoul, Wullie phoned Doddie to confirm what they had done and what had been reported to them.

"Apres moi le deluge." – Porter

Chapter 41: The Return of the Wolf of Badenoch

Wullie was instantly awake. The time on his bedside clock revealed just after 3.00 a.m. The telephone on his bedside table was buzzing with "clinkum-bell," a disharmonious jangle from a deep sleep. Wullie reached for the receiver and, ever polite, announced his name. Jimmy apologized.

"But I've just seen a light coming from the castle on the loch. I was up at the toilet and looking out the window. It was only a quick flash, and it was gone. But, Wullie, my eyes do not deceive. There's somebody on the old Wolf's island in Red Comyn's lair and no mistake. Can you come?"

"Aye." Wullie was already reaching for his shirt. Martha stirred and opened one eye, and Wullie explained as he dressed.

"Be careful." She rolled over and went back to sleep. She was used to Wullie and his adventures. As he pulled his jacket on and approached the Land Rover, he phoned Doddie. The long litany was expected. He knew that after "hanging is too good fer you," Doddie would get to the point. Wullie explained the situation and that he was headed to Lochindorb. He asked to meet him there.

"And bring help," was his final instruction.

Of course, the road was dark as befit a night in late winter. The only lights were when he drove a deserted Grantown street and was out the other side and onto the moor, where the gloom added a certain numinous quality to his drive. It wasn't long before he reached the Dava turn off and was soon pulling up to the front of the lodge when Jimmy appeared with a torch.

"Any more signs?" Wullie enquired as Jimmy guided them to the boathouse to get a better look at the place.

"No, none."

They made it onto the dock and looked across to the dark silhouette of the ruined castle on the island. Wullie explained that help was on the way from Inverness but thought they should row out there at first light to investigate, even if at that point, Doddie had not arrived. They were careful not to have their flashlights turned on but sat down in the cold at the edge of the dock to watch. They were shivering slightly. The waters lapped gently, ironically belying the excitement and tenseness of their feelings as surges of adrenaline coursed through their veins. A slight breeze off the loch chilled them as they peered out at the dark outline of the castle crenellations, not so far distant away. To Wullie, it was as if they were back seven hundred years previously, awaiting the return of the banditry from the terror and havoc they had wreaked on the worthy town of Elgin. Jimmy began to move with the first glimpses of light coming up from the east.

"We could use the outboard motor, but I think that the silent approach is best." Jimmy was standing with two oars, one in either hand. Wullie stood, and they moved to the rowing boat moored at the dock by the prow. He then manoeuvred his way to the stern. Jimmy placed the rowlocks and oars, Wullie cast off from the stern. They moved away from the land with Jimmy dabbing the water gently with the oars. It took ten minutes or so before they could come to a landing spot on the island. Silently and cautiously, they tied up the boat and crept over the long grass, being careful not to stumble on the fallen building debris that caused an overgrown uneven service beneath. They paused at the corner of a ruined wall and peered into the darkness. They remained still and silent for the best part of five minutes. Hearing nothing, they edged their way forward still without the use of their torches. They heard it before they saw it. The gentle flapping of a tarpaulin so obviously out of place in this ancient abandoned ruin. It was rigged up as a makeshift shelter. This confirmed that, at the very least, there had been a human presence here relatively recently. The natural light of the early morning revealed a sleeping bag and cooking area and the detritus of a campsite that had been left sometime before. They abandoned all caution and clicked on the flashlights. Wullie checked the camping stove for warmth; it was ice cold. Jimmy felt no heat inside the sleeping bag; the abandoned cup of tea was almost frozen. Whoever had been there was there no longer. They decided to circle the island going in opposite directions. When Wullie reached the perimeter closest to the shore, he saw a police car pull up, and sufficient light revealed the profile of Doddie accompanied by two police constables. Wullie shouted over to Jimmy that he would row over and pick them up.

It was full daylight when Doddie, Smith, and Davidson arrived. Doddie had woken them early, and they got out of their respective flats. He told them to come prepared for a hike on the moors, so they were clad in sturdy boots with woolly bonnets, gloves, waterproofs, and layers.

The site was covered in the debris of a recently evacuated campsite. It looked as though somebody had spent some time at the place. By the sights and sounds of it, the person had left hurriedly in the night. Doddie pulled out his high-powered binoculars and scanned the edge of the loch methodically. Nothing appeared at first glance, so he decided to concentrate on likely landing areas. Again, nothing appeared, so he decided to give the binoculars over to the younger eyes of Smith.

"See yon patch of woods on the far side of the loch, beneath the cottar on the hill? Jimmy tells me that's where the boathouse is, where the fishers pick up the boats for a day on the loch. See if you can spot anything unusual around that area."

Smith played and adjusted the focus until he was satisfied. He panned back and forth a few times and suddenly stopped and craned his neck forward like a giraffe reaching for a high branch. He then handed the binoculars to Davidson.

"See what you see, just beneath the group of three silver birches in the shape of a "W."

Davidson took over.

"I think it's a bike."

Smith grabbed the binoculars back and moved closer to the edge of the loch, reaching forward with his whole body as if to touch the other bank.

"Aye, aye it is."

Doddie turned to Jimmy.

"Why would somebody have a bike on nothing but a moor?"

"There's an unpaved road to the cottage that leads back to the B-road here. If we head back to the lodge, we can pick up yer Land Rover and drive over for a closer look."

They all clambered back into the boat and rowed briskly to the shore.

Doddie frowned.

"If somebody were living rough here on the island and popping over to the shore there occasionally, would not the occupant of the croft have noticed their comings and goings?"

Jimmy shook his head.

"Aye, normally, Murdina Moore would, but she spends winters wi' her sister in Edinburgh."

Doddie climbed into the front of the Land Rover with Wullie while the three others made the best of a tight fit in the back seat. They drove the short half-mile to the junction and turned left onto the dirt road. There were so many holes and ruts that Doddie asked Wullie to stop, and he and the three others left Wullie to manufacture slow progress while they walked on ahead. Doddie soon realised that he had not the pech of his youth and was quickly out of breath, so he ushered the other three to run ahead. He would catch them up. Davidson arrived first at the site, and his suspicions were confirmed when he looked down at a newish mountain bike that obviously had good recent usage. Proudly, he picked it up and began to ride back towards Doddie.

"Get aff that, ye daftie, it might be evidence."

Davidson did as he was bid and dropped it by the side of the road.

When they arrived at the boathouse, there were obvious signs of a break-in. The locks on the chains of the boats had been cut, and, carelessly, the cutters had been left leaning against the boathouse wall.

Doddie sat down on the dock and tried to formulate a plan. He thought about calling in a helicopter but knew he could not justify the expense at this point. Besides, it like the weather would sock in, making visibility difficult. He looked towards the Monadhliaths, the range of small peaks that guarded the moors. Ominous black clouds were gathering, promising rain and storm. The wind was starting to get up, making the showers likely to be horizontal rather than vertical. If the person had been in the process of leaving when Jimmy saw his light, then he had a good head start. He would be the needle in a haystack; the hope of finding him without a full-blown search party would be more by luck than good management. Doddie ran through this with all of them.

"Let's cut our losses, return to the lodge, and call in the SOCO team. About time Scene of Crime earned their keep."

So, they made their way back to the main road as the Land Rover hobbled along behind them. They reached the road as the storm broke, dashing to get into the vehicle before they got a soaking.

Back at the lodge, over tea and buns, Doddie called Inverness and arranged for a SOCO team to get up as soon as possible. He decided that little could be done further, so he and the two constables drove back to Inverness, Wullie drove home, and Jimmy prepared himself for the arrival of the unaccustomed crowd.

"The critical period in matrimony is breakfast time." – Alan Herbert

Chapter 42: Petty

Dermot and Monica departed Inverness for their new residence at Petty on Saturday at 10.30 a.m. Dermot had solicited the good offices of Davidson and Smith to help them move. Monica had looked alarmed when Dermot told her.

He smiled. "Yes, I know. You're worried about them dropping and breaking. I've promised them beer and pizza when all is delivered safely. You and I have boxed everything up. All they have to do is pick the stuff up, drop it in the back of the rental van, and deliver it. What can go wrong?"

Monica looked doubtful. "It's the 'dropping it' that worries me."

But sure enough, Davidson and Smith were at Dermot's suite on Saturday morning, and, after they had supped the tea and eaten the cakes that Dermot's landlady had made for them, they got their heads down and went for it.

"Such nice young fellas," Mrs Macrae had confided quietly to Dermot as they watched a chest of drawers being marched up the garden path and unceremoniously banged into the gate post on the way.

Dermot looked like he was not so sure and was glad Monica was not there to witness it, having decided to pack up her few belongings and make several journeys in her car. Dermot had thought ahead and picked up and copied the keys for Petty a couple of days before. The plan was for Davidson and Smith to follow Dermot in his car as he drove. So, after a tearful farewell with his landlady and a large unnecessary package of cheese and tomato sandwiches being thrust into his hands, he took his leave.

Slowly checking his mirrors, they drove through Inverness and onto the main Aberdeen road. Dermot was reassured that the truck behind had done the difficult part and left town without too much trouble—all was well. Dermot indicated left to turn off the main road and was surprised when the truck hurtled past, careering along the road at a rate of knots. He pulled over into a layby and waited ten minutes, feeling sure they would realise their mistake and turn back. He phoned Smith's mobile, but there was no reply. Baffled, he headed on to Petty, where he knew Monica would be waiting.

He reached the garden gate to find Monica putting down a box and opening the front door. He rushed forward to pick it up for his pregnant partner, but she was having none of it, explaining for the umpteenth time that pregnancy was not a disease. Dermot knew better than to argue. She went into the bedroom, and Dermot disappeared into the kitchen and put the kettle on. As they sat sipping their orange and ginger herbal, looking out over the well-manicured garden and down onto the bay, Monica asked the question Dermot had been dreading.

"So, where's Smith and Davidson?" After Dermot had explained, he noted Monica biting her lip, determined that she would not have an "I told you so" moment.

"I'll try phoning them again." Dermot dialled, but there was still no reply. But at that moment, he heard the slow progress of the truck and saw the two unlikely movers and, hopefully not shakers, pulling up beyond the gate.

Dermot shouted cheerily to Monica, "They're here," and ran up the garden path to greet them.

"What happened?"

Davidson looked sheepish and reddened.

Smith said, "Well, we're here now."

They went to the back of the truck and flung open the doors. Dermot did a double-take because there seemed to be some boxes he didn't remember packing.

"Must be losing it," he muttered to himself and thought no more of it.

Smith and Davidson were eager to get going, especially since Davidson saw the icebox with some lonely-looking cans of lager wanting company and having heard that the pizza was ordered for 2.00 p.m. So, they unloaded with a will. Dermot had to say that he was impressed with the speed and care they took. He decided to leave the unpacking of the boxes until after they had left so that he and Monica could do it at their leisure.

So, after the sweat of the unloading was complete, and the ropes were tidied, and the doors were shut on the empty, hollow shell, they settled in the living room, sat on the floor, and opened a can. Smith and Davidson were proud of themselves; they were happy to be of use.

Punctually, there was a knock at the door, and Monica went to pay the pizza delivery guy. Everybody was hungry, and after they had wolfed down their food, Smith stood and said, "Well, we should get the van back to the rental company."

Dermot and Monica stood at the door, arms around each other, and waved as the two constables pulled off. They decided to delay the unpacking by taking a walk down the bank to the water and out to the point of a little cape that overlooked the Moray Firth. When they reached the headland, they both felt the breeze strengthen and knew it would be a race back to the house before the rain came. They turned and jogged along the road with mackintoshes raised over their heads as big drops started to fall. They had just reached the front door when the heavens opened.

Monica went into the front room, where most of her boxes lay unopened, and Dermot took himself off to the bedroom. Monica heard him begin to rip the tape. She sat up when she heard a surprised shout, followed by a shriek of indignation. "Those fucking eedjuts; I should never have trusted them."

Monica dashed into the room to see what the problem was. Dermot was raging and dashing around, ripping tape off boxes here and cursing his discoveries there.

"What is it?" Monica frowned.

"This is NOT my stuff." Dermot was running his fingers through his hair.

"How could this be? Those lunatics have somehow managed to deliver the wrong stuff. How the hell could that happen?"

"What's his number? I'll phone Davidson right now." Monica was all business.

A surprised Davidson picked up the phone. "Monica? Long time no see. What can I do for you?"

"You and your buddy need to get over here right now. The contents of the van are not Dermot's contents; they belong to somebody else."

Davidson laughed. "That can't be right. You're joking."

Monica yelled over the phone, "Pick up that lunatic mate of yours and get over here right away." She hung up.

It was not so much a welcoming party when Davidson and Smith arrived back at the house, but more of a lynch mob. Monica and Dermot hauled the two miscreants into the kitchen, where Dermot had unpacked four chairs and a table, not his own, and sat them down, ready to be interrogated. Monica started.

"I'm going to ask the questions. Where did ye go when Dermot lost you on the main road?"

Smith began to speak.

"Well, we realised that we had lost Dermot and took a right turn further down the road and found ourselves in a place called Loch Flemington. We were totally lost, so we pulled into a driveway to ask for directions. We parked up next to a van exactly like ours—the same rental company and everything. A very kind old gentleman pulled out his map and showed us where we had gone wrong. On the way out, I spotted our van keys in a bowl by the door, grabbed them, and we got into the van and drove here. It is true that I didn't remember putting the keys in the bowl, so we must have picked up the other set and taken the wrong van."

As he finished speaking, he reached into his pocket, and his eyes lit up with delight as he pulled out a set of keys.

He smiled broadly and said, "And here's the other set of keys."

Monica groaned and raised her right hand, putting it across Dermot's chest as she sensed he was just about to grab Smith by the throat and pull him over the table. Davidson stood up and, pulling Smith to his feet, they both retreated to the door.

"Don't worry. We'll fix it." They ran out of the front door and down the garden path before Dermot's explosion looked likely to open up a second murder inquiry.

"When the tide goes out, you can see who has been swimming naked."

– Warren Buffet

Chapter 43: Manhunt

The SOCO unit had found an abundance of fingerprints at the campsite. They believed they could get samples of DNA from an unwashed teacup, but all of this gave them no clue to the identity of the missing camper. The National Database revealed no match for the fingerprints, telling them this person was not a known criminal. Doddie tried desperately to convince himself that this was an unknown person. He had always preached to his team the dangers of assumption getting in the way of effective detective work. But in his heart of hearts, he was convinced that their fugitive was Purbright. It hadn't helped that the weather had been socked in for two days, so they had not been able to get a helicopter up to see things from the air. Wullie had raised his mates in the local Search and Rescue teams, and they had been out on the moors using all their expertise and experience to find the mysterious camper amongst the wilderness of the Monadhliaths. No luck.

Finally, the weather lifted and the sun came out on the Monday after Dermot and Monica's move. Immediately, Doddie was up in the police helicopter, scanning the area for signs of life. Nothing and nobody appeared in this remote wilderness. Doddie returned to Earth, frustrated and flustered.

Wullie was out on the moor with several locals stretched on a line across the heather when suddenly he stopped dead in his tracks. He asked the others to proceed up the hill and returned to the Murdina Moore's cottage. He was giving himself a mental kicking because nobody had thought to search the empty cottage in their assumption that the missing person was somewhere out on the moors. Wullie walked around the building, peering into the windows. If he noticed nothing untoward, he did realise that Murdina Moore had left her house spic and span. He tried the front and back doors, but they were both locked, and he was reluctant to force an entry. He noted the two stone outbuildings and some disused and rusting farm equipment. He managed to prise open one of the doors, which was almost off its hinges. A tractor was garaged there, and the place smelled of oil and maintenance. He looked up and saw an old hayloft. Looking around, he found a ladder and propped it up, and he ascended slowly. There was a different smell as he reached the top. He paused there for a moment and caught sight of what looked like an old sports jacket. As he crawled closer, he realised what the smell was. The buzzing of flies confirmed what he suspected. There before him were the cold, dead eyes of a man. Beside him was a pill bottle. Clutched in his right hand was an envelope. Purbright was missing no more.

"There is no such thing as madness,
just varying degrees of sanity."
– Midsomer Murders

Chapter 44: The Dilemma

Sitting in their front room, looking out over the garden still manicured with the loving ministrations of their landlady and landlord, Dermot and Monica had enjoyed their traditional Saturday morning fry up. Dermot noted inwardly the gusto with which Monica hoovered down the contents of her plate and was up helping herself for more even before he had pierced the yolk of his first egg. He said nothing, having read copiously of the minefield that is the pregnant woman's mind. He was unusually quiet as he washed and dried the dishes as Monica rested with her feet up on the window seat, looking out and sipping her cup of herbal tea.

As he put the last plate away in the cupboard, he said, "I think I'm going to walk down to the bay."

"Great. I'll get my boots on."

Dermot shook his head and said, "Sorry, love, I have some things that I need to get straight in my head, and I need to be alone."

Monica frowned.

Dermot came over, put his arm around her, and kissed her forehead.

"Nothing to worry about; I just need to give some more thought as to whom I am going to ask to be my best man. I just don't want to offend anybody, that's all."

He grabbed his coat off the rack by the door and reached for a precautionary umbrella.

As he walked down the steep hill to the water's edge, he noted how still the day was, not a breath coming off the water, only gentle lapping on the shore. Dermot had good friends back home in Ireland, but times had been hard for them, and he couldn't justify the expense of them coming over. They would feel obliged, of course, because he was a mate, but still, he did not want them to have the expense. Then he felt he couldn't even ask them because if he asked Jimmy Toolan, then Brian Mahoney would be offended; the same went for Peter Armstrong and Geoff Turnbull. Then, of course, there would be the added expense of the stag night. He thought it best to keep the wedding a secret from them and just invite his mum and dad. He thought about the possibilities of his new friends in Inverness. Davidson and Smith came as a duet, and he felt uneasy at times about some of the music they played. Doddie was spoken for as he was giving away the bride. Mental Martin would work, but he couldn't come to terms with what the speech might sound like. McIvor might have been good value, but he didn't really know him. Rowlands was too much of a boss.

When eventually he decided to turn back home, an idea suddenly came to him. Before he had gone another fifty yards, there was a skip in his step and a smile inching its way onto his face. Dermot reached for his phone and dialled. After about a five-minute conversation, he switched off his phone and jogged up the hill to the house with a light-hearted bounce and a twinkling eye. Monica greeted him as he was taking off his coat.

"Is everything straight? Gonna tell me about it?"

"I think not, o' beautiful bride of mine. You'll learn about it nearer the day."

Monica swung her right arm, aiming for the back of his head, but he ducked and grinned back at her.

"We live in a world of continuous partial attention." – Linda Stone

Chapter 45: Backtracking

Dermot was a wee bit surprised to be given the task but figured it was not for him to reason why. The simple message in Purbright's suicide note said cryptically: *I love my wife.*

That was it. Nothing more. Dermot saw reasons for his desperate act there, mainly if the love of his life was leaving him for somebody else. There seemed to be no link between the act and the murder other than the commonality of Welwyn Garden City. He shrugged and was more interested when Doddie changed direction and asked him to contact the Cairngorms and ask for CCTV footage around the time of the death, showing a group of teenage boys.

"What am I looking for specifically, Boss?"

"A small group of teenage boys," was the reply.

So, Dermot contacted the mountain and was dismayed when it was explained that the footage was likely long gone. He was clear about the dates but could almost see, certainly imagine, the shaking of the head at the other end of the line. It was a dead-end street, so Dermot gave up that idea. He had put the phone down when a call came through from the Cairngorms barely fifteen minutes later.

"A colleague of mine took a picture of a group of adolescents around the dates you were talking about. I'll have him fax it down to you asap."

Dermot expressed his appreciation and got off the line. A few seconds later, he heard the whir of the fax machine and leapt up, moving over to it quickly. Ever so slowly, the picture appeared. It was a posed picture of five young men, a couple of which Dermot recognised. He snatched it up quickly and walked briskly to Doddie's door, barely able to contain his excitement.

Doddie was in the process of looking through Davidson's and Smith's files and was shaking his head. He looked up as Dermot entered.

"Ye ken that expression 'the walls have ears,' nae doot. Well, in the case of these twa bampots, the ears have walls. Setting them on the right path to success is like herding cats. What can I do ye for, oh bright-eyed and bushy-tailed one?" he said with a grin.

"You can look at these, Boss. A cell phone picture from an alert employee of the Cairngorms around the time of the murder of Dr Ross."

Doddie stood up and stared down at the picture with intent.

"Get on the phone to Sinclair; tell him we're on our way to the school to see him."

He grabbed his coat and headed for the door.

"Pistol and DS Richards, come with me now."

Monica looked up from her desk, vaguely insulted to be ordered out in the same breath as Doddie's dog. But she saw the glint in his eye and the purpose in his stride and decided to let it go. There was a brief conversation in the elevator as they descended to the ground floor so that Monica was au fait with the purpose of their visit.

On arrival at the school, Dermot explained to the receptionist that they were expected, and he flashed his ID. There was no real need for either because Sinclair had already informed her.

Sinclair did not get up to greet them but peered over his glasses suspiciously at Pistol, who was renewing his acquaintance with his office and had begun sniffing around the bookcase.

"Don't worry, Mr Sinclair, Pistol has done his business several times this morning. It's safe enough. I need young Stewart down here right now. Can you get him for us?"

"Aye, I'll send for him," and he reached for his phone. Doddie was shaking his head.

"Na, na, Mr Sinclair, in this case, we want you to go and fetch him. Ye can take Constable Long along wi'ye."

Sinclair was used to getting others to do such mundane tasks, so he was a bit taken aback. Then he noticed Pistol sniffing around his bookcase and figured that discretion was better than valour. He stood up, and Dermot followed. Within minutes, they had returned with a very worried-looking seventeen-year-old boy. Monica directed him to sit down next to her. She had been obviously delegated as the interrogator. She explained as gently as she could that Stewart did not need to answer any of her questions without a social worker or parent present, but given that he despised the one and was terrified of the other, she felt he would be happy to cooperate. Stewart nodded.

"Tell us about your hiking trip to the Cairngorms."

The boy looked confused and started to shake his head, at which point Doddie produced the photograph and pushed it in front of him.

"We know you were there, Stewart," Monica pressed the point.

His head drooped, and he knew there was no point in denial.

Doddie spoke. "You're still a minor; the more you cooperate, the easier it will be for you." Stewart realised he was caught between Scylla and Charybdis, a rock and a hard place, and began to open up.

"Mr Mickelthwaite and Mr Lombard thought it would be good for our futures if we were to become part of the Duke of Edinburgh's Award Scheme. So, he arranged for us to have a few days in the holidays to go on a trial expedition. So, the plan was to take a mini-bus to Aberdeenshire and hike up the Lairig Ghru frae Mar Lodge. We would walk ahead of Mr Lombard, and Mr Micklethwaite would drive the bus back to the other side and pick us up after our day hike. It began as a great day. It was a bit of a lark, but we were all getting tired as we got close to the Pools of Dee. We had a wee bitty to climb when we ran into this older guy sat on a rock having a snack. He smiled and took a shine to us and could see that we were struggling, so he started to encourage us and even gave us some of his snack. He seemed like a nice guy, and pretty soon, he was part of the group. We were happy when we reached the Chalamainn Gap, but we hadn't bargained on this difficult part of the path, right at the end of the day, but yer mannie there encouraged us and got us through most of the hard stuff without too much bother. I cannae remember how it came up in conversation, but somehow, we took an interest in what the guy did for work. He smiled at us and told us he was a paediatrician at some town in the south of England. We stopped dead in our tracks at that, surprised that somebody would confess to such a thing. He explained that he loved working with children. We all looked at each other, and before any of us had any time to think, Hamish Brown had clenched his fist and smacked him on the jaw. He looked surprised for a second and then went down. Then we were all kicking him and hurting him. It was soon obvious that he was unconscious, so we left him and walked away ahead. We only meant to give him a kicking; we never meant to kill him."

"Why would you give him a kicking in the first place? I thought you had befriended him," Doddie said quietly.

Stewart dropped his eyes; the others in the room could feel his guilt.

"Aye, well, it was only efter we heard on the news that we learned that a paediatrician was a doctor who helped children. We all thocht he was a paedophile. We didn't think he was that bad; it was when we reached the road and were sat around waiting for Mr Lombard that we realised we had killed him."

"Then what happened?" Monica's eyes were intense.

"Mr Mickelthwaite arrived. We dropped our packs in the van, walked back up the trail, and rigged up a stretcher and a tarp to carry the body down. We drove back to Inverness with the body lying between us in the back of the bus. We were all silent and shocked. Mr Lombard and Mr Mickelthwaite swore us to secrecy and promised they would dispose of the body and that they would protect us. They dropped us all back hame and took off. We never knew what had happened until the body of Dr Ross turned up in Munlochy. What will happen tae us, mister?" He turned to Doddie.

"That's up to the courts, laddie, but better late than never, you've done the right thing."

"Find a way to get out of my way." – Grant Davidson

Chapter 46: The Truth Will Out

Umbago and Morgan Mickelthwaite were not difficult nuts to crack. Yes, they had been using information purloined from Mental Martin's records to "frighten" paedophiles off, but both knew that such behaviour was unlikely to work since the illness was so much a part of that type of person's being, and it would take a great deal more than a kicking in a back alley to see off the perversion. Doddie became flustered very quickly with the details of their crimes against the sex offenders and was eager to move on to the murder case. It was Morgan Mickelthwaite who led the way on the explanation.

"I arrived at the scene after the boys had met me at the end of the trail. They were not in a good mental state, but I persuaded them to come back up the trail with me and search out the body. I understood that when we found Dr Ross, it would be imperative to get him away from there so as not to implicate the boys. We arrived at the body splayed out on the rocks and assumed that the beating had killed him. I was in no doubt that my boys had done this and swore to them that Umbago and I would take care of it and somehow keep them out of it. We managed to conceal the corpse in the tarpaulin, and, not without difficulty, we reached the trailhead. Umbago returned with us, and together we managed to get the body to the trailhead. We dropped the boys in Inverness, emphasizing all the way home that they had nothing to worry about. We reached the Black Isle, and it was there that things started to go awry. The mini-bus hit a rock, and a tyre blew out, so we had to pull over. It was still dark, but somehow, people arrived to help; two guys who had been drinking turned up and offered us advice. They would not leave us alone, and they made so much noise that lights came on in the local houses. The neighbours were not happy, and one had threatened to call the police, so as soon as the punctured tyre was removed and the spare fixed, we drove off speedily and in a blind panic with the belief that we would be pursued by the police and the body would be found. We had no idea where we were going but found a farm track, drove down it, hastily dumped the body, and skedaddled out of the village and back to Inverness. We were very surprised that nobody had taken the number of the bus and that it was not followed up when the body was found. Umbago panicked when you brought him to see me. I knew he would head to Bruach. It was me who arranged the hideaway on Orkney, although I knew it would only be a matter of time before he was caught. He was too good of a person, too nice of a guy to hide the truth forever. We are so sorry that our boys killed Dr Ross."

Doddie nodded but said nothing. He debated whether to tell Morgan Mickelthwaite that his "boys" had not killed him. It seemed that he was unaware of the knife wound. However, he decided to keep that neither the kicking nor the knife had killed him a secret. Dr Ross had died of a congenital heart complaint, possibly, it was true, brought on by the kicking. The stabbing had happened post-mortem. Nobody was directly guilty of murder in this case. The truth would come out soon enough in the court case to follow.

"A person should keep his eyes wide open before marriage and half-closed afterwards." – Ben Franklin

Chapter 47: Happy Days

Now that it looked like the murder inquiry was ending, Dermot and Monica decided to set a date for their wedding. So, they agreed that the venue would be the garden of their rental place at Petty. Spring had come to the Highlands, and whilst that had not guaranteed good weather, they decided to risk it. April showers may dampen the day, but they would have a tent if that came about. Accordingly, the stag and stagette were set for the weekend before.

Monica had told Dermot that whatever he had planned, it was not to occur in Tomintoul. She had been in touch with Wullie and Martha. They had invited her to stay with them in the village, Wullie volunteering to take her and her friends on a scenic tour of the area. Monica's fitness level was so high that she was carrying her pregnancy well. She did not seem to have many girlfriends, but she had kept in touch with a couple of girls from school and had one close friend from her time in Turriff.

Dermot had weakened. He realised how much he wanted some friends from his hometown to be there on their big day. He decided to invite three close friends, who flew in from Belfast on the Friday before his stag weekend with plans to remain for the whole week and attend the wedding on Saturday. This surprised and delighted him to the extent that he was ashamed he had not asked one of them to be his best man.

This was still shrouded in mystery. Davidson and Smith had expected that one of them would be asked, but no such offer was forthcoming. All they knew was that the best man had organised a bus and booked them all into the Coylumbridge Hotel near Aviemore. Monica knew this much and was slightly concerned that the "stags" and "stagettes" may well run into each other, but Dermot assured her that they were going fishing on the Spey and had no intention of heading away for a hike in the National Park.

Dermot brought his fellow Ulstermen into the police station when he picked them up at Dalcross on Friday so that Doddie, Davidson, and Smith had the chance to meet Seumas, Ian, and Sean, three acquaintances whom he had known for a long time. He explained that they would meet his best man up there as he was coming directly from the east. At 4.00 p.m. on that evening, Doddie would arrive as the driver of the hired mini-bus, and they would leave the station and head up to Aviemore. The first stop would be the Happy Haggis for fish suppers, and they would then book into their hotel for the night.

Doddie had always been a stickler for punctuality, so everybody who had him as their boss was there on time. However, the three Irishmen had gotten themselves lost in the streets of Inverness, so it was 4.30 before they hit the road. "Hanging had been too good" for the Ulstermen, according to Davidson and Smith, who preened themselves on the journey up to Aviemore. The other part of the trip was spent inquiring of Dermot as to the identity of his best man. However, Dermot was not forthcoming, explaining they would meet him soon enough. Davidson and Smith had thought well enough ahead to bring along a carry out of Tennents Lager with some non-alcoholic equivalents for "Doddie the Driver." There was initial consternation about having their boss along on this stag, let alone as their driver. The feeling was that he would restrict their antics and get in the way of a fully-fledged frolic. Secretly, that was the reason Dermot was keen to have him. He did not want to end up stripped naked up a hotel flag pole only to be arrested by the local police force and awaken in the morning in a police cell with wee elves jack-hammering their way through the inside of his skull. But then he smiled as he ruminated on that because his choice of best man would likely cause more consternation than Doddie's presence.

The journey was uneventful. It was 6.00 p.m. when they hit Carrbridge and at 6.45 when the Irish contingent was lined up outside the chipper, trying to make themselves understood to the teenage lassie who was trying to decipher their orders. Dermot had called ahead to his best man and was surprised when the order came through for a deep-fried Mars bar "with all the trimmings." He failed to understand what "all the trimmings" might be for such an appalling combination of batter and chocolate but the server seemed to better understand that than the "sachs fush sappers" that Seumas had ordered and eventually paid for. There was silence as Doddie drove them over the bridge and the few miles to the Coylumbridge Hotel. The aroma and the silent munching spoke volumes about the hunger of the occupants of the van. They remained in the van eating as Dermot headed off to the hotel reception to sign them in. They could just make out another figure with him as he arrived back as they were finishing up the feast.

"Right you lot, I would like to introduce my 'best man' Dr Veronica Richards, Monica's mum."

The new arrival smiled at the group of young men whose mouths were now agape, the occasional chip in limbo hovering with uncertainty between lap and mouth. Nobody spoke. The sight of Dr Richards, mother of the bride, was so incongruous, given that this was a stag weekend. It took Doddie to break the ice. He smiled broadly and pulled himself out of the driver's seat and onto the tarmac, hastily wiping the remnants of greasy chips off his hands on his shirt before extending his right hand for Dr Richards to shake.

"Trust this dumb Irishman to pull a stunt like this. Pleased to meet you; I'm Doddie Macfarlane, this bampot's boss."

"Of course, you are. I've heard an awful lot about you, all of it, well, some of it, maybe a wee bittie of it, good," and she laughed a deep catching belly laugh that caused the other occupants of the bus to le.

"Where's ma deep-fried Mars bar and all the trimmings? Ah cannae drink on an empty stomach like yon smytrie of wee doddie weans that you've brocht alang for a weekend of daftness and drunkenness."

With that, they all retreated to the bar to let the weekend begin.

Meanwhile, in Tomintoul, Monica and her friends had arrived independently. They had gathered at their hotel, and Monica led them down the rural road on a walk to meet Wullie and Martha. The warmth of the greeting was not simply that from the AGA, but pots of tea and home baking were set forth. Martha noted Monica's condition and beamed when Monica invited her to the wedding.

"Don't ye worry, lassie, I will make my Wullie presentable in his kilt. He will fit in. As for that young Irishman, I hope he realizes how lucky he is. Where are they, by the way?"

"They're in Aviemore with strict orders to keep well away from the hills. I think they're going fishing." Monica was forceful in her language.

"One hint is worth two bushels of advice." – Farmer's Almanac

Chapter 48: The Trial

"Sorry, ye cannae can ye, let's head over to the café. I need to talk to ye." Monica pointedly looked at her watch and sighed. Doddie produced his best hangdog expression and put his head down with deliberate exaggeration.

"It winna tak lang, lass, I promise you."

Monica was already walking towards the coffee shop. She reached the counter first and ordered and paid for a pot of tea and a couple of muffins. Doddie pulled up a chair by the window and waited for her to bring them over. When she sat down, Doddie got straight to the point.

Monica was sceptical.

"What the fuck does cock a snoop mean?" She asked, smiling.

Doddie returned to hangdog mode. She sighed.

"Okay, supposing that you have a point and these are not the ravings of an idiot who has just spent a weekend on a drunken jolly with my future husband, where do we go from here?" she asked.

"Go, Monica, go? Is it no obvious? We head down to Welwyn Garden City and chat to the local police, maybe even pop in and give our condolences to Mrs Ross, and we dig a lot further and a great deal deeper. This case is not yet done and dusted, lassie. I'm off to see Rowlands to get money for a flight released for us."

Monica was shaking her head and had her hand raised as if she was on traffic duty.

"Stop right there. I'm now very pregnant and getting married on Saturday unless it had escaped your notice. If you want to head off on some hair-brained mission like this, take that man o'mine and get him out of my hair for a few days." Suddenly, she was beaming. "That's it. Get on the phone, get him out of his scratcher and get him out of here. He'll only be sat at home with a 'woe is me' wimpy sore heided mope on."

"All truth passes through three stages. First, it is ridiculed. Second, it is violently opposed. Third, it is accepted as self-evident." – Arthur Schopenhauer

Chapter 49: Welwyn Garden City

All was quiet at Petty at midday. Dermot, who had the day off, was still lying abed, luxuriating in the peace. His hangover had been remarkably gentle, considering the battering his liver had been put through on the weekend. He preened himself at his stroke of genius at selecting Dr Richards as his best man. He knew with his Irish mates that they would be more restrained in the presence of a woman and that they were probably not happy with his choice, but he didn't care. He was more concerned about Davidson and Smith, a couple of loose cannons if ever he had met them. He hoped they would be so intimidated by having their boss along that their high jinks would become low jinks. He had been right; Doddie had headed them off at the pass when the shopping trolley appeared on their fishing trip to the Spey River. The river wardens would not have approved of salmon fishing using anything other than a rod and line. Dr Richards was able to turn a blind eye to the naked swim in a small hill loch, but not without medical comments about shrinkage. They had reddened when they emerged, and she flung them towels with which to dry and were unable to resist a smile when she produced a set of binoculars and zoned in on their parts, shaking her head at the inability of the magnification to produce a larger picture. She had turned her nose up and ventured, "still not much to see here" and "wish I was in the lab; where's a microscope when you need one?" Davidson had looked confused when she said, "A man of great parts is sure to rise."

Dermot smiled at the thought and rolled over in the double bed, wondering if he would miss the unaccustomed space when two of them were in it all the time. He then sat bolt upright when he realised there would likely be three of them there on occasions, albeit one pretty wee squirmer, when his baby arrived.

Dermot's phone rang, and he groaned as he realised that it was Doddie calling.

"Pack a case, laddie; we have a flight to catch." Doddie explained the situation, and suddenly, Dermot's interest was sparked.

"And dinnae worry, Monica has given the okay. You'll be back to face the music on Saturday."

The police station at Welwyn Garden City was welcoming, and everyone there was relieved that the two visitors were not Davidson and Smith. The following morning, Dermot and Doddie drove out of the hotel car park with the loaned police car and the sat-nav showing them a route out of the town. They were headed for Ayot St Peter, a wee village where Dr Ross and his wife had resided. Doddie was happy to drive and was in a talkative frame of mind.

"Did yer lass ever tell ye about Lewis Grassic Gibbon?"

"No, is it a disease?"

"Aye, well, she'll know of him, maybe even have read him. One of Aberdeenshire's favourite sons, James Leslie

Mitchell, died in his early thirties but not before making an enormous contribution to Scottish literature. *Sunset Song* and *A Scots Quair* are just a couple of his wonderful books. He is one of the great Scottish socialist minds of the 20th Century. His pen name was Lewis Grassic Gibbon."

Dermot looked puzzled.

"What's that got to do with today?"

"Nothing at all, except that he and his wife left rural Aberdeenshire and settled here in Welwyn Garden City."

Dermot nodded and retreated into his reverie, eventually saying, "Boss, why are we really here?"

"The truth and a hunch are the point, Dermot. Nane o' us like lies, particularly when they lead to injustice. When we meet Mrs Ross, let me do the talking."

They were on a rural road washed clean by recent hard rain. The hedgerows glistened with the freshwater, the fields were a typical English patchwork, too early now for the crops to be harvested, but burgeoning growth promised a goodly harvest to come. Spring flowers, bluebells, daffodils, and primroses gave occasional bursts of colour. The very English woman's voice on the sat-nav informed them that they were one hundred yards from the house, which should appear on their left. Doddie slowed as an open wooden gate appeared with a short gravelled driveway, up which he drove. He saw Mrs Ross at the kitchen window with an apron on and seemingly doing the washing up as he pulled in. She waved, reached for a towel, and came to the back door, which was really a side door. She recognised them from her visit to Inverness and ushered them through the house to the front room that looked out on a very English garden. Roses abounded; there was a well-manicured lawn with floral borders destined to produce an abundance of colour when the summer's heat had done its work. She offered them a seat and went to fetch the promised pot of tea. As soon as she left the room, Doddie did what he always did and stood up and examined many of the photographs settled on the mantelpiece and top of the TV set. He turned when the tray of tea things arrived.

"You have a beautiful house and garden, Mrs Ross."

"Yes, we moved here a few years ago. George was very keen to get out of the town when he wasn't at work. He loved his job but felt he could give it more of his all if he could retreat at the end of every day and every weekend. I always feel the calm when I come home here, and I always saw the calm descend on him as soon as he entered through these portals."

"What have you been doing since his death, Mrs Ross?"

"Oh, I have been keeping busy. I have my job as a fitness instructor and, as you know, I like to run and, well, keep myself busy. I do miss him, particularly at night." This last part of the speech tapered away unconvincingly. Both Dermot and Doddie sensed, for the first time, a lack of sincerity in Mrs Ross.

Doddie was suddenly all business.

"Do you know Mrs Purbright, Mrs Ross?"

"No, should I?"

"Would you recognise her if you saw her?"

Mrs Ross hesitated and thought before answering, "I think that I would; after all, her picture was in the papers and on the news and Welwyn Garden City is not that large of a place."

Doddie nodded.

"Well, that'll be all for now, Mrs Ross. Constable Long and I will be in town for a few days. Please contact me if you should think of anything that might be relevant." Doddie handed her his business card. He and Dermot stood up to leave, and as they moved towards the door, Doddie stopped and turned around.

"I nearly forgot," he smiled. "May I have the address of your gym, please?"

Mrs Ross looked stunned and delayed her reply.

"Why would you want that, Detective Inspector?"

Doddie was casual in his answer. "Oh, I don't know; just a bit of follow up I might want to do. Besides," Doddie reached down and gripped his overhanging stomach, "the awning over the playground could do with being retracted a smidge, might go for a workout." Doddie grinned what he thought was a most winning smile but what was instead a ghastly baring of his teeth sort of grimace.

"Let me know when you think you would like to come. Here's the address, and a list of my various workouts. I don't recommend the "Kinetic Killer" at this point at your level of fitness, but maybe "Jolly Jogging" to start with, which, as you see, is on Thursday morning."

Doddie took the handout, and he and Dermot continued to walk to the door. Dermot thanked her and said, "We'll see ourselves out."

As they drove back to the town, Doddie announced that they were not going to their hotel but would drop in on Mrs Ross's gym. Yet again, the sat-nav came into play.

They found the gym just behind a shopping centre in the middle of the town.

"Let's be brazen about this, Dermot. We show our IDs; we are coppers down from Inverness, investigating a suspicious death. I want Mrs Ross to know we've been snooping."

They entered a modern building with a large reception area. A well-planned gym with treadmills, bikes, cross trainers, and free weights was to the left. To the right was a room with a panelled wood floor with what looked like a yoga class taking place. They approached the front desk, where the young woman smiled her greeting. She looked alarmed as they flashed their IDs, but the smile resumed quickly, belying the honesty of the expression. Doddie asked for a guided tour, so the girl paged a colleague who bounced in from another part of the building, clad in a tracksuit and trainers, every move supple and athletic, every facial expression filled with energy and good intentions. She looked a little bit askance at the physical disaster in front of her, but her professionalism soon returned as she led Doddie firstly into the weight room. Dermot had been instructed to nose around on his own. He began by looking at the photographs of various activities on the wall. He had glanced at one of a muscled man and woman, working out at the gym when he was distracted by the picture next to it. While perusing it closely, Dermot reached for his phone and dialled Doddie.

Doddie was being taught how to plank on a mat in the weights gym when his phone rang. He informed his guide that the tour was over, and together they returned to the reception hall, where Dermot was still studying the picture on the wall. He pointed at two people in the picture, one woman leaning over the other, smiling and giving advice to a customer. They were posing and obviously hamming it up for the camera, the body language suggesting the two women knew each other.

Doddie and Dermot returned to the police station, went into the boss's office, and asked if she could have Mrs Ross picked up to come in and answer a few questions, no hint of an arrest, just an appeal for help to clean up a few issues regarding her husband's death. Mrs Ross was ushered into an interview room at the station within the hour. Dermot began the interview.

"Mrs Ross, you told us that you only knew Mrs Purbright from pictures you had seen in the newspapers and other media."

"That's correct."

"Yet, we have just visited your gym and saw a picture of you and her on the wall, having a conversation, which suggests that you know each other quite well. Do you still deny knowing Mrs Purbright, Mrs Ross?"

Doddie watched her closely as she replied. There was a moment's lapse in her demeanour, and her eyes quickly looked to her left, but then she was back with her head upright and staring straight ahead.

"Never seen her before in my life."

"But we can return to your gym, Mrs Ross, and show you the picture. A picture which you pass every day of your working life."

"True, but I have posed with many people while trying to promote my gym. The fitness business is competitive, you know, so we are always trying new ways to attract people. If I am posing with Mrs Purbright, it is one of many promotional pictures I have done over the years. I never really associated any of the pictures with anybody I might recognise on the street."

Doddie sat back in his seat.

"Okay, Mrs Ross, thanks for coming in."

"I may go?"

"Of course, thanks for your cooperation." He and Dermot stood up and reached across the table to shake her by the hand. A constable escorted her from the building. Doddie turned to Dermot.

"I want you to follow her."

"How can I do that? She's gone."

"True, but there's a tracking device attached to her car. Grab the car awaiting you out front and get going."

"Are you coming with me?"

Doddie smiled.

"That's a job for the young and athletic; I think I'll away back to the gym and do some physical jerks, get myself an appetite for a good old Ruby Murray the nicht. There must be a good Indian restaurant here in the town. Aff ye go."

Dermot did as he was told, all the time muttering about a fool's errand and how hanging was too good for Doddie, thus giving his opinion on capital punishment and detective inspectors in the same breath. He expected Mrs Ross to go home and was surprised when the tracking device revealed that she wasn't there. He found her car parked in a residential area and wasn't sure where she had gone. Just at that moment, she appeared from a garden gate, retrieved something from her car, and went back into the house. Dermot wasn't sure how to proceed. Should he phone this in to his boss? Should he knock on the door on some pretext and be surprised at the coincidence of finding Mrs Ross there? Should he sit in the car and wait? After some thought, he decided there was no hurry, and he should give her some time to reappear.

After thirty minutes, Dermot was becoming impatient, and after an hour, he resolved to be bold. He opened the car door, got out, locked it behind him, unlatched the gate, and walked up the garden path. He noted that "God Save the Queen," the National Anthem, rang out as he pressed the doorbell. It seemed to be playing the whole verse. It was about a minute before the door was answered. There was something familiar about the woman who stood before him, but before he could process this information, he felt the floor coming up to meet him. He turned as he fell, just in time to see the clay plant plot come crashing towards his forehead and then oblivion.

Meanwhile, Doddie had mustered a pathetic twenty-minute stroll on the treadmill at Mrs Ross's gym and felt that it was sufficient to justify the onion bhajis, chicken korma, and rice he would order at the Bombay Duck, which the desk sergeant had suggested to him was the best Indian restaurant in town. As he walked out of the gym, showered, with a red glow to his features and holier than thou because of his exercise regime, he decided he had better give Dermot a call. When there was no reply, he surmised he had switched his phone off and was probably in the thick of something important. He thought no more of it and settled in for his curry with the requisite pint of lager.

It was dark when Dermot awoke. His head throbbed. His mouth was taped shut, and his arms and legs were both bound with well-tied rope. Looking around, Dermot realised he was in a small broom cupboard. Dustpan and brushes, a vacuum cleaner, the smell of polish and disinfectant were all there. As he slowly made sense of what had happened, he realised that the woman who had opened the door was Fred Purbright's wife. Slowly, he noted a connection between Mrs Ross and this woman. He could not figure out why, but he knew he was in trouble, perhaps, he thought ruefully, because he had just been hit on the head, tied up, and locked in a broom cupboard. He heard no movement outside in the house, and he struggled to get comfortable. Minutes dragged into hours. It was to no avail that he tried to undo the knots. Finally, he heard movement outside the cupboard. A lock was undone, and his eyes squinted as he was exposed to the lights outside. As he became used to the light, he gazed up and recognised the faces of the two women standing in front of him.

Never would he have believed there could be such a transformation. Mrs Ross, who had appeared as everybody's image of a bereaved loving wife, glared down at him with pure hatred. Her open eyes, so sad in her earlier grief, seemed to look through him, and her lip curled in pure malevolence. Dermot realised then and there that this woman had killed and could easily do so again. Standing behind her was Mrs Purbright, a willing participant in whatever dire fate they had in store for him. Dermot's heart sank as he realised nobody was coming for him and his chances of escape were in his own hands. He also realised it was now dark outside and that it would not be here wherever his death was to take place.

Mrs Ross reached for a knife and cut the rope around his ankles. She then grabbed him by the hair, put the knife to his throat, and ordered him to stand up. Dermot had no choice. He was quickly frog-marched through the kitchen and out the back door, where the open trunk of a car awaited him. He was bundled in without ceremony and was suddenly back in the dark again. The engine started, and the car moved off. He recognised that one faint hope was that it was Mrs Ross's car and would still likely have the tracking device attached.

Meanwhile, Doddie was on his second pint of lager and was reaching for a poppadom. The curry had arrived, and he was taking his first bite. Gone were the days of his youth when he would be out with his mates, competing over the hottest vindaloo they could eat. He decided to finish his repast and then give Dermot a call to see how he was doing. He decided against the third lager as he thought he might have to drive somewhere. After paying the bill, he waddled through the car park and called Dermot. He was a little surprised when there was no answer but had every faith he would call in when he had something to report. But he was not surprised when he received a call from Monica.

"Hivnae heard from Dermot in a while; what's he up to?"

"Och, he's fine, just have him tailing Mrs Ross at the moment 'cos I am suspicious of her, as you know."

There was a sharp intake of breath on the other end of the line.

"If you've put my man in harm's way, Doddie Macfarlane, I'll not forgive ye."

Doddie laughed.

"Och, naething to worry about, Monica, just me delving into the fine print of this case."

He tried to sound reassuring.

She hung up.

Back in the car's truck, Dermot was starting to cramp up. He could not straighten his legs to ease the pain. It wasn't long before he felt the car slow and start to bump over what was obviously an untarmacked track. Dermot was almost relieved when it drew to a halt—almost because he had long since concluded there would be no good outcome in this journey for him, and he would somehow have to act soon if he was to save himself.

Doddie was about to drive back to his hotel when his phone rang. He was surprised to see Davidson's name appear.

"Aye, what do ye want?"

No preamble.

"Smith and I are here to help."

"Whit? What do ye mean, 'here?'"

"We both had a week off and figured you and Dermot might need a hand, so we flew down. We're waiting for ye at yer hotel."

"Fuckin' hell."

"Aye, I hope they do, I hope they do, Boss."

Doddie hung up.

He arrived in the hotel foyer to be greeted by the grinning inanity of two sloppy Labradors who doubled as policemen.

"I hope that youse twa realise that this is at your own expense. There's nae money comin' your way from Police Scotland."

They nodded.

"Okay, let's give Dermot a buzz and see what he's up to." But before he could act, his phone rang. A short monosyllabic response from Doddie, and he hung up, looking worried.

"That was the local police. Dermot's car is parked outside Mrs Purbright's house. He's not there, and Ross's car has been traced to some woods near Ayot St Peter. A car is coming to pick us up and take us there." At that moment, a blue flashing light appeared around the corner and pulled up. They exited the hotel at a run, the sirens opened, and they were off to the woods.

In his dark, cramped space, Dermot heard the approach, felt the key in the lock, and suddenly, he had a view of the stars. The overhanging branches and stillness told him he was somewhere outside the town. Mrs Purbright held the knife at the ready as Mrs Ross pulled him out of the car. Dermot overbalanced, but Mrs Ross had him up in a flash while Mrs Purbright was quickly behind him with the knife at his throat. Dermot lost all hope when he saw Mrs Ross reach into the back of the car for a pick and a spade. His back was being pushed, and he was being forced to walk into the darker woods, where he knew his fate would be sealed and there would be little chance of him being found. For some reason, he remembered reading somewhere of a person in crisis, where they lost all hope and, as a result, felt much better. He even managed a smile beneath the duct tape at that.

Now he had his legs free, hyper-alertness made its presence felt, and Dermot resolved that he would pick his moment and make a break for it. His moment came sooner than expected. Mrs Ross was leading the way through the woods with the help of a small hand-held torch when Mrs Purbright suddenly stumbled on a root and plunged forward. Dermot suddenly felt the knife fall away from his throat and threw himself sideways, at the same time feeling a sharp pain in the upper reaches of his arm. Initially off-balance, he quickly recovered and stumbled off into the darkness. Mrs Ross and her flashlight were slow to respond, partly distracted by the crack and shriek from her partner that suggested a twisted or broken ankle. By the time she could give chase, she could not see Dermot but could only hear him crashing through the bushes as he tried to distance himself from the two women.

Dermot was lucky. Considering he was stumbling blind, he had managed to keep upright but knew he could not ride his luck for long and would have to find a place to hide. Soon, he noted the shape of a fallen tree trunk. His luck was in as it lay across a hollow bank with ferns. He stopped and carefully managed to manoeuvre himself under the trunk and behind the ferns without creating too much disturbance in the surrounding vegetation. As he lay there, safe for the moment, he knew this was only a temporary respite. The motivation of the two women to find and kill him was very high. He had hoped the cavalry would arrive but knew from his time growing up in Belfast that independence and self-reliance were more likely to work than the forlorn hope of last-minute rescue. This was not a movie; there was no seventh cavalry. As he lay there, he could see the intermittent scanning of the torch and the movement in the bushes as his foe or foes approached.

Meanwhile, the police had found the car. Doddie got out at the same time as Davidson and Smith got out of the back seat. Doddie had to do a double-take as he looked over at his two constables.

"What the fuck have you got on yer heids?"

"Night vision goggles, Boss."

"Where the fuck did ye get those? Okay, forget I asked."

Almost as he spoke, Doddie heard a moan from somewhere in front of him. Davidson spotted the body on the ground almost simultaneously. They moved cautiously closer to Mrs Purbright. Doddie looked down on the prone figure from above, "Mrs Purbright, I presume?"

"Well, I'm not David fucking Livingstone," she growled up at him.

"What seems to be the problem?"

"I've broken my soddin' ankle," she winced with the pain.

"Okay, we'll call an ambulance. Where's my constable and Mrs Ross?"

"Aaargh, somewhere in the woods."

Smith said, "You stay with her, Boss; we'll find them." Before Doddie could answer, the two young coppers had activated their night vision goggles.

Doddie shouted after them as they sprang from tree trunk to bush like over-caffeinated ninjas. "She may be armed". There was no reply from the flitting figures in the shadows.

Dermot was no longer resigned to his fate. He saw hope on the horizon. One of his kidnappers was now disabled, leaving the other vulnerable, as far as he was concerned. They came to a clearing in the forest where Mrs Ross stopped and scanned the locale. She led Dermot over to a tree, reached into her backpack, which Dermot noticed for the first time, and produced a hefty length of rope. Still with her knife close to him, she pulled him over to a tree and tied four or five revolutions around his shins. She firmly anchored him to the tree, where he could do nothing. She went back to the clearing and started to dig. She had been going for about ten minutes when Dermot received the shock of his life: a hand appeared around the side of the tree and gripped him firmly by the mouth. Suddenly in front of him appeared the prominent features of Davidson, signalling him to remain quiet. He felt his hands being untied and the rope falling from his legs. Then Davidson grabbed Dermot's hand and pulled him behind the tree. Dermot watched in amazement as Davidson edged closer to the digging Mrs Ross, who was now totally absorbed in the task.

Suddenly, Davidson leapt out of the shadows in front of her and pressed a button on his belt. There was a sharp crack, and from somewhere on his body, around his belly button, a net catapulted out, exploding forth like that of a Roman gladiator in combat. The surprise was complete. Mrs Ross felt the netting land on her from above; such was the mesh that she was soon tangled. The more she struggled, the worse it got. Smith arrived, toppled her over by the side of the hole, and tied the bottom of the net below her legs so that she could not escape. Mrs Ross struggled and swore, but it was to no avail. Dermot, now free and talking, grabbed an end of the rope, and the three of them dragged her back towards the waiting police car, which had, by now, become many. When they arrived, the ambulance was there, and Mrs Purbright was being loaded aboard.

Doddie watched as his three constables arrived on the scene like Neanderthal hunters with a netted deer.

Once again, he was speechless.

"I dream a dream that dreams back at me." – Toni Morrison

Chapter 50: The Wedding

The sun shone on Nairn Beach on the Saturday of Monica and Dermot's wedding. The two of them could not decide where they wanted the ceremony to be, so it fell to Doddie to make the decision. Petty had vanished from the wedding venue radar when they realised there would not have been room indoors if the weather had been wet. Dermot's parents had arrived the day before, and Doddie had picked them up at the airport and whisked them off to his house at Loch Ruthven, where he insisted they spend the night. By the look of Mr and Mrs Long, red-eyed and pale, they had been victims of Doddie's whisky-based hospitality. Dermot looked aghast as they walked onto the beach.

"Ye've aged ten years in as many months, so ye have," he whispered to his dad as they shook hands.

"It's not us, son; it's yer boss, so it is. How many different brands of whisky do ye have in this country, and how came they all find their way into yer boss's house? Any of yer mates there gat any spare brain cells they can let us have, yer ma and I sure need them, so we do," and with that, he slumped down on the fold-up deck chairs that Davidson and Smith had provided.

Dermot spoke to his best man, and she nodded.

"Did those eedjuts gang a' the way to Brighton to get they deck chairs; looks like a beach postcard frae the 1950s and no a weddin'? Yer a guid man, Dermot Long, but ah dinnae ken whare ye find yer freends."

"Aye, I hope Monica arrives before the congregation has handkerchiefs on their heads and are licking ice cream cones."

Doddie's car belched and farted its arrival. He got out of the driver's side, looking surprisingly dapper in his kilt and jacket. He dashed around to the passenger side, opened the door, and out popped Monica, resplendent in green with a bouquet in hand. Dermot turned and looked at her, and she smiled at him.

"Oh, God, the dimples!" he muttered, not thinking that her mother heard him. But she did, and she smiled at him.

"Aye, those dimples have broken mony a hert," she said.

Then suddenly, the dimples were gone when Monica realised who Dermot's best man was.

"My mither?" she exclaimed too loud not to be heard.

The ceremony went off without a hitch apart from the occasional sound of collapsing deck chairs and muttered oaths of guests who had fallen victim to Davidson and Smith's "great deal" on seating arrangements and the attempted savaging of Pistol by a couple of large mongrel dogs over which the owner and dog walker had no control. Doddie looked over from his position next to Monica with a wry smile as his dog matched savagery with savagery and sent the two miscreants yelping into the distance with a frantic owner giving chase.

The reception was a lively affair with Dermot's Irish mates having set themselves up as DJs, playing plenty of Irish folk tunes. Of course, bride and groom were first on the floor, but Doddie and Mrs Richards followed on closely. Doddie expressed two concerns; one was that the Davidson/Smith marquee was looking pretty frail, the second was the fact that it was protecting some low lying grassy dunes, the dance floor was lumpy sand, the DJ's turntable looked likely to tip over backwards at the slightest wrong move.

There was to be no honeymoon for the newlyweds as attendance at next week's court case involving Mrs Ross and Mrs Purbright was coming up. They were being involved in collating evidence in the coming week. The two women had been transferred to Inverness and were awaiting an interview. The crimes against Dermot were enough to imprison them, but Dermot would himself admit that the police had bigger fish to fry.

Later that evening, the married couple were driven back to Petty by Monica's mother, who had insisted on doing so. She saw them off at the lychgate and turned to drive back to her hotel, so she didn't witness Dermot's failed attempt to carry his heavily pregnant bride across the threshold.

"The trouble with trying to escape from yourself is that you take yourself along for the ride." – Salman Rushdie

Chapter 51: The Great Collusions

The written statements by both Mrs Ross and Mrs Purbright had wide-ranging consequences, not all of them bad. They had plotted the killing of Dr Ross, ostensibly for his failure with the Purbright baby, but in Mrs Ross's case, because she was in love with Mrs Purbright. She had lived the lie of her marriage for a few years previously, thus the separate holidays that had been manipulated so that the two women could be together. They were very much in love with each other, so the plan was for the good doctor to be murdered and Fred Purbright blamed for it. Fred Purbright loved his wife so much and had always wanted her happiness, so he agreed to go along with the farrago of this murder in hopes they would all get away with it and in a pathetic attempt to curry favour with his wife and renew their love. It was never likely to happen.

Doddie had been unable to come to terms with the grieving wife he had first met in Inverness and the bitter, selfish, twisted woman he had watched confess to murder. But then, he partly understood because he had met Mrs Purbright, who was grieving the loss of the child whom she had never had time to get to know. The power and strength of collusion—the fact that the crime may never have materialised if the person was destined to act alone became possible when more than one person was involved—was very real. Added to that, the sexual content and the cocktail was ready for drinking. Doddie always shook his head at the influence and inspiration of the singular sexual act, an event which took seconds rather than minutes, to change people and impact their lives almost irrevocably. He shook his head at the behaviour of the cuckolded husband.

The details of Dr Ross's killing were simplistic in the extreme. The two women had booked into accommodation under false names; they knew where Dr Ross would travel. They did some ETAs and set off from the Loch Morlich side of the path to meet him. They ran into the teenagers fleeing the scene, found the unconscious doctor, and stabbed him, thinking he was still alive. If they had not touched him, they would have been home free. But the world, Doddie reflected, is full of "ifs." "If yer aunt had testicles, she'd be yer uncle" was something an old sergeant of his used to say when he was a junior soldier. Mrs Purbright and Mrs Ross would serve time for their crime, but it wouldn't be much.

That other great collusion was between Umbago and his mother. The police interviews prompted an investigation into the whereabouts of Umbago's dad. Eventually, a search warrant led to a dig in the back garden of their Edinburgh home and the finding of a body. Dental records and DNA proved that he was Umbago's father. The cracked skull revealed that it was likely he had been murdered. The obvious culprits were the mother and child, but they were lucky that there were records at Social

Services of how badly they had been abused, so prison time was unlikely.

The exploitation of the teenage hoods by Morgan Mickelthwaite was perhaps more of a crime. Morgan Mickelthwaite resigned from his position as a bank manager. He was tried and convicted of encouraging and perpetrating acts of violence.

Some years after Morgan Mickelthwaite came out of jail, Doddie observed a homeless person setting up a tarpaulin under the bridge where Colin had his homeless shelter. Something about the unshaven man in a long ex-military jacket caused Doddie to stop and take notice. It was Morgan Mickelthwaite, now divorced, now jobless, now down on all the good luck that had been his since his terrible days in the children's home. Doddie remembered what he once was and how he had helped him get his mortgage. He found room for the ex-bank manager at his house at Ruthven. The only condition for him staying there was that he make himself scarce when Doddie was spending time with his god-daughter, Millie Long-Richards, who visited with her parents but not nearly as often as Doddie would have liked.

As for Morgan Mickelthwaite's group of teenage miscreants, Doddie had fought hard to keep them out of the headlines, away from being a part of the delinquency system. He had found them all part-time jobs. Stewart was helping Mr Patel by becoming a stacker of shelves in the wee corner store. To mixed results, he also introduced all of them to Highland Rugby Club, where, after the initial shock of having to get fit, some were starting to enjoy the game.

One Sunday, Dermot and Pistol were out in his garden pottering about when he heard a car pull into his driveway. He recognised it as Dermot and Monica's battered old vehicle as it came into view. It was an unexpected visit but nevertheless welcome. Dermot retrieved Millie from the baby seat and thrust the squirming character into the waiting arms of Doddie. After an initial awkwardness when this had first happened to him shortly after Millie's birth, Dermot looked forward immensely to holding this little piece of squirming life in his large hands.

"To what do we owe this visit?" he asked as he lifted Millie up and down above his head, eliciting smiles and chuckles.

"We have some news for you." Dermot smiled broadly.

"You'd better come in, and I'll get the kettle on." Dermot led off with Pistol following close behind.

As they sat around the kitchen table, Monica, now breastfeeding her hungry child, opened up about how much Dermot and she loved having Doddie as a boss. Doddie was quickly shaking his head.

"Get to the point, lassie."

"I've applied for a post in Aberdeen and succeeded in getting it. I am going to be a detective superintendent in the city. Dermot has a post as a village bobby in Methlick and the area. My mum is semi-retired and has agreed to help out in looking after Millie."

Both Dermot and Monica kept to themselves the good attempt at the brave face, which Doddie was putting on for their benefit. Doddie set a smile on his face, fixed the smile on his face, and forced the smile not to leave.

"Aye, well, that's great news. I'm very happy for you both."

"I knew you would be," Dermot said unconvincingly. "Hopefully, you'll make the drive over there to spend time with Millie and us. Dr Richards would be more than happy to put you up since space is limited at our new place on the edge of the village."

Doddie looked down.

"I guess that I'll have to have some sort o' Doric immersion lessons, eh?" And he raised his head, and this time, the smile was genuine, and the twinkle had returned to his eye. Doddie stood up.

"Awa hame wi'ye. Pistol and I have our weekend walk to get in. When will ye be leaving Inverness?"

"At the end of the month."

"Och, well, I'll have to activate Davidson and Smith to get the farewell party arranged."

Dermot and Monica replied quickly and in unison. "Please don't." And they moved towards the car, and Doddie and Pistol moved off up the hill.

FINISH

Epilogue

The school gym was full of students, and a stage had been set up at the front. Conversation was exciting and excited. The students were ignorant about why they had all been called into an impromptu assembly, but they did not have to wait long. Soon, Sinclair, resplendent in his academic gown and mortarboard, arrived, leading a procession that included Umbago, Morgan Mickelthwaite, Stewart, and a couple of senior school teachers. They took their seats on the stage, and Sinclair moved forward to take the microphone.

Sinclair, sometime resident of Castlebay, Barra, full of his little self as a headmaster of some standing in the town of Inverness, short in stature, long in windedness, stood and marched forward on the stage to where stood a dais and a microphone. There was silence in the auditorium. Nothing now could be seen of him as he was behind the dais. Eventually, the crowd saw a hand appear and tilt the microphone downwards, and a voice, as if from nowhere, said, "Welcome to our special assembly and our special guests." He introduced them one by one with a pointed finger, and each stood and bowed as they were applauded. There was the sudden appearance from one of the sports cupboards off to the side of the gym where Ms Forbes, the maintenance woman, appeared carrying a wooden platform. She walked onto the stage towards the dais and dropped it on the ground, at which point there was a yelp of pain, and Sinclair hopped to one side, holding his foot. The platform was adjusted, and Sinclair limped over and mounted it. Now, he towered above the crowd and had to bend considerably to reach the mike.

"I would like to introduce our special guests, Detective Inspector Doddie Macfarlane and Colin Pettigrew."

Doddie entered first, then came Colin. Doddie had at least tried to dress for the occasion, but Colin was in a tracksuit that used to be red. It had flared bottoms with a black and white stripe up the side. The students who were close as they walked up the aisle noted it was a Jamaican Olympic uniform from the 1976 Montreal Olympics, and they also noted that there was a foul odour of rotting vegetables as they passed by. The two men mounted the stage. Doddie moved forward to Sinclair and shook his hand. Colin did the same, but Sinclair had quickly turned away. Doddie stood on the rostrum and found himself a dizzying height away from the microphone, so he stepped down and shuffled the wooden structure to one side.

He stood before the gathered throng and spoke, "Aye, aye, that's better, not so short in the arse as yer headmaster. My name is Detective Inspector Macfarlane, and I am here today to address the homeless situation in our town. This is my friend, Colin Pettigrew; he lives under Kessock Bridge amongst other less salubrious local shelters."

Colin grinned, revealing an assortment of teeth but more a mouth where his pearly whites used to be but were no longer. His unshaven features, broken nose, and unkempt greasy brown hair confirmed his status as one of many street dwellers.

"Colin is not going to speak to you today. He is here to simply make us all aware of the fact that there are many good people out there who are down on their luck, who have fallen away from the norms of society but are still human and worthy beings. I am proud to call Colin Pettigrew my friend. All we are doing here today is creating awareness so that nobody looks down on such as him, that we pass a few words of politeness when we pass them on the street, that we give them the odd chip from our carryout or slip them some loose change when we have some. The other two men on the stage are Umbago Lombard and Morgan Mickelthwaite, who are on day release from prison to speak to you. They agreed to talk to you today about their childhoods and how they grew into adulthood with a misconceived idea about dealing with people whom they believed were paedophiles. They will talk about the silence they kept for so many years and how the festering wart of their upbringing led them to commit crimes. Their message is one of opening up, speaking about problems, and sharing deep-seated personal issues. I have already stolen too much of their thunder."

Doddie dropped Colin Pettigrew back under his bridge. Colin's silence on the stage had spoken more loudly to the audience than any oration. He had cajoled all three of his guests into doing what they did. It had gone well.

He returned to the station, picked Pistol up, and drove home to Loch Ruthven with Bruce Springsteen's "Dancing in the Dark" at full blast. The summer evening was light as only light can be in the far North of Scotland in June. It was over eighteen months since Dr Ross had been killed. He still marvelled how the two women had somehow gotten away with murder and been given a custodial sentence for manslaughter. A mere five years in the prison at Peterhead, and they would be free again to pursue their lives.

Doddie wound up his window and wound down the "Boss." He reflected on the fallibilities that existed all around him, including so deeply, in his own character. It was easier for him to turn a blind eye to the likes of Davidson and Smith, Rowlands's yoga, which wasn't working, the battered and bruised childhoods of Umbago and Morgan Mickelthwaite that made them use teenagers to avenge their own childhood, Fred Purbright with too much devotion to the idea of a flawed marriage, and Mrs Ross who decided to murder because of her sexuality. These were extremes. Reflecting on his love for Monica and Dermot and affection for Pistol, Doddie realised that they had all inadvertently helped him come to terms with the scars of his wartime experiences.

"Less than fatal frailties, there but for the grace go I," he said out loud and reached over to Pistol and affectionately patted his head.

The RSPB car park was full as he drove past. He had read that there was a rare visitation to the loch from mainland Europe, but he could not tell whether it was a grebe with a great chest or some species with lesser spots. Doddie liked the idea of a hobby and liked the thought of bird watching, considering where he lived. But like all hobbies, it was a future plan that would likely remain a future plan until his dying day. He and Pistol saw the familiar car as they pulled up at the front of the house. A rather irritated-looking Monica was pacing up and down beside his front door while a tired-looking Dermot was pushing a wailing pram back and forth along the gravelled driveway.

"Whit the fuck, Doddie Macfarlane, ye invite us for the weekend, and you're awa' ben countin' sheep or worse when we arrive. Did ye forget or something? Fa's yon welcome, yon ever open door ye're always braggin' aboot?"

Doddie smiled sheepishly, "Slow down, I cannae understand you Doric speaking fairmers at the best o'times. Besides, is that onywy to speak to yer boss?"

"Boss, schmoss, ye're no my boss ony mair." And with that, she came up to him and gave him a great big hug.

"Away wi'ye and let's hae a keek at my bonnie wee god-daughter." He shook Dermot by the hand, reached down into the pram, and was greeted by a blue-eyed chuckle.

"Och, Millie, you could teach yer ma and pa a few things about good manners."

Doddie smiled with pure pleasure. He reached down into the pushchair and picked her up.

CPSIA information can be obtained
at www.ICGtesting.com
Printed in the USA
LVHW040946120722
723290LV00003B/141

9 780228 872870